A FAMILY AFFAIR

A FAMILY AFFAIR

HARPER
BLISS

ladylit_ publishing

OTHER HARPER BLISS NOVELS
The Duet
And Then She Kissed Me
That Woman Next Door
About That Kiss
At Your Most Beautiful
A Breathless Place
If You Kiss Me Like That
Two Hearts Trilogy
Next in Line for Love
A Lesson in Love
Life in Bits (with T.B. Markinson)
A Swing at Love (with Caroline Bliss)
Once Upon a Princess (with Clare Lydon)
In the Distance There Is Light
The Road to You
Far from the World We Know
Seasons of Love
Release the Stars
At the Water's Edge
High Rise (The Complete Collection)

THE PINK BEAN SERIES
THE FRENCH KISSING SERIES

Copyright © 2022 by Harper Bliss
Published by Ladylit Publishing – an imprint of First Page V.O.F., Belgium
ISBN-13 9789464339215
D/2022/15201/06
Edited by Cheyenne Blue
Proofread by Claire Jarrett
Cover design by Caroline Manchoulas

CHAPTER 1
KATE

E ven though I designed every gorgeous detail of this place, I don't want to live here. I'm almost forty and I'm moving into my mother-in-law's pool house. This was not how things were meant to go.

"Do you need a hand?" Stella shouts from her lounge chair by the pool.

When I glance back at her, she hasn't even looked up from the script she's studying—lest anyone in this family forget she's auditioning for a big part alongside Nora Levine in a few days.

"Here you go, babe." Kevin hands me a bottle of water. "It's only for a few weeks." He squeezes my shoulder. "Our house will be ready and beautiful in no time. Trust me."

I want to trust my husband so very badly. I want to trust him with the same passion I felt when I said 'I do' at our wedding. But so much has happened—and hasn't happened—since that day.

"I'm not asking again," Stella shouts.

"We've barely moved in," I hiss at Kevin, "and already your sister's getting on my nerves with her entitled ways."

"Cut her some slack," Kevin says, predictably. "She's preparing for—"

"No need to say it." I take a deep breath. "And I'm sorry." None of this is Stella's fault, although she's still a spoiled brat, convinced, as she has been since the first day I met her, that her big break is just around the corner.

"I'm going by the house one last time to pick up the rest of our stuff." Kevin pecks me on the cheek. "Try to get settled in." He flashes me a grin. "Or hang out with my lovely little sister by the pool."

I roll my eyes and sigh, but none of that makes any difference to my current situation. I glance at Stella, who is talking to herself, running lines, as though she's all alone in her mother's backyard.

"I hope I'm not bothering you too much," I say, just to vent my frustration.

"You could never bother me, Kate." Stella puts down the script and pushes herself up. Her smile looks genuine enough. She knows why we're here. Perhaps she's not so self-absorbed that she can't muster a smidgen of compassion for her brother and his barren wife. "It's great that you and Kev are staying here. The more, the merrier, now that Mom has moved Keanu in."

I walk over and sink into the chair next to hers. "As long as you don't expect me to make you dinner."

Stella shakes her head. She fixes her gaze on me but remains silent. Her shirt has fallen open and all she's wearing underneath is a skimpy bikini.

"Just a heads-up," Stella says after a few seconds. "Keanu's cooking us a big family dinner tonight." Keanu is not Mary's boyfriend's real name, but Stella has taken to calling him that because of his resemblance to Keanu Reeves in his *Point Break* days, laid-back surfer vibes included. "That should be fun." To say that Stella doesn't approve of her mother's choice of partner is an understatement—probably because she has to share her mom's attention. But I say, good for Mary. And Keanu—whose real name is Nathan—is very easy on the eye.

2

"That sounds like fun, actually," I say.

"Kevin's not too crazy about him either, you know."

"I know." But Kevin's mature enough to not let it show every time he gets the chance. Kevin respects his mother enough to just let her be happy with whomever she wants to be with. But that's too much to ask from the likes of Stella, who still lives at home at twenty-eight because she claims she can't afford her own place until she gets that 'big break'. While LA rent is steep, Stella could move out if she really wanted to, but she's too spoiled at Mary's. Case in point, she's rehearsing poolside for her upcoming audition.

"How's that going?" I nod at the script because I don't feel like talking about Nathan behind his back any longer. If that means indulging Stella, then that's what I'll do. At least that way, I also don't have to talk about myself, and the reason Kev and I ended up here.

"I've never been so nervous in my life." Stella sounds pretty confident to me. "Not even when I had to kiss Faye Fleming."

I try not to roll my eyes and, despite myself, giggle like a teenage girl at the mention of Faye's name. The urge to giggle wins out because I've always had a soft spot for Faye Fleming and my irritating sister-in-law got to play her lesbian lover on screen—a fact she likes to remind me of every chance she gets.

If it was anyone else, I'd offer to run lines with her, but this is Stella, Kevin's exasperating little sister, and today of all days, I can't bring myself to do it.

"I'm sure you'll smash it," I say on a sigh.

"Hey, Kate." Stella's voice goes all mellow. "Are you okay? Today's pretty rough, I bet."

I run a hand through my hair and take a deep breath. "Kev just really wants to do this. To create some sort of impossible clean slate. To give us a different house to return to after..." It's still hard to say, but Stella knows.

"That's Kev. He needs to be busy. He needs to build something. It's how he processes."

3

I nod.

"How are you… processing?" Stella asks.

I'm not, so I just shrug.

The touch of Stella's hand on my shoulder startles me. "Faye and Ida are hosting a cast party the day after the movie premieres next week. Would you like to be my plus-one?"

"Faye Fleming and Ida Burton?"

"Yes." Stella flashes me a big smile. Maybe she's not as bad as I thought. Maybe I've been too caught up in my own struggles to give my sister-in-law the benefit of the doubt.

"You want to take me to their party?" Incredulously, I bring a hand to my chest.

"I sure do." She looks at me in a way that allows me to see, maybe for the first time since I met her, that Stella Flack could be a movie star in her own right. She has the kind of commercial smile that dazzles Hollywood executives, and the girl-next-door-with-a-little-extra air about her that moviegoers can't resist.

"Hell, yes!" I shout. "Thank you so much."

"That's what family's for," Stella says. "To make each other feel better."

CHAPTER 2
STELLA

I've yet to meet anyone more intelligent than my mother. She has built the most outrageous architectural marvels all over the world, yet she can't pick a suitable man to save her life. I get what she *sees* in Keanu, though. He's eye candy. A gorgeous man on her arm when she goes to a cocktail party. Like a trophy wife in reverse—and thank goodness they aren't married. Sure, Keanu's hot, but he would be. He's barely older than me. One year and seven days to be exact. He could be a guy I hang out with at one of those achingly hip East Hollywood hotspots. All he's missing, really, is a man bun. Instead, his hair is suavely draped along his cheeks, nineties style, so he can tuck it behind his ears with one of those cute gestures Mom goes crazy for—I know because she has told him so in front of her own children, one of whom is older than him.

The whole situation is infuriating, but as my brother put it not so long ago when I was off on a long rant against Keanu again: I don't *have* to live here. I could get a place of my own, which might allow me to deal with my mother's toy boy better. I wouldn't have to see him in the morning wearing only his boxers, pecs all taut and biceps perfectly sculpted. But this is my house, too. I grew up here. I've lived here all my life, and as far as I'm concerned, Keanu is the intruder, so he should be the one to leave.

Mom walks to the dining table. "Darling," she says while grabbing me gently by the shoulders before planting a kiss on my cheeks. "Just so we're clear. I'm bringing Nathan to your big premiere next week."

I'm of half a mind to wiggle myself out of her impromptu embrace, but the mention of the movie I have a small but not insignificant part in softens me. My mother knows how to play me. She raised me. She knows better than anyone which buttons to push.

"Guess who scored an invite to the after party at Faye Fleming and Ida Burton's?" Kate all but screams. She points both of her thumbs at her well-shaped chest. "Moi!" Totally out of character, she blows me a kiss. I'm well aware my sister-in-law isn't my biggest fan, but she and my brother have been through a lot. Life hasn't been going their way and they're family.

"Wow." Mom gives my shoulder a squeeze. "You're not taking Hayley? She'll be upset."

"Hayley's not my girlfriend. I don't have to take her every-where I go."

"Fair enough," Mom says, before a short silence falls.

"My mom still plays old Lady Kings records all the time," Keanu says, clearly not caring how that refocuses the attention on his scandalously young age.

How does Keanu's mother feel about her son dating a woman almost twice his age? I scan Mom's face for distress at Keanu mentioning his mother but find none. All the qualms that she doesn't have about their affair, I have a thousandfold.

"I hope Kevin can make it." Mom checks her watch ostenta-tiously. She can deal with just about anything, except for people being late, especially to a dinner her boyfriend cooked. She follows up with a sigh.

We all know Kev's going to be late because he got sucked

into the remodel of his and Kate's house—which is already perfect because he and my mother designed it—and lost track of time. Because, right now, it's the only thing that makes him forget he's not going to be a dad—at least not any time soon, or maybe never. For that same reason, Mom has already forgiven him for being late.

I eye Kate. She seems resigned to the fact Kevin's not here. That he said he was going by the house to pick up some stuff three hours ago and still hasn't returned. That he's leaving her to deal with her feelings about all of this on her own. That's my brother for you. But he'd better make it to my premiere, although if he didn't, I'd have to forgive him for that instantly as well.

"I can't believe I'm going to meet Faye Fleming." Kate has her own way of dealing with her emotions, so it seems. Although she has always been very vocal about being 'gay for Faye'. "I think it's only now sinking in that you played her lover." She fixes her gaze on me.

I smile at her, then run a fingertip over my lips. "These lips were on Faye's." I love nothing more than putting on a show, than being the center of attention, and this family needs all the distraction it can get right now. Maybe that's why my mom has always supported my dream of becoming an actor. We already had enough left-brained, ultra-serious people in our family.

Kate plays along and clasps her hands to her mouth. "Stop right there, Stella. Don't tease me like that."

"Can't wait to see your movie, darling." Mom sits there grinning. She has always been such a good sport about everything. I should really try to return the favor when it comes to Keanu—to Nathan—but it's hard. I'm probably not mature enough yet. Besides, my bedroom's on the same floor as hers, and I'm not deaf. I hear things a daughter's ears should never be subjected to. I should have moved into the pool house as soon as she brought Keanu home, but that's no longer an option now.

"It's hardly *my* movie, Mom." My voice drips with false modesty. My part as queer rock legend Lana Lynch's much younger lover may be small—Cleo Palmer hasn't been with Lana long enough to get a lot of screen time in a movie about her life—but it's big in its own way. Cleo is nothing less than Lana's redemption. And I got to kiss Faye Fleming. If that's the only thing my sister-in-law can respect me for, I'll take it.

"Still, I can't wait to see you play an older woman's much younger girlfriend," Mom says, while draping an arm around Nathan.

"Touché," Kate adds.

I can hardly say the movie's fiction. It's a biopic based on Lana Lynch's life, and there's nothing fictionalized about it. "Fine. I'm a hypocrite." I throw up my hands in supplication. But it's not the same when it's your mother. Lana Lynch doesn't have children. All things I can't say out loud, but are all nothing but the truth.

"Do you all know I'm auditioning for this super-hyped Nora Levine project next week?" I'd rather they mock me for my self-absorbed ways than for my inability to accept Nathan into our family.

"It's hard to forget, darling," Mom says.

Kate just sighs one of her more spectacularly disdainful sighs.

The only one who shoots me an encouraging smile is my would-be stepdad, Nathan.

CHAPTER 3
KATE

Maybe because of the current circumstances of our lives—me with the barren womb and my husband with his incapable seed—I've counted down the hours to this movie. It's not every week you get to attend a premiere of a movie your sister-in-law has a part in, especially not a movie with Faye Fleming as its star. Faye and Ida aren't the only A-listers I've spotted. Lana Lynch and The Lady Kings are here. And Lana's girlfriend, Cleo Palmer, and her band, The Other Women. And I could have sworn that earlier, when the celebs were ushered into the theatre after we, mere mortals, had been seated for more than half an hour, I spotted *King & Prince*'s Sadie Ireland. Re-runs of that show have been an unexpected but immense comfort to me during all the sleepless nights after my hopes of motherhood got crushed.

Best of all, tomorrow Stella's taking me to Faye and Ida's house in Malibu for a star-studded party. Shallow as it may be, I can do with the distraction. Unlike most girls I went to school with, I never harbored secret dreams of becoming an actor. I was always too busy redesigning my bedroom and, if I got bored with that, the living room or my parents' bedroom. All I've ever wanted to be is an interior designer—and a mother.

One dream has come true. The other decidedly has not. So why not lose myself in the absorbing life story of Lana Lynch? It's unlike anything I've ever seen. Faye Fleming's almost unrecognizable with Lana's funky hairstyle and leather rock star garb. But she sure does Lana justice. I wonder what it's like for Lana to witness herself being portrayed on the big screen like that. Maybe I'll get to ask her at tomorrow's party.

"This is it." Mary, who is usually the very picture of level-headedness, has been beside herself since we left the house. "Stella's big scene." Maybe it's more elation at her daughter finally playing a role that consists of more than a few lines. Or maybe she's just insanely proud of Stella, who got picked to play Cleo Palmer out of thousands of hopefuls. It must be thrilling for a mother—no, I'm not letting my thoughts go to the child I might never have, and the motherly pride I may never feel. Instead, I nod at Mary and refocus on the movie.

On screen, Faye and Stella, as Lana and Cleo, are singing a duet and sparks are flying. When Stella was shooting this movie, more than a year ago now, Kevin and I were going through another round of IVF and I was too hyped up on hormones to pay much attention to my sister-in-law and her tales of upcoming Hollywood glory. I also had a big-bucks refurb going on that I was channeling any remaining energy into. Truth is, I never paid much attention to Kevin's sister at all. Until now.

She can hold her own next to Faye Fleming, who is dazzling even on an off day. I don't know why, but up until very recently, I never looked at Stella and believed she could be a movie star. Yet here she is, on screen at the Dolby Theatre, pretending to sing this sultry song with Faye Fleming, and she looks damn fine doing it. She looks like she was born to do it.

"That's my baby," Mary whispers next to me.

Kevin curls his fingers around mine. This is a big day for the Flacks. For better or for worse, I've been a Flack for a while now. And our family could do with a day like this, when things look up, or at least seem like they might go our way for a little while. Stella has done that for us.

We've reached the final act of the movie and things are progressing quickly between Lana and Cleo. They're in a dressing room backstage somewhere. They're approaching each other. Their lips are so close, they're almost touching. The camera zooms in on Cleo's face and it's as though Stella's looking right at me. And then, my sister-in-law, the girl I always believed wouldn't amount to very much, kisses Faye Fleming on the lips, and I know I will never think of Stella in the same way again. Because that's some kiss. There's no doubt in my mind that Lana and Cleo were deeply in love—and lust—with each other at that point in their lives, because Faye and Stella make me feel it in every fiber of my being.

———

"It should be illegal to see your sister do that," Kevin says in the car on the way home.

"Don't be such a prude," Mary chimes in from the driver seat. "It's art. That's all."

"Art my ass." Kevin looks at me, possibly for backup, then just shrugs when he doesn't get any.

I've been pretty much speechless since the movie ended. Lana's life story was amazing. Faye Fleming was reliably astounding. But I can't stop thinking about that kiss. I can't stop thinking about Stella kissing Faye.

Mary and Kevin go at it for a while, the way they do—the way a parent and a child who work together and therefore spend too much time together, do—but I tune them out.

For the first time since Kevin and I decided not to go through another grueling, and quite possibly entirely fruitless, round of IVF, my mind doesn't naturally drift to the nursery we set up in our house, which has been ready to welcome a baby for years. To the empty crib. The useless rocking chair. The lovely but infuriating pastels I used in the color scheme. The bottles lined up in the kitchen cupboard. The tiny clothes that will never be worn by our child.

Instead, my mind keeps going back to Stella. She was playing a part, I know that. This isn't even about Stella. It's about how watching her kiss Faye—or Lana, if you will—made me feel. It felt like something real. Something tangible. Something to hold on to in this phase of my life where everything seems up for discussion, where everything I've ever wanted is up for grabs. Where I don't even know who I am anymore if I'm not going to be a mother—if I'm going to be a woman who has never carried her own child inside herself.

All I want to do is hold on to that feeling the kiss brought, just so I don't have to descend into the black numbness of my brain again. It's an easy choice to make. Relive Lana and Cleo's on-screen kiss again and again and ride the small but pure wave of joy it ignites, or deal with the fact that I have a hostile womb and Kevin's sperm is not welcome there. And with the painful fact that the IVF worked twice, that I was actually pregnant twice, but only for a few weeks each time. Kevin and I hurled ourselves into a cycle of hope and despair every time, only to come out more bereft. The toll that takes on a marriage is immense. The silent blame. The secret guilt. All the things you can't say and the things you do say but shouldn't.

The choice is easy. It's not an issue for me that I have to use my sister-in-law to experience a few moments of reprieve from my grief. She's family. That's what family's for—she said so herself the other day. It's just a thought, anyway. It's a movie. An illusion. A pretend kiss that makes me feel all sorts of pretend emotions that feel just real enough to take the edge off my pain. It's perfect, really. Like a drug with no side effects. It's not even a crush—although I've had a celebrity crush on Faye Fleming forever. Since long before she got with Ida Burton and adopted—

Adoption. That's more than enough to rip me from whatever

spell I've been under. I don't want to think about adoption right now. For all the right and wrong reasons, I'll just think about myself for now. And how to move on from this. How to rebuild my life—the way Kevin is rebuilding our house.

When we get home, Mary goes straight upstairs, dragging Nathan with her. She's an obnoxiously early riser and she probably has a dozen big meetings tomorrow—she always does.

"I'm exhausted too," Kevin says, which is no wonder, seeing as he has given himself an extra full-time job. "Are you coming, babe?"

"I'm just going to sit outside for a bit. Have some wine by the pool to unwind."

"Sure." He folds his arms around my waist and pulls me close. He buries his nose in my hair. "Are we good?" he asks.

"Always," I say, unsure whether I'm lying or not. But it doesn't matter. He's my husband and sometimes I have to tell him what he needs to hear, even if it's not entirely true.

CHAPTER 4
STELLA

When I get home, I'm too amped up to go straight to bed—and I want to be certain Mom and Nathan are fast asleep. I pour myself a stiff celebratory drink and head outside. I find Kate with her feet dangling in the pool. I got swallowed by the press after the screening and I haven't been able to ask my family face-to-face what they thought of the movie—although Mom sent me a couple of texts before they headed off to say she couldn't be more proud of me. But my mother was always going to love it. I'm much more curious what my sister-in-law made of my first movie part worth the name.

"Hey." I take off my shoes and join her. "It's late. What are you still doing up?"

"Waiting for you, actually." Kate gives me a funny look.

"Me?" I bring a hand to my chest in mock surprise. "What-ever for?"

Kate juts her elbow lightly into my biceps. "You're a movie star now. I can't just go to sleep in your mom's pool house like it's any other day of the week."

"Now that you've seen me kiss Faye, you mean?"

She draws her lips into a grin and nods. "Fuck, yeah."

"Is it going to be a problem for you to meet her tomorrow?"

It's nice to be able to shoot the breeze with Kate like this. She and I never had much of a relationship, which I've always good-naturedly chalked up to us being in different stages of our lives—her trying to have babies and me trying to get my career off the ground. Although I've never been able to entirely shake the notion that she simply doesn't like me very much.

"I'll be the best-behaved party guest you've ever seen."

"Nah." My turn to bump my shoulder into hers. "Let your hair down. Let's have a gay old time."

"Seriously, though, Stella." She turns to look me in the eye. "You were amazing. You really were. I wouldn't say that if I didn't believe it with all my heart. Kev was a bit miffed about seeing your character kiss and fondle another human, but you know, he's your big brother."

"Thanks." Somehow, it means a lot coming from Kate—at least more than from someone I'm related to by blood. "I'm glad you liked it."

"What's the dress code for tomorrow?" Kate sips from her wine.

"Come as you are."

"What does that mean?"

"In your case, I wouldn't worry about it. You have an amazing wardrobe. You look good in anything, so."

"For real?" Kate asks.

"Yeah. Duh." An image flashes in my mind. "That cream suit you wore at Mom's sixtieth, for example. That was the bomb."

"I'm sorry, Stella. Are you messing with me right now or are you being serious?"

I furrow my brow. Why would I be messing with Kate? And why would she think so? "Pale colors suit you. They accentuate the dark lusciousness of your hair."

"The dark lusciousness of my hair?" Kate shakes her head. "Now I know for sure you're messing with me."

"You have amazing hair. Always have had. Don't you

remember how Mom used to fawn over it? Ask you for all kinds of tips on how to get hers to be as shiny as yours? I guess I've been fixated on your hair ever since."

Kate chuckles. "That was years ago. Mary hasn't talked about my hair in a long time."

"I've always remembered. I don't know why. Maybe because she was right. You have awesome hair." Kate's hair always looks perfect, like she has a hairdresser on standby. I take a sip from my drink to stop myself touching it.

"Here's to my hair, then." Kate holds up her glass. "And to my cream suit. I hope it still fits, what with all the hormones I've been on."

"No matter what you wear"—I tilt my glass in Kate's direction—"you'll look amazing and you'll fit right in. The only issue I foresee, what with me being such a big lez and all, is that other guests may confuse you for my girlfriend, which might be awkward, since you're married to my brother."

Kate chuckles again, then brings a hand in front of her mouth. "I don't want to wake Kev. He's been working like a maniac."

"I think Mom's cutting him some slack at the firm, to give him a bit of breathing room now that he has to renovate your house with his bare hands."

"I know." Kate cups her hands around her almost empty wine glass. "It's how he deals."

"Yeah. It's all very manly of him." I know my brother's hurting. It's written all over his face, but he's not the type to confide in his little sister about that. "How are you dealing?"

"Just, um… living life, I guess."

"In your mother-in-law's pool house."

"Thank goodness I decorated it myself," Kate says, her voice strained. "Can we, um, talk about something else, please? I just… can't right now. Maybe some other time."

"Of course."

17

"You taking me to that party tomorrow means a lot to me. It's the perfect antidote for my non-baby blues."

"It's odd." I pull my feet from the water so I can turn to her and look at Kate directly. "I'd never, ever pegged you for the type to go nuts over a celeb party. Truth be told, I always got this rather dismissive vibe from you when it came to my career."

"I'm sorry about that." Kate puts her glass down and leans back on her hands. "I can be a bit of an asshole."

"We all can, so there you go."

"Seriously, Stella." She tilts her face toward me. "I have ridiculed your career choice. I grew up with girls like you. They were a dime a dozen and, as far as I know, none of them ever made it. But that doesn't give me the right to judge you. And I did, so I'm sorry for that."

"You need a lucky break and I got one. Although I say that now, but it may all be over after this one movie." It's what keeps me awake at night the most. As an actor, you have no control in the movie business. It's all up to the people who are in charge of the money.

"No fucking way." Kate shakes her head vehemently. "If Nora Levine sees that movie, she's going to demand you get the part you're auditioning for in her new show."

Kate's adamance flatters the hell out of me. And I've already had such a big night. "Thank you for saying that."

"I will also say this." She flashes me her own kind of movie star smile. "If someone does mistake me for your girlfriend tomorrow, it would be my honor." She throws in a chuckle. "I promise I won't make it awkward."

"And here I was thinking you were only ever gay for Faye."

We both burst into stifled laughter.

"Seriously, though, you'd tell me if that was in any way offensive, wouldn't you?" Kate asks.

"Some people might take offense, but I don't. Just, um, maybe don't go shouting it from the rooftops tomorrow."

"You have my word." Kate gives me a solemn look.

"Just out of curiosity, though... what does it actually mean? If push came to shove, would you?" We're deep enough into our midnight conversation for some gentle needling.

Kate's eyes widen. "What do you mean?"

"I mean... is it more than just something you say? Have you thought about it? Indulged in the fantasy?"

"The fantasy?" Kate's cheeks pink up. "Um. I don't know. I—"

"It's okay. Now I *am* just messing with you."

"Have you ever had a man crush?" She recovers quickly. Maybe what she's been through with Kev has made her excel in the art of deflection.

"Only ultra-platonic ones. No fantasies. Nah. Not for me." I look her in the eye, but I don't really want to know about my sister-in-law's possible girl-on-girl fantasies. Kate's married to my brother and it's not my business.

"And Toni? Are you totally over her now?"

That was a bit out of left field. "I've had a few years to get over that."

"But you haven't pursued anything serious since?"

I give a slow shake of the head. "Would you? If the woman you wanted to marry fell in love with your best friend?"

"I'm sorry I wasn't there for you when all that went down." Kate puts her hand on my knee and gives it a brief pat.

"It wasn't your job to be there for me."

"But still. I could have been more than the distant sister-in-law."

"Don't worry about it." I haven't thought about Toni in forever, although a tiny part of me hopes that when she and Sheena spot the movie poster for *Like No One Else*, they experience a pang of guilt for what they did to me.

Kate suppresses a yawn. "I'm going to bed. I need to look my best tomorrow."

"Thanks for coming tonight." I push myself up as well. "It meant a lot to have you all there."

"Does that include Keanu?" Kate's grin is infectious.

"For an age-inappropriate dude, he is rather sweet." I shrug. I don't want to think about Nathan. I just want to bask in the afterglow of my big Hollywood premiere.

"Night, Stella." Kate reaches for me and presses a kiss on my cheek. "See you tomorrow."

CHAPTER 5
KATE

My business partner, Skye, is the opposite of me. She lives for the glamor of LA. Like so many others, she moved to the West Coast with the sole purpose of working in the movie business—instead, she ended up with me.

Who's to say why we vibe with certain people and couldn't care less about others? Despite our differences in temperament and pastimes, Skye and I have been inseparable since we met in college and bonded over our shared passion for curtain fabrics and paint colors.

"Tell me everything about last night." She pats the seat next to her on the patio bench outside our office where we drink our morning coffee. "I made you a flat white, just the way you like it."

"It was amazing." I plop down. "I keep wondering how I can be thirty-eight and have lived in this city for twenty years and never have attended a glitzy Hollywood premiere before."

"You've certainly changed your tune."

"I know, but it's… well, you know." Skye's aware of every detail of my personal life.

"Better than the support group I suggested."

"I may do that too, but it'll have to be without Kev. He's

21

much too busy distancing himself or, as he himself would call it, processing while keeping very busy."

"He probably just needs some more time."

"It's okay. I'm good with him doing what he's doing. For now. I don't even mind staying at Mary's. I guess I'm glad for the company."

"It's excellent timing, now that Stella's career is finally taking off and you can unleash your inner Faye Fleming fangirl."

"I can't believe I'm going to be at her and Ida Burton's house tonight." I check my watch. "In less than eleven hours."

"Do you need the afternoon off to prepare?" Skye jokes.

"I might." I'm not even kidding.

"I'll keep on repeating myself." Skye leans her shoulder against mine. "Take all the time you need. I've got your back."

Tears prick behind my eyes, just like when I was on a high dose of fertility hormones and I'd spontaneously burst into tears in the vegetable aisle at Whole Foods. But the only hormones coursing through my blood today are my own. Out of sheer defiance, I've even stopped tracking my cycle. If my body won't work with me, as I recover from its ultimate betrayal, I'm going to ignore it as much as I can. "Damn." I quickly catch the drop that threatens to spill down my cheek.

"It's okay." Skye wraps her arm around my shoulder and pulls me close. "Just let it out. I know it's hard."

There's nothing I can tell her without repeating myself a million times, but it still helps to say the words out loud rather than letting them fester inside me into something even more impossible to deal with. "What kind of woman am I if I can't even bear a child?"

"None of that misogynist bullshit at our casa," Skye says. "As if women aren't good for anything else than popping out babies."

Some days, it's enough to just hear another person say those words to me, to break the spiral of doom my thoughts have been caught up in. Today is one of those days—probably because Stella's taking me to Faye Fleming's house tonight.

"You popped out plenty for both of us," I joke, as I always do.

"You're welcome to take the twins off my hands for the next ten years," Skye replies, as she always does. "They're a nightmare. In fact, can you tell Stella that your best friend could do with some glitzy distraction as well. Do you know what it's like to be the only female in a family of six? The toilet seat is never down."

"I'll take Thiago. That cutie-pie breaks my heart every time I see him." It wasn't that long ago that Skye brought her youngest boy to the office a few days a week. I miss seeing his adorable little face, his tiny fingers grabbing my bigger ones, his eyes always sparkling. I walked around with that baby in my arms for hours on end, not because he was fussy, but because I could.

"I'm sorry, babe. I'm going to have to hold onto that little bambino a little longer."

"I get it." I try to muster something resembling a smile.

"The boys miss their Aunt Kate." Skye drains the last of her coffee. "You and Kev should come to dinner soon. Gabriel has set his sights on the junior version of *Knives Out*. Let him cook for you for a change."

"Gabriel's only nine."

"Tell me about it."

I can't help but chuckle—tales of Skye's kids have made me cry with laughter plenty of times.

"I'll talk to Kev." I get up as well.

"When you're ready."

"I hope to invite you to our freshly renovated home sooner rather than later."

"Remember what I told you. Don't just let him do whatever he wants to the house. Check up on him all the time. Make sure he stays in line and doesn't build you an extra floor you don't need just because he can't process his emotions. Men are funny like that."

"Roland isn't."

"Ah, my lovely beta-man. So many women are all about the alpha, but let me tell you, they have no clue what they're missing out on."

"I always considered Kevin more beta than alpha, but this not being able to make a baby has him veering into alpha territory much more than I expected. Like he has to make up for something."

"It's a spectrum, I guess." Skye holds out her hand for my empty coffee mug. "He'll come back to you once he's done some more healing. Meanwhile, you can become best friends with Faye Fleming."

"You know what Stella asked me last night?"

Skye shakes her head.

"I've always joked that I'm 'gay for Faye', right?"

"Hm."

"Stella asked if I'd ever had any actual fantasies about Faye. If the attraction was real, basically."

"And?" Something in Skye's eyes lights up.

"Maybe once or twice. Or, I don't know, five or six times, but I wasn't going to tell Stella that."

"Why not?"

"Because… She's Stella. She's family."

"Either way, we all do it, babe. So don't feel bad about any of that." With that, Skye carries our mugs inside, and leaves me to ponder what she meant by that. Then I check my watch again. Only ten hours and thirty-six minutes until I meet Faye.

CHAPTER 6
STELLA

I shouldn't have reminded Kate of her cream suit. She looks like a million bucks. She looks ready to walk down the aisle of her very own lesbian wedding. She most certainly looks ready to steal all my thunder. But she may look the part, I know that beneath her sparkling exterior hides a world of hurt. So I let her have her moment of walking into Faye and Ida's place and turning more than a few heads.

I introduce her to Charlie Cross, who wrote the movie based on Lana Lynch's life, and her ridiculously attractive wife Ava Castaneda, who, I could swear, raked an appreciative gaze over Kate's shapely body.

"Oh my god." Kate squeezes my arm. "I'm doing my best to stay calm, but Skye was just talking about *Knives Out* earlier and it didn't even occur to me that Ava Castaneda would be here."

"Ava and Faye are best buds," I say matter-of-factly, as though, just because we kissed on set, I know everything about Faye's intimate relationships.

"Oh my god," Kate exclaims again. "There she is." She stops in her tracks, as though she's devoutly religious and an angel has descended from the heavens and appeared before her. She clings to my arm. "She looks even better in real life. How is that possible?"

"Stella! Hi." Faye has spotted me and walks over. It's not as though I'm immune to any of this. If Faye is A-list, I'm C-list on a good day—on a day I'm on set with her. Before this movie came out, as my friend Hayley likes to remind me, I was decidedly F-list—as in f-off already, you mere mortal non-celeb. "So glad you came." Faye grabs me by the waist and kisses me on both cheeks—real pecks, not just airs and graces.

"Thank you so much for having us." Kate is squishing my biceps so hard, I expect to find my skin bruised. "This is Kate, my sister-in-law and a huge fan." I wisely refrain from outing Kate as 'gay for Faye'.

"You were so good in *Like No One Else*, but also in *Twice Bitten, Once Shy*." Kate continues to list movies Faye has starred in. "And in *A New Day*, of course." She takes a breath, then beams Faye a wide smile. "You've made me laugh so many times when I needed it most, so a heartfelt thank-you for that."

"Aw." Faye brings her palms to Kate's shoulders and proceeds to kiss her on the cheeks. "Thank you so much. I really appreciate it. And welcome to our house. I hope you have a good time."

"Kate's an interior designer so she'll have a great time just looking around," I say.

"Are you? How great. Do let me know what you think. I had to make a few, um, concessions when Ida moved in, but luckily not too many."

"Did I hear my name being called?"

Kate, who has grabbed my arm again, as though she can't get through this parade of stars without holding onto something for dear life, presses her body against mine as Ida Burton joins us.

"You remember Stella," Faye says.

"I remember every other woman you've ever kissed, sweet-ie." Ida is all wild hair and dazzling smiles. "But job well done. I was a touch jealous, which means your on-screen chemistry came across loud and clear."

"This is Kate," Faye, truly the hostess with the mostest, continues. "Stella's sister-in-law and an interior designer. I was just about to tell her about the cold, stark, all-white house you lived in before you met me and I painted your life all the gorgeous colors of the rainbow."

"Slight exaggeration, but I'll let you get away with it since this is your party," Ida replies.

"Thank you, babe." Faye slings an arm around Ida and pulls her close. She pins her gaze on me. "I've been getting questions about you. I told the PR people they should involve you in the promotion for this movie. Are you shooting anything right now?"

"Um, no." *I wish.*

"Stella has a big audition next week," Kate chimes in.

"Which project?" Faye seems genuinely interested.

"The new Nora Levine show," I say.

"Oh, wow. That sounds big," Faye says. "I hope that goes well for you, Stella. Keep me posted, okay?"

"Sure," I say, as though Faye and I are friends. "Let me know if you need me for anything."

She nods, her face serious. "Someone from the studio will be in touch. I think we can all make good use of you."

"Not too much use," Ida says. "Not to play the part of the obnoxiously jealous wife." She flashes us all one of her Ida-smiles.

"Stella's way too young for me, sweetie," Faye says, obvi-ously taking great pleasure in playing along. "I like my women more seasoned, like you."

Ida pretends to be greatly offended by this. "We're the same age, for your information." The glee in her voice betrays how she really feels. A man I don't recognize approaches them and steals Ida and Faye away from us.

"Pinch me, please," Kate says. "Did that really happen?"

"Fuck, yeah."

"They're so… utterly pleasant and lovely." Kate finally lets go of my arm.

"What did you expect?"

"More… I don't know. Fake friendliness and snobbery, perhaps. Like they would make us feel that they're better than us."

"But they're not. Not in the ways that count. Granted, I live with my mom and her toy boy instead of in a Malibu beach house, but that doesn't say anything about me as a person."

"Your mother's house is extremely nice so that just tells me you like nice things."

"If I wanted more independence, I'd move into the pool house, but it's already taken."

"And what a pool house it is."

"Don't feel as though you have to leave any time soon, Kate."

"I wouldn't want to cramp your style." Kate puts her hands on her hips and grins at me. She really does look stunning tonight. What's my brother doing, not paying any attention to his wife right now?

"You could never. I swear."

"What about Mary?" Kate drops her arms, but it was great to see her really sparkle for a few moments, to see her like she was before she and Kevin became obsessed with having children—before she paid much attention to me at all. "She must have a thing or two to say about us moving in."

"You know Mom. You know what she's like. Sure, living *and* working with Kev might be a bit much, because he can be an insufferable bastard sometimes"—Kevin's my brother, so I'm allowed to say things like that about him—"but he's her son and you're her daughter-in-law. Besides, she's too busy with

Keanu and work. I think she and Kev are off to Washington D.C. next week, so at least, if you're there, it won't just be me and the boy toy."

Surprise crosses Kate's face, but she quickly regroups. "Does Keanu cook you dinner when Mary's away?"

"I prepared one failed meal for you, Kate. One, in all the years I've known you. It's hardly fair that that should follow me around forever. I *can* cook and I will prove it to you."

"I very much look forward to it." She huffs out some air. "Either Kev didn't tell me or I forgot he and Mary are traveling next week."

"Kev probably—" I start to say, but Kate's eyes grow wide.

"It's like my television has come to life," she mutters under her breath. "Leona King just walked in. Or did someone call the police?"

"Oh, Kate. You are too cute." It's adorable to see her like this.

"It's Sadie Ireland from *King & Prince*."

"Not anymore."

"She will always be King to me," Kate says.

I follow Kate's gaze as she stares at Sadie Ireland and her gorgeous partner. This place is teeming with hot queer women tonight. And I had to go and bring my straight sister-in-law.

"I'd pegged you for more of a Detective Prince adept."

"Prince is hot, there's no doubt about it, but I'm all in for the sisterhood and I've always had a soft spot for Leona King."

"Don't tell me you're gay for King as well. I might start asking myself some questions about you."

"It's not gay. It's just appreciation. Leona King has been on our TV screens for decades, showing us, in prime time, what women can do. That their only purpose is not to serve men or make their male co-stars look better. It's the same with Lana Lynch. The fact that she's queer doesn't have anything to do with what she stands for and all the roads she paved for the women coming after her."

"Hear, hear." I should really get to know Kate better. I might end up liking her more. We might even become friends.

"Hey, Stella." Raimy, who played one of my character's band mates in the movie, walks up to us. "Long time no see. How have you been and what are you up to?"

CHAPTER 7
KATE

I try following Stella's conversation, but the woman she's talking to is getting a bit too flirty with my sister-in-law for me to be comfortable with. I step a few paces away to give them some privacy and glance around the room. It opens up to the deck overlooking the ocean by way of some spectacular bi-fold doors. The bling is kept to a tasteful minimum, but it's subtly there, giving the space a luxurious touch. I wonder who designed this house. To be let loose on a mansion like this with a limitless budget is any decorator's dream.

"Hey." A woman I've never seen before sidles up to me. "Inquiring minds would very much like to know… are you with Stella?"

"Oh no. I came here with her, but we're not together." An involuntary giggle rises up from my throat.

"Good." The woman nods at me. "Can I get you another drink?" She eyes my empty glass. "You look a little dry there."

"Oh, um, sure. Thanks."

When I hand her my empty glass, her gaze as well as her fingertips linger on me. Wait a minute. Is this woman hitting on me? I try to flash her my wedding ring, but she has already gone to fetch us more drinks. I look around for Stella in case I need to be rescued, but she's still in conversation with her cast mate. I guess there are worse things than being hit on by a woman at Faye Fleming's house.

When she returns, I try to get a good look at her face to see if I recognize her from the movie, but her appearance doesn't ring any bells.

"I'm Dax," she says, handing me a flute of champagne. "And you're dazzling."

I can't help but chuckle. Is she for real? Does that line actually work on women? I make a mental note to ask Stella later.

"Nice to meet you, Dax. I'm Kate and I'm married to Stella Flack's brother." I make sure she gets a good look at my wedding ring now.

"Oh." She holds up her free hand. "My bad, but let me tell you, Kate, that suit looks damn fine on you and, well, I just had to come over and say hello. Is Mister Kate here? Am I going to get into trouble for this?"

Dax looks as though she wouldn't care one bit if she came face-to-face with Kevin.

I shake my head. "I'm Stella's plus-one. Were you in the movie?"

Dax shakes her head. "I'm someone's plus-one, too." She waggles her eyebrows. "It would have been nice if we could have plus-one'd together."

Something about Dax's easy manner cracks me up. It's like she has gotten the message loud and clear but can't help herself regardless.

"Hey." Stella joins us. I make introductions, as though Dax and I have had much more than a conversation of a few minutes.

"Oh, you were amazing in the movie. Getting it on with Faye." Dax is nothing if not hyper-enthusiastic.

The three of us chitchat for a bit, until Dax has had enough of the dead end she walked into and slinks off.

"I believe we were both just being flirted with," I say to Stella when it's just the two of us again.

"You certainly were." She pulls her face into a funny expression.

"So were you."

"Nah. Raimy's just like that."

I shake my head vehemently. "Raimy is very much interested in you, Stella. Take my word for it."

"I didn't really get that impression."

"Oh, Stella."

"Tell me about your own adventures in flirtation." Stella cocks her head. She looks like the glossy version of the quintessential girl next door again. Her blond hair just the right amount of disheveled. Her blue eyes inviting as hell. In those hip-hugging jeans and that barely-there tank top, she looks as though she didn't bother to dress up for this—she really did come as she is—yet she fits in perfectly.

"I guess it was nice enough to have someone walk up to me like that and get me a drink. It's been a while since I've had that experience."

"It's that cream suit," Stella says. "And the hair, of course. It rivals Ida Burton's luscious mane of extravagant curls."

"Wow, Stella." Somehow, it feels as though I'm still being flirted with. "Keep the compliments coming. In fact, feel free to keep on going long after we leave this party."

"And it's just the two of us by the pool again?"

"Why not?" Stella's life is very different from mine. This is a very different experience for both of us. Her life's on the up, while mine is going through a definite rough patch, but tonight, at this party, surrounded by all these beautiful people, and Stella, I feel like better things might still be around the corner for me. It's all I wanted to get out of this night. A glimmer of hope. A stranger smiling at me with appreciation in their glance. I hadn't anticipated that someone would flirt with me, or that I would have that chat with Faye and Ida. I just wanted to come here and soak it all in—and get a peek inside a Malibu mansion. Stella made that happen for me.

It might only be a minute step on the long road I still have to walk down, but every step counts. Every time I don't feel like a complete failure as a human being, and the pain of missing something I never really had stops consuming me, is a big win.

I knock back the champagne Dax gave me, look at Stella, and say, "Let's have another because I really am having a gay old time."

"You're so much more fun than I ever gave you credit for." Stella's gaze lingers on mine, then skitters away as a waiter walks past as though we summoned him, and offers us more champagne.

"Now, about Raimy," I say. "Why aren't you into her?"

"What are you even talking about?"

"Sometimes I wonder why you're single." I've had a few and there is so much unexpected delight in needling Stella. "I get that it took you a while to get over the whole Toni debacle, but, come on. A woman like you. Granted, I'm no expert, but you're hot. You're talented. And, as it turns out, you're a lot of fun as well. No wonder Raimy's grabbing her chance while she can."

"Jesus, Kate. Did Dax put something in your drink?"

For a moment, because of the times we live in, I'm worried that she might have. But Stella's just deflecting.

"Come on." I grab Stella by the hand and lead her to the deck. Even though it's filled with people and Stella nods at a few of them, we find privacy in a corner facing away from the ocean. Before I address Stella, I take in my surroundings. This place is as stunning as its inhabitants. Maybe, instead of rebuilding our old house, Kevin and I should get a beach house like this. But who am I kidding? Mary might be wealthy, but she's not movie-star rich. And Kevin and I can only dream of a place like this. I refocus my attention on Stella. "I'm not just anyone. I'm your family. You can confide in me."

"About what?" A smile I can't decipher—is it smugness? Aloofness? Something else?—plays on Stella's lips.

"About why you're not interested when a hot woman puts the moves on you."

"Does there have to be a reason?" Stella draws up her eyebrows.

"No, but there usually is." I bump the tip of my foot against Stella's. I need her to know I mean well. That I care about her, even though I haven't done the best job of showing her in the past.

"I'm just not… bothered. Ever since Toni, nobody has even remotely made me feel the way she did. I was all in with her. She had my whole heart. And then she tore it to bits. And I don't think I'm afraid, because I've asked myself the same question. I just haven't met another person who makes me feel like that."

"Fair enough." Even though I was asking for an honest answer, I hadn't expected Stella to open up to me like that. Toni was another aspect of Stella's life I didn't pay much attention to. The fallout of their break-up was hard to ignore, although I steered far enough away from that as well. Come to think of it, I've been a pretty awful sister-in-law. The perfect example of a privileged woman absorbed by only her own issues. "So, what you're saying is that with Toni, it was instant? You saw her and you knew?"

Stella nods, a wistful expression on her face. "Toni was just… I thought she was the one. Not when I met her, then she was just someone who blew my socks off, but after we fell in love, I just knew that I wanted to be with her for the rest of my life. I don't want to waste my time on anything but that. It doesn't interest me."

Toni and I knew each other when she and Stella were together, but I don't remember her being that spectacular. But of course I could never see her in the same way Stella did. Just like

I never really knew Stella was the kind of person I could have such a wonderful time with.

Stella takes a deep breath and straightens her spine. "Now let me ask you something, Kate. What are you doing quizzing little old me when you could be hanging out with Faye and Ida?"

"Fair point," I reply.

"Come on. We can shoot the breeze any time we want in my mom's backyard." She curls her fingers around my wrist. "Time to cozy up to some serious A-listers."

CHAPTER 8
STELLA

When we get out of the Uber at Mom's house, Kate still has her palm pressed against her cheek where Faye kissed her goodbye.

"Do you need a Xanax or something?" I joke. "Something to take the edge off so you can get some sleep?"

"Stellaaah!" Kate wiggles her body around as though she doesn't know what to do with herself.

"Shhh." I hold a finger to my lips. "Let's tiptoe outside."

"This is what happens when one for the road becomes a second, and a third, and a fourth," Kate whispers. "Like they didn't want us to leave." She takes hold of my hand again, as though we're best friends on the playground. As soon as we're poolside, Kate slips out of her blazer and drapes it over the back of a chair. She brings her fingertips to her lips, plants a kiss on them, then touches them to her cheek. "I guess I'll give Faye a final kiss goodbye."

I burst out laughing. I will never let her live down this night.

Kate looks down at her pants, a befuddled look on her face. "Is it okay to take these off in front of you?"

"Why wouldn't it be?"

"Coz you're a lesbian. Duh." Kate sounds as though she's actually serious, although she's far too tipsy for that.

"I think my big old lesbian heart will be able to resist your naked legs."

"It's not your heart I was referring to." Without further ado, Kate unbuttons her pants and slides her long legs out of them. "Swim?"

"Let's just sit for a bit. We don't want to wake the others."

"I don't even know if Kev's home. The other night, he slept at the house so he could get some work in before he went to the office." She sinks into one of the lounge chairs. "More often than not, these days, I feel as single as you are."

Maybe I should talk to my brother, but surely he knows. Although, I guess grief can make people do things they shouldn't.

"I'm sorry about that, but Kev's a good guy. The best. We both know that."

"Your brother is an amazing man." Kate leans back into the chair and stretches her legs in front of her. "But I'd actually like to see that amazing man from time to time. Who knows, maybe go on a date? It seems totally out of the question right now. He's almost unapproachable. I want to give him the time he needs. I have no choice, anyway. But sometimes I want to scream that I'm here, too. I hurt as well. And I need him, but he's gone off on some self-declared mission and he doesn't want me there. I'll be lucky if I get him to myself for half an hour this weekend."

"How about tomorrow, we go over to the house together?" I offer. "See what he's up to."

"For all I know, he has torn the place down and he's building a brand-new house from scratch."

I wish I could say something to make Kate feel better. At least I know she had a wonderful night and we've made some memories she can cling to in darker times.

"Thank you, Stella. For being there. It's such a comfort to me that you're here, just in case you didn't already know that."

"If Kev's busy all weekend, I'll prepare you a feast tomorrow night."

"Argh," Kate groans. "I want to say thank you and yes please, but don't you have anywhere to be on a Saturday night? A town to paint red? This is LA. Isn't there a brand-new Silver Lake lesbian hotspot for you to try out?"

"Downtown's the place to be these days, but no. I was out tonight and, in case you missed it, I have a big audition next week. I need to look and feel my best."

"I can run lines with you if you want. Maybe I can finally find out if I should have been an actor all along."

"I've spent weeks going over all the lines I need for this audition and know them by heart. I'm more worried about keeping my nerves in check on the day, and forgetting my lines, even though I know them like the back of my hand."

"So the trick is to relax you, then."

"There's no way to relax before an audition of this magnitude. There's so much riding on it for me, and the time is so right, you know? I'm so ready for this. I don't know what more I could possibly do to prepare."

"Don't do anything more. If you're ready, you're ready. Do less, instead." Kate could be uttering the biggest bullshit I've ever heard or dispersing the wisest advice, it doesn't make any difference to how I feel. I want this part so badly, I'm just going to have to find a way through the whole process and hope my best is good enough. And be a nervous wreck all weekend. Maybe cooking for Kate can take my mind off what's to come.

"Mom is meeting Keanu's family tomorrow."

"Oh, to be a fly on the wall in that house." Kate chuckles. "But he's a good dude. I know you think he's too young for your mom, and I get that, but he adores her, and she clearly enjoys being with him."

"Are you asking me if I want my mother to be happy, no matter who she chooses to be with?"

"I guess." Kate lies there smirking at me. "It can all be so fleeting. In the spirit of get it while you can, I say: go Mary!"

"I suppose I should trust her judgment, but... I don't know. It's hard not to suspect a much younger boyfriend of some good old gold-digging."

"You think Keanu's after your inheritance?" Kate's eyes sparkle. She's enjoying this. I suppose, for her, it beats discussing her faltering marriage to my brother.

"I wish I didn't, but it's hard not to."

"Money always does funny things to people."

"Mom's got a nice chunk of change in the bank. Keanu must know that. And in my mind, it's hard to not let two and two equal four."

"But you see them together. You see what he's like with her. He's so affectionate and some things you just can't fake, like the way he looks at her."

"In his mind, he could be looking at a juicy pile of money."

"Either way, Mary would never marry without a sturdy prenup."

"You say that now, but you never know."

"No wonder you're not giving him a chance. You think Mary is Nathan's sugar mama." Kate bursts out laughing.

"I don't want some dude who's barely older than me to become my stepdad."

"I think you should give him the benefit of the doubt."

"Or put a PI on him." I'm only half-joking.

"Oh, fuck, Stella." Kate covers her mouth with her hand to stifle her exuberant chuckle. "Stop it. You're killing me." Her laughter stops abruptly. "Something just occurred to me. Roland's niece recently broke up with her girlfriend." She sits up. "Don't worry, she's age appropriate. I know that's extremely important to you." The smile she sends me is devilishly crooked. "Maybe you should meet her. She's got Roland's family's good looks and if she's anything like her uncle, she hasn't let it go to her head."

40

"You want to set me up with Roland's niece, just because we're both lesbians?"

"Is that offensive?" She knots her eyebrows together.

"It's more ludicrous than offensive."

"Where's my phone? I have a picture of her from one of the many parties at Skye's house. She's great with kids, for your information." Kate looks around. "Can you reach my purse? I'll show you what she looks like, then we can either continue this conversation or not."

"Let me get this straight." Because my curiosity's been piqued, I reach for Kate's purse. "You think setting me up with someone is going to get my mind off Keanu's possible darker plans with my mother? That's your genius ploy?" I hand Kate her bag.

"Ha. There! You said it. Genius, indeed." She digs for her phone, then scrolls through it for a few moments. Triumphantly, as though she is solely responsible for this woman's very existence, she shows me the screen.

"She's hot, sure, but how shallow do you think I am?"

"You have to start somewhere if you ever want to feel that spark again."

"Fine. How about we start with her name?"

"That's a bit of a problem for me right now. Skye has so many children and Roland has so many siblings and nieces and nephews, it could be just about anything."

"Meaning that you barely know this woman."

"I've spent time with her."

"Up until last week, you'd spent time with me. Plenty of time, actually, though you didn't know all that much about me."

"But that's my point exactly, Stella. Spend some time with someone. Get to know them. See what happens."

"Like what we're doing."

"Yeah. I guess. Isn't it fun?"

"Sure." I glance at the woman in the picture again. If I'm

going on a blind date, it might as well be with someone my sister-in-law vaguely knows—and Roland's niece is very pleasing to the eye.

"So I can set it up?"

"How about I double confirm in the morning."

"Fair enough." Kate stretches her arms above her head. "We could both do with a good night's sleep. I'm beat. Who knew meeting celebrities was so exhausting?" She narrows her eyes and fixes her gaze on me. "What am I going to do when you're famous?"

"If it's up to you, I'll be taking Roland's niece as my plus-one to any future parties."

"Oh fuck. I've just royally screwed myself. I call dibs on the first party you're invited to at Nora Levine's house."

"You say that as though you're certain I'll get the part."

"That's because I am." She pushes herself up and sits facing me, her bare knees touching mine. "I know you've got this, Stella. Because I know how amazing you are." She taps her phone against her knee. "And I'll make sure Roland's niece, whatever her name may be, knows all about that, too."

CHAPTER 9
KATE

"Hey, bro." Stella bumps her fist against Kevin's impressive biceps. "'Sup."

Kevin told me that, after their father died, when Stella was only nine and he was already in college, as time progressed and Stella grew up, he felt more fatherly duties than brotherly ones toward her. That he was so glad he had decided to attend UCLA, where his mother was teaching at the time, instead of shipping off to the other coast for college, just so that he could be there for Stella. For that reason, despite their large age difference, they're closer than most siblings would be. They each think the world of each other, although, until recently, in my uninformed and very biased opinion, both Kevin and Mary coddled Stella for way too long, indulging her every whim, letting her get away with not working while trying to become an actor.

"You know how hard it is to go from rejection to rejection?" Kevin said to me once after I'd pointed out his sister's obvious laziness again. "Do you know what that takes? How strong you have to be to take that time and time again?"

Kevin playfully elbows Stella's shoulder. Seeing them together, for a moment, reminds me of how Kevin would be with his child—and how I'm not able to give him the one thing he wants the most.

"You haven't torn the roof off," Stella says. "That's something."

Kevin grunts something, then turns to me. He's dusty and sweaty, so unlike the suited-up version of him I've grown accustomed to.

"Hey, babe. Sorry I didn't come home last night. I just really wanted to get that wall done." He holds out his arms for me and I happily let him gather me in them.

"I missed you." I push my nose against his neck and inhale his scent. "Please come home tonight." Never mind that we're actually standing in our home—and that 'home' is now his mother's pool house.

"I'll try."

"Stella's making dinner."

I delight in the shudder of Kevin's body as he chuckles. "I'll be damned."

"If you're going to gang up on me, you can forget about it. I'll just get take-out," Stella says.

"How was the big party?" Kevin lets go of me.

"Your wife didn't embarrass herself too much," Stella says, shooting me a wink.

"My behavior was exemplary, is what she actually means to say." I reach for Kev's hand, wanting to feel a little more of him for a while longer. "It was awesome. Faye Fleming is so friendly and just plain nice. And the house. Skye's going to wet her panties when I tell her about that."

"Do you know who built it?" Kevin asks. Mary's firm, where he's worked since graduation, used to draw up plans for big movie star mansions, but they have since pivoted to eye-catching designs for public buildings—which reminds me.

I shake my head. "Are you going to Washington next week?"

"Oh, yes. Did I not tell you?" He gives my hand a squeeze.

"I forgot, but yes, we have a big pitch for the Bernheim Institute. Mom and I leave Monday night, after Stella's audition. It's a big week for all the Flacks."

If my last round of IVF had worked, I would have been six weeks pregnant—then it would have been a big week for me as well. But I'm happy for my family, of course.

"When are you coming back?"

"Thursday," Kevin says. "You know Mom. She wants to do some schmoozing while she's there. She has a bunch of lunch and dinner dates scheduled."

"And she loves parading Kev around." Stella taps her chin. "Maybe soon, she'll take Keanu instead of you."

"Last I checked, *Nathan*'s not an architect." Kevin makes a point of emphasizing Nathan's real name.

"But he is very good with his hands," Stella says, impersonating Mary.

Kevin shoots her a shut-up look. "He's coming over tomorrow to help me out with those great hands of his."

"Kev, if you need me to do anything, you know I'm no slouch either," I offer.

"I know, babe, but your time will come. I need to just remove a couple more walls. Just let me do my thing for now."

"For the record, I'm not offering any help," Stella says, probably to lighten the mood.

"I wasn't expecting you to."

"Should I set you a place for dinner?" Stella's gaze has softened on her brother. She can probably see it too. How he's running himself into the ground doing something completely unnecessary.

"I'll text you later. See how I get on. I'd like to finish the demolition works before I leave for Washington."

"Whatever you say, bro."

"Hey." Kevin pulls me to the side, out of earshot of Stella. "I need to do this on my own. I can't really explain it any other way, but being here, doing this, it makes me feel... better. Like I

45

can cope. Like I can… maybe find a solution, or a right thing to do, if I put in the time."

What about me? I don't say it, because I can give him this. And, strangely, I've got Stella by my side now. "It's fine," I say, instead. "I get it."

"Are you okay?" he asks, his tone of voice so pleading, I fear it might break his heart even more if I dared to tell him the truth. If I dared to say no.

"I'll be fine. I've got work and Skye and your family's been wonderful."

"I always told you Stella's a great kid." He smirks at me, then runs his hand through his salt-and-pepper locks, leaving them in even bigger disarray—a bit like my heart.

"I hope to see you tonight." I kiss him on the lips, but even as I do, I can feel parts of him slipping away already, into that place he needs to disappear to make himself feel whole again. I know he won't be home tonight. It'll just be me and Stella again.

———

"We're going." Mary's gaze lingers on me a little longer than usual, giving me the distinct impression she's more worried about me than about dinner with her possible future in-laws —although, to be fair, no one has alluded to marriage yet. "Keep an eye on Stella. Make sure the kitchen doesn't catch on fire."

"I heard that," Stella shouts. "Why is everyone acting as though I can't cook to save my life."

"Maybe because there are days when I think I should have you admitted to hospital with a DoorDash-thumb," Mary says matter-of-factly. "Get your thumb straightened because of all the food ordering you do on your phone."

"This is LA. The food choice is amazing. You'd be a fool to not take advantage of that." Stella defends her case adamantly. "For the record, the time and energy it takes to cook a meal from scratch is not worth the effort if you can just have someone deliver it to your doorstep."

"We can have this discussion as many times as you like," Mary says. "But at some point, you're going to have to accept that your dear old mom doesn't understand everything that comes natural to generation Z. If it's any consolation, it was the same thing with my mother, and with hers before. A never-ending cycle of misunderstanding, although, in my defense, these days technological innovation is much harder to keep up with."

The way Mary's rambling, I do detect a hint of nerves. She might be Mary Flack, but that doesn't mean she doesn't get anxious about what matters—and Nathan matters to her, that much I know.

"Have fun, Mom." I wasn't expecting Stella to walk over to Mary and kiss her goodbye-and-good-luck.

"You girls have fun, too." Mary kisses us both goodbye. Nathan gives us a quick wave.

"What was it like when Kev brought you home to meet Mom?" Stella takes position behind the stove.

"Not as intimidating as you'd expect meeting Mary Flack to be. But only because Kev told me she liked my work, although we'd never dealt with each other directly, only through him." I grab a bottle of wine from the fridge and settle at the other side of the kitchen island. "I knew she liked me as soon as she asked me to redecorate the living room, although I still suspect Kevin might have had something to do with that. They both deny it to this day, but I have a hunch I can't shake off." I pour us each a glass of white wine and slide one in Stella's direction. "Call it female intuition."

"Toni was quaking in her boots when I brought her home the first time. Can you imagine that? Toni, who was never afraid of anything, not even getting the hots for my best friend, was scared to meet my mom." Stella drinks from the wine.

"I guess your mom can come across as scary, but only to

people who don't really know her. It's her image. It comes with the territory of being a very successful woman in a man's world."

"My dad died so long ago, I barely remember him, but I always had Mom." Stella sounds wistful. "And what a mom she is. I couldn't dream of a better mother. Or maybe it's because she had a knack for picking out the absolute best nannies."

I think about my parents in Iowa, whom I haven't seen in too long. We FaceTime regularly, but when you mostly have bad news to share for an extended period of time, you start to subconsciously associate FaceTime with your mother as a time for crying and feeling sad.

"To Mary." I raise my glass. "I can't wait to hear all about her evening."

"Maybe Nathan's parents are the ones who are intimidated by her and not the other way around. Maybe Mom's not the first woman of a certain age he's brought home." Stella snickers. "Maybe it's his thing and they're like, here we go again with a brand-new cougar, at least this one's a renowned architect."

We share a moment of glee and it takes my mind off my own issues a little more still.

CHAPTER 10
STELLA

"Once again," Kate says, "I have to admit that I've taken you for granted, Stella Flack." She points her fork toward her plate. "This is delicious."

"Thank you." I tip my head. I didn't make anything elaborate. The internet's not only good for food delivery. There are so many easy but tasty recipes available, made fool-proof for people who've lived with their mother their entire life and don't cook much. "Not bad for a mommy's girl, I believe you mean to say."

"You took the words right out of my mouth." A shadow crosses Kate's face.

"What is it?" We've spent enough time together lately for me to let my guard down and just blurt out whatever I want. To just ask her what's wrong.

"All this talk of your mom makes me think of your dad. Having lost his father so early, and seeing you grow up without one, even though your mom did an amazing job, really made Kevin want to be one. It's just one of those things that's such a part of him that it's become unshakable." She waves her hand about. "But let's not go down that conversational route again."

"It's okay," I assure her. "We can talk about this. I want you to talk about this with me. He's my brother and you're his wife. I love you both. You can talk freely."

"Thanks." Kate spears a morsel of grilled zucchini on her fork. "Honestly, Stella, if I had known you were such a great person, I would have spent more time with you from the get-go."

"I've always been this great, you know." I bat my lashes, just so Kate knows I'm not that full of myself.

"That's the thing. I didn't know. But I should have. It's my own fault, for having my head so far up my own ass. It's our ages as well, I guess. We're what? Ten, eleven years apart? It's not a huge gap, but at the time we met, it seemed bigger."

"It's okay, Kate. You can be frank and tell me you considered me a rich woman's spoiled brat of a daughter, whose brother treated her with kid gloves because their daddy died when she was only nine. I get it. I never made much effort for you to think of me otherwise."

"If you put it like that, it sounds truly awful." Kate's cheeks actually pink up.

"I was busy doing my thing and you were busy doing yours. It's how life is, or can be. Let's just leave it at that, and toast to our budding friendship."

In response, Kate refills our wine glasses.

"I saw how Kev was today. Maybe he gets that from our dad, I don't know. The silent, brooding thing. Mom certainly isn't like that, and neither am I. But I get that he's grieving." I pause. "Maybe it's not my place to say, but there are other ways to become parents. In the queer community, we have to be more inventive about having children."

"I know. It shouldn't be the end of the road. There's surrogacy. Adoption. Maybe it's selfish, entitled even, for us to have wanted what we wanted. But it's still what we want."

"It's not selfish or entitled. It's biology. It's evolution. It's what humans have always done because procreation is in our DNA."

"Maybe what hurts the most is that Kevin and I together are the worst possible combination. Maybe if he'd married another woman with a more hospitable womb, his swimmers would have stood a chance. And maybe if I'd married—" She doesn't continue. I suppose there are limits to the things you can confide in your sister-in-law.

"But Kev and you are great together." I hesitate before popping the piece of pappardelle on my fork into my mouth, in case I have to comfort Kate more. "You'll get through this. You'll find a way that works for you, that makes you happy."

Kate nods but not with conviction. "It's going to take some time. While I wait for that to pass, this is not a bad place to stay." She musters a smile. "The food and company are excellent."

Mom was looking forward to being a grandmother, that much I know. And I was hoping to become an auntie to my brother's child, but our disappointment is nothing compared to what Kevin and Kate are going through.

"So... next week," I say. "It's going to be just you, me, and Keanu at the house."

A genuine grin appears on Kate's face. As much as I dislike my mother dating this much younger man, he is a good topic of conversation.

"You're welcome to stay with me at the pool house," she says. "It's more like a bungalow, anyway."

"There's only one bedroom."

"So?" Kate shrugs.

I shake my head. "I'm not letting Keanu chase me from the house I grew up in." This is my house, I want to say, but that's not true. It's Mom's house, and she's been very generous letting me live here for as long as I want. Like many people of my generation, I can't bear the thought of checking out of Hotel Mama. "But maybe you should stay at the main house while Kev's away. There's plenty of space."

"I'll think about it, but what happens if you go on your blind date with Elena?" Kate has found out the name of Roland's niece. "And you want to bring her home?"

"I'm not going on a blind date next week."

Kate nods, as though she's entirely on the same wavelength as me.

"My audition's on Monday and I hope to get a callback. I don't need the extra stress of a blind date."

"Did you want me to take the day off and drive you?" Kate offers.

"That's so sweet, but not necessary." Nerves tear through my stomach and I drop my fork altogether. "I may need you for moral support on Monday evening. I'm not sure I'll want to cry on Keanu's shoulder in case of a disaster."

"How about Hayley?" Kate asks.

"She's out of town until Tuesday." I cock my head.

"You can count on me, Stella. I'll be there for you."

"Thank you."

"Only returning the favor."

"Is it even a favor when you're family?" I ask.

"Maybe not when you're family by blood—"

I snicker in response. "It is when you've been shoved together by your relatives, hoping for the best, like us."

Kate lifts her glass of wine. "Exactly."

We clink rims. "Has Roland's niece been told about me yet?" I ask, because it's the weekend before an audition and, despite the inevitable nerves, the air is also full of possibility. Hope still reigns supreme because anything can still happen. They haven't rejected me yet.

"I was planning to talk to Skye on Monday, but I can move up my matchmaking timeline if you want." Kate grins at me. "For the record, you'd make a hot couple."

"High praise from my sister-in-law." I shake my head. "No need to speed things up, I was just curious." I have been in a big movie. Maybe Elena has heard about me.

"I'm at least happy for you that you've decided to... take a leap again. Just take a chance."

"Hm, I'm beginning to suspect you're looking to do a bit of vicarious living through me, what with you having been hitched to Kev for a decade. I can't even imagine what that's like." Although, at some point, I had serious plans to ask Toni to marry me. "To be with someone for so long."

"It's pretty great, but yeah... it does happen that the mind wanders." Kate covers her mouth with her hand. "I'm sorry. I'm not sure that's something I should tell you. It just came out, because of the, uh, nature of our conversation."

"It's okay. It's not because he's my brother that you can't confide in me. This friendship doesn't come with conditions because of Kevin. We really can talk about anything."

"All right. In that case, I am curious about something..." Kate fixes her brown-eyed gaze on me. She's always had very kind eyes. It was the thing I said to Kev when he asked me what I thought about Kate and I didn't really know what to say because I didn't really know her and Kate never made any effort to change that.

"Oh, god. Should I brace myself?"

"Maybe." She purses her lips.

"Go on then. Ask me." I square my shoulders in anticipation.

"Have you been with anyone since Toni?" Her eyes seem to grow kinder still.

Because it's Kate asking the question, I know she's not prying in the way my mother would—desperate for her youngest to find love again. I can even give her an honest answer. "I've been on a few dates, but I never felt that thing, you know?"

"That elusive spark you referred to last night?" Kate asks.

"It's not that elusive."

"I think it is, especially if you're passively waiting for it."

"What do you mean?"

53

"I was with you last night, Stella. You're a hot, single woman. You're a young, exciting actor on the cusp of a massive breakthrough. I saw how some women were looking at you. The one who tried to hit on you, for example. What was her name? Raimy?"

"I wasn't the only one being hit on. Remember?"

"But I'm not single and I'm not gay. I'm not looking. There's a big difference."

"Why do I get the impression I'm being told off for something I didn't do?" Kate's tone is confusing most of all. Her words don't match how she's looking at me.

"I wouldn't dream of telling you off. I'm just... infinitely intrigued why you're single."

"Infinitely intrigued, huh?" Kate does keep bringing the conversation back to my relationship status, while it's not something that bothers me all that much. "Truth be told, if loving someone can hurt that much, I'm not sure I'm game any longer. I'm not sure it's worth it."

"You mean how much Toni hurt you with Sheena?"

"They both hurt me and... Yeah. I like myself plenty. Yes, I live with my mom, and I know how that makes me look, but I don't care, because, frankly, living with Mom is awesome. It certainly has been up to now. I'll have to see how things go with Nathan."

"It's not just about where you live, though..."

"I guess I don't fall in love that easily anymore. I'm sure fear has something to do with it as well. But people my age, we don't automatically go for coupledom anymore. We question everything, especially the lesbians." I throw in a smile. "For your information, Hayley and I tried the friends-with-benefits thing, but that did not work out at all."

"How so?" Kate leans back in her chair, relaxed. She's enjoying this, that's for sure—much more than I ever enjoyed my friends-with-benefits arrangement.

"She's Hayley. I can't go there with her."

"Who suggested that you try?"

"She did."

Kate's shapely eyebrows arch up. "Did she have a crush on you?"

"No."

"I guess it's tricky when you're two, um, gay women."

"It's not. When there's something more, you know. When two women feel something for each other, you just know. There's a charge in the air that exceeds friendship. I never had that with Hayley, that's why I couldn't have sex with her. If that's what I wanted, I'd date her properly."

"But who's to say she didn't want to date you?"

"Me." Is Kate being deliberately obstinate about this? "When we kissed, she was the one who giggled the most."

"Giggles can be deployed to hide all sorts of things." She purses her lips and nods, as though she has all the answers. Strangely, it doesn't annoy me. I don't even think she's trying to rattle my cage. She's just trying to coax some information out of me that I don't easily share. Maybe to make up for all the things I know about her marriage to my brother.

"Hayley and I are never going to be a thing. I love her to pieces, but we are different in a way that makes us utterly incompatible for a romantic relationship." I give a slight shake of the head. "If you want to see some heads turn, you should try taking Hayley to a lesbian shindig. Her mere appearance is like catnip to the average woman looking to hook up with another woman."

"Really?" Kate sinks her front teeth into her lower lip, as though pondering what Hayley looks like.

"Fuck, yeah."

Kate taps her fingertips on the tabletop. "I'm going to tell you something, okay? Something I was too bashful to tell you the other night."

"Be my guest." My turn to paint on a satisfied smile, although I have no idea where this is going.

"When you asked me if I'd had, um, actual fantasies about Faye Fleming…" It's like Kate has found an extra reservoir of confidence tonight. Her voice is firm and her declaration almost straightforward.

I nod encouragingly, but don't say anything.

"I *have* fantasized about… that. Even though I told you I hadn't when you asked me."

I probably shouldn't have asked Kate that question. "Okay." What am I meant to do with this confession? I guess this is girls-night-out talk, when you confide things in each other that should never leave the room. "Good for you." *Good for you?* Wow. While I like myself plenty, I'm not crazy about that response. Is that really the best I can come up with? "I mean, um, Faye is as gorgeous as they come."

"I don't know why I didn't just come out and tell you. That is what 'gay for Faye' implies, anyway." Kate's words have a bit more hesitation in them.

"And, um, is Faye the only woman you've had such… thoughts about?" I ask. I might as well satisfy my curiosity now.

CHAPTER 11
KATE

The evening has taken a turn. It's like my brain has lost control of what my mouth is saying. Or, maybe, I'm just enjoying Stella's company so much, I can truly speak freely. I can just be in the moment.

"Maybe not," I reply to her question, even though I'm not sure what I mean by that. Although, on some level, I'm starting to get an inkling. Because, truth be told, last night's party notwithstanding, I haven't had this much fun in long, long months—maybe years. Part of me is glad Kevin isn't here because, even though I long for his company, it would have made the night heavier. The two of us being in the same room, all our faults bubbling to the surface like water coming to a sudden boil, has that effect these days.

It's why he has come up with a good enough reason to avoid me, basically dumped me here with his mother and sister so he knew I would at least be taken care of—as long as he didn't have to do the taking care of. He hasn't said it as such, but the two of us together don't make much sense right now. He's got his house to rebuild; I've got Stella. That's why I'm here, letting words slip from my mouth that really shouldn't. Maybe I feel like demolishing a wall as well, albeit a metaphorical one.

Maybe I feel like doing something dangerous, something reckless. Like breaking something. I make a mental note to buy some cheap crockery at the dollar store for the sole purpose of smashing it, of watching it splinter into a million pieces in front of my very eyes.

"Who?" Stella's face is all innocence, and why wouldn't it be? Lovely, glorious, easy-to-be-around Stella. Out of all the billions of people on this earth, and the couple of dozen I actually know, she's the one I prefer to spend time with, because she doesn't have any children. She's single and kids aren't even a blip on her radar. She's just the right amount of self-absorbed for me to be around. And she took me to Faye's party. When I watched her kiss Faye on screen, it undid one of the many knots in my stomach, and it's a feeling I'm desperate to experience again.

"I can't say. Don't ask me again, because it's really impossible."

"What are you talking about?" Stella leans over the table. Of course she's not having any of this. "You started this and now you're going to shut me down? Now that it's about to become juicy?" Something sparks in her eyes. "I know we're talking about women, but just to be sure, it's not Nathan, is it? I guess he's dreamy in a straight woman's eyes. Maybe I could even see it. He is—"

I hold up my hand to stop her mid-sentence. "It's definitely not Nathan."

"Phew. That would have been too complicated." She leans backward again. "Do you want me to keep guessing until I get it right? Provided it's someone I know, of course."

I lock my eyes on Stella's. They're blue and sparkly and inviting. Her shoulder-length hair is pulled away from her face in a messy top-knot. All the Flacks are so ridiculously good-looking, but it's the fact that they seem to be unaware of it, or attach zero importance to their looks, that makes them even more attractive. Stella might even take it as an insult to her

58

acting skills if I told her that with looks like that, she's bound to hit the big time soon. I wouldn't mean it as an insult, though.

"I'm sorry, Stella." I have to put a pin in it. "I was just kidding. I shouldn't have. There's no one." I get up and take our plates. "Let me clean this up. It's the least I can do after you cooked me such a delicious meal."

Stella gives me a funny look, but then just shrugs. Maybe she's chalking up my erratic behavior to what I've been through —the mad non-mother.

"Wanna hit the hot tub? It's a great night for it."

"Sure," I say without thinking.

"Bring another bottle of wine." Stella's already unbuttoning her shirt. Wait a minute. Isn't she planning on going upstairs to put on her swimsuit?

"Are you going in naked?" I nearly drop the plates at the prospect.

"Oh, damn." She slaps her palm against her forehead. "I'd best change my ways now that Keanu lives here too." She continues to unbutton her shirt. "Keanu's not here, though. But I get that it would make you uncomfortable." She shoots me a wink. "I am a movie star now, after all." She gets up and takes the salt and pepper shaker from the table. "And with all your movie star fantasies of late." Chuckling loudly, she walks inside the house, leaving me to ponder my choices. I can't bail now.

———

"Now that we're fully covered by water, do you mind if I take my top off?" Stella huffs out some air as though putting on a bikini in her own backyard is the biggest sacrifice she's ever been asked to make. "I hate wearing swimwear in the hot tub." She wrinkles her nose. "Oh, damn. That's got me thinking about Mom and Keanu in the hot tub. Without swimwear. Quick, Kate, put another thought in my head to erase this one. It's unbearable." She covers her face with her hands. "Argh."

I can't help but chuckle while scrambling for a chaste thought to replace the one currently torturing Stella. I try to think of a joke, but as usual, when you need it most, it's never there.

"Think of Elena," I blurt out.

"She's too hot," Stella replies, but removes her hands from her eyes. "It's okay. I'm over it." She proceeds to take off her bikini top and catapults it onto the lawn.

I glance away quickly and focus my gaze on the back of the house. "What a view." It's easy enough to see why Mary installed the hot tub in this spot. The outside lighting scheme illuminates her house in a way that makes it look even more spectacular. Although the house Kevin built for us is nothing to sneeze at, I should still count my lucky stars that I get to stay here—albeit for all the wrong reasons.

"Ah, yes. In case you hadn't noticed, the Flacks really, really, really like to build things. Well, apart from one Flack."

"It's a beautiful house," I muse, taking in the glass wall connecting the back of the house with the garden.

"And you wonder why I never left. I don't think I will ever leave. Maybe that's why Toni cheated on me with Sheena. I didn't move in with her at the exact time when she wanted me to, because I was living here."

"As a designer I get that you can be attached to a place, but you shouldn't be so attached that it keeps you from moving in with the woman you love. That has a touch of the unhealthy about it."

"I was just kidding, Kate. It's not like I didn't move in with Toni because I liked it here so much. I just didn't think the time was right. We'd only been together a few months when she first asked."

"Yet you wanted to marry her."

"I could see myself marrying her and I would have moved in with her eventually. Of course, I would have. I just don't like to be pressured and then, I appeared to have missed my chance."

"I think that sometimes two people can fall in love, despite the person they're already with, and how much they love them, or how wonderful they are. That sort of thing happens all the time."

"That didn't give them the right to cheat on me, though."

"Agreed."

Stella pushes herself a little higher and her nipples are only half covered by the surface of the water. She doesn't seem to notice. I guess she feels as comfortable with me as I do with her, although my levels of comfort are quickly starting to fall.

"Have you had a crush on anyone else since you've been with Kev?" Stella asks. "A real one, not a celebrity crush."

"Only so fleeting that I barely remember."

Stella nods. "I just wonder what it takes to go from that initial feeling of maybe just liking someone a little bit more than you would a friend, of noticing them more and in different ways, to actually acting on it, and betraying the person that you love." She runs a hand through her hair, baring even more of her breasts in the process. "I was obsessed with finding out after Toni told me she was leaving me for Sheena. When did it happen and why didn't I notice? What kind of a fool does that make me? My girlfriend and my best friend?" She fills her cheeks with air, then lets it escape. "It just goes to show how far I have my head up my own ass. Toni said as much at the time."

"If that was her defense, Toni was full of crap. She was probably trying to make herself feel better."

"The other day, I was wondering if she was going to see *Like No One Else* with Sheena, not knowing I was in it, only to see me kiss Faye Fleming on screen."

"Would you get a kick out of that?"

"Fuck, yeah."

"Was she a Lana Lynch fan?"

"Find me a lesbian who isn't," Stella says. "And who isn't into Fida big time."

"Fida?"

"Faye and Ida. Two massive A-listers getting together, making a lesbian movie, and coming out is still a big deal. I wish it wasn't. I wish it was just a trivial anecdote, but it's not. Every lesbian I know ships Fida because of what they've done for the community, although, and I actually talked about this with Faye on set one day, they are so privileged, and if not them, then who? Although Ida saw things very differently all those years she was in the closet."

"Times change, I guess." I'm sure Stella isn't waiting on my particular privileged opinion on any of this.

"I'm well aware of my own privilege, of course. Look at where I'm sitting. Look at who my mom is. And, according to my sister-in-law, I'm hot as hell on top of all of that."

Maybe it's the temperature of the water, but a flush rises from my core to my cheeks. "Don't put words in my mouth, Stella. I never actually said hot as hell."

"You didn't?" Stella grins at me. "That's how I remember it."

"That's not to say you're not." My gaze drifts to the swell of her breasts. The evening's taking a turn again, at least it is for me. But I want nothing more than this feeling to last well into the night, well into the days that follow, so that the first thing I think of when I wake up is not that I can't have children, that my husband isn't there with me to process that or to talk through different solutions or outcomes, that I'm alone and sad, and the only person who is really there for me, albeit through circumstance more than intent, is Stella. Who is drop-dead gorgeous and truly hot as hell and the best company I've had in ages. So what if the boundaries in my troubled brain are getting a little blurred? So what if I'm flirting with my sister-in-law? What does it even matter? At the moment, I don't feel as though I have anything more to lose. "You are Hollywood-movie-star-level attractive. Toni was a fool to let you go. Elena is so lucky that she gets to go on a blind date with you."

Stella lowers her body so only the top of her shoulders remain visible. "Are you okay?" She pauses. "Is it the wine in combination with the hot tub? Some people react funny to that."

"It's none of that."

She narrows her eyes as though trying to read in my face what on earth I'm playing at.

Under the water, I stretch out my legs. I hook my calf behind her ankle. I'm no longer thinking straight—I'm no longer thinking at all.

Stella cocks her head, huffs out a little air, but she doesn't say anything. She doesn't shut me down and it's enough for me to dip into the last ounce of courage lurking somewhere inside me. With our legs intertwined, I pull her close.

"Kate," Stella whispers. "What are—"

I don't let her finish. Instead, I touch my lips to hers. And the urge to do so hasn't been consuming me for days, nor have I developed a crush on Stella while I've been staying here. All I know is I want to kiss her. That I want to feel something so powerful, it blots out all the other feelings inside of me.

Before this kiss can go anywhere, Stella pushes herself away. "No. No. No," she keeps repeating. "Oh, no. No way." Quick as lightning, she pushes herself out of the hot tub and balances on the edge. "What the fuck, Kate?" She shakes her head. "I wasn't —I didn't—Just no."

"I'm sorry." *Oh shit.* One moment, one split second of not caring about anything else other than what I wanted at that moment, and I've gone and ruined everything again. I've pushed away the person who comforted me the most.

Stella covers her chest with her hands while looking around for a towel. It's on the other side of the hot tub. She gets up and, without saying anything, walks away. Dripping with water, she disappears inside the house.

CHAPTER 12
STELLA

I don't know what to do. I feel like a prisoner in my own home because of Kate's presence outside. What the hell was that? Were we flirting? I wasn't. I *wouldn't*. She's my brother's wife. I take a quick shower just to gather my thoughts and throw on as many layers of clothing as my body can handle. Is it because I took off my bikini top? I touch my fingertips to my lips where Kate kissed me. What the holy fuck? Why did she kiss me? Was there a vibe that I missed? Maybe a little one. The conversation was perhaps a bit more intimate, a bit more playful than before. I did serve her dinner by the pool. But I didn't mean anything by it. I was just trying to be a good sister-in-law, trying to take her mind off all the things that have been going wrong in her life.

I'm afraid to look out the back windows. I close the blinds. What the hell was she thinking? I pace through the living room. What time is it? Mom and Keanu might be back soon, or they might not. I don't know what Keanu's parents are like. They might all be getting on like a house on fire. Where the hell is Kevin when I need him—when his wife needs him the most?

Should I go out and talk to her? Clear the air before it gets too muddled? Maybe that's a good idea. Maybe we should put this behind us as quickly as possible so that we can pretend it never happened. I'm not a huge fan of denial because it always catches up with you, but sometimes, it's the only way. Kate and I are family. She's living in the pool house. I won't be able to ignore her.

I go out the back. There's a light on in the pool house. She's probably mortified, wondering what on earth came over her.

I softly knock on the door. "Kate. It's me. Can we talk?"

I hear footsteps. As soon as the door opens, Kate hides her face in her hands. "I'm so sorry," she mumbles. "You have no idea."

"It's okay."

"I don't know what came over me."

"Hey." I take her wrists and lower her hands. "It's fine. It's just one of those things. But it doesn't have to be a big thing. We can just pretend it didn't happen. It was nothing." Unless it wasn't, but either way, it can only be nothing.

"Okay," Kate whispers. "It was nothing. I promise you, Stella, it was nothing. It was a moment. It was—"

"Nothing. Good. I'm glad we agree."

"Don't tell Kev. Don't tell anyone, please."

"There's nothing to tell as far as I'm concerned."

"Thank you. So much. I feel terrible…" Kate pulls her robe tightly around her body before sinking into a chair. She lets her head fall against the back rest. "Oh, fuck. It's all just been such… shit. Look at me? I'm all alone in this wretched pool house, which is actually lovely, but that hardly makes a difference."

"I know things are bad right now." I crouch next to her. "But it won't be like this forever."

Kate swallows hard. She gives a terse nod. "Oh, fuck." She pushes the heels of her hands against her eyes. "You're the only one who makes me feel better," she says between sniffles. "I—" More tears, only interrupted by sharp intakes of breath.

"It's okay. Let it all out." I make sure the tap on the knee I give her is as chaste as possible. "Just let it out."

And she does. Kate cries and cries, perhaps expelling all the tears she has kept inside for way too long. I don't remember much from the time my dad died, but I do remember that, for the longest time, I couldn't cry. It took a nasty spat with Kevin, a physical brawl that started as something playful between siblings but spiraled into physical aggression, for me to finally find the tears that wouldn't come before.

I cried and cried, as Kate is doing now, and afterward, for a while, I felt a little better. As time went on, I kept on feeling better. Mom channeled all her grief into her work and kept getting bigger and bigger commissions. Kevin met Kate and got married. I worked on my dream of becoming an actor, perfecting my skills in the dark art of rejection and working on ways to pick myself up faster after each one—and there have been many.

So, despite what happened, or maybe because, I let Kate cry as long as she wants. Until my muscles cramp up and my legs start shaking. I sink onto the floor next to her, my hand on her knee, just so she remembers that I'm there, and I let her cry for all the things she's lost and all the things she will never have. For the dream she's had to let go of, for the life she always wanted but that's not on the cards for her. I let her forget about that kiss—if you can even call it that. Our lips barely touched before I put a stop to it. When you really think about it, we don't even have to pretend that it didn't happen, because it might as well have never taken place.

I find a tissue box on the cabinet behind me and hold it out for her. Kate pulls out tissue after tissue until there's a collection of crumpled white balls on the floor in front of us.

"Don't stay here tonight," I offer once Kate's cheeks look reasonably dry. "The guest room's always made up. Stay at the house. Maybe you won't feel so alone."

"Maybe." Kate's eyes fill with tears again as she looks at me. "You are so incredibly kind and considerate. You are—"

"I can easily go back to being the brat you always thought I was if you want me to," I joke, not knowing whether the timing is right for that. But some light relief is always welcome.

"I don't think you can. I don't think you were ever that person."

"Come on." I push myself up. "Do you need me to grab anything for you?"

"It's okay. Just give me a few minutes." Kate looks around the room as though she doesn't recognize any of her stuff.

"Take all the time you need." I head to the door. "I can talk to Kevin. Make him understand that you're not okay."

"I think Kevin knows that."

"Just let me know if there's anything I can do."

"You do so much already, Stella." With that she turns away from me and disappears into the bathroom.

———

Nathan has just offered me a pancake as Kate appears in the kitchen. "Morning, Kate," he says. "The more, the merrier."

"I understand you need your privacy," Mom says, "but that pool house is only good for a few nights. I'm glad you decided to stay at the house."

Kate and I exchange a glance. She joins me at the kitchen island, in the same spot where she sat looking at me last night.

"Thanks," I say to Nathan as he deposits a stack of pancakes in front of me.

"Have some fruit with that, darling," Mom says.

To them, this is just an ordinary Sunday morning.

"How was dinner?" Kate asks. Her voice is a bit raspy. Maybe she didn't get much sleep. Neither did I, for that matter.

"Great," Nathan says in his nonchalant way, as though he and Mom had dinner with friends instead of his parents.

"Harry and Hope are great," Mom says. "We'll be having them over to the house soon." She casts a loving glance at Nathan. Great. Their bond has been strengthened by this whole meeting-the-parents thing. "How were things here? No kitchen fires?"

Not in the kitchen, I think.

"Your daughter is an excellent cook," Kate says. "It was delicious. We had a great time."

"Good." If only Mom knew what really happened—even though, last night, we concluded that it didn't really happen.

Nathan's made more pancakes. Without asking, he puts a stack in front of Kate.

While from the outside, this could be seen as a perfectly lovely Sunday morning family tableau, it's anything but. My mother's boyfriend is still too young for me to fully accept. Kate still can't have children. My sister-in-law tried to kiss me in the hot tub last night and my brother's still flagrantly absent.

"I don't suppose Kev made an appearance?" Mom can't hide the tension in her voice.

Both Kate and I shake our heads.

"I'll be spending a lot of time with him this week. I'll try to break through whatever he's hiding behind." She fixes her gaze on me. "But first, my darling daughter." She's already beaming with pride as though I got the part. It's too much pressure, I want to shout. "Big day tomorrow."

I take a bite of pancake. Nathan's are better than Mom's, but now's not the time to tell her that. "Hell, yeah," I say, instead.

"Are you nervous?" Nathan asks while he cuts up fruit.

Mom stands next to him and presses her hips against him. I don't know how I'm ever going to get used to this. Probably by being exposed to it on a Sunday morning like this.

"Super nervous," I admit. "My agent keeps saying that the odds are very much stacked in my favor. The script is great. It's not one of those run-of-the-mill comedies, even though I wouldn't say no to one of those either. It's more like a dramedy, which are all the rage these days, and to work with Nora Levine…" It's as though my brain can't even go there. This show might be dubbed 'the new Nora Levine project', but it has two equal leads: Nora's part and the one I'm auditioning for.

"Do you need me to be here for you tomorrow night?" Nathan asks. "While your mom's away?" Is Keanu going to play daddy for me now?

"That's okay."

"When will you know if you get a callback?" Kate asks.

"It could be straightaway, or it could be later that day or even later that week. It all depends on a million things that are completely out of my control."

"I'll be here for you, Stella." Kate briefly touches her hand against my back. Before last night, it would have been a completely normal gesture between supportive sisters-in-law, but this morning, I could interpret it differently. It also turns out that pretending that half-kiss never happened is more difficult than expected. But I have to focus on my audition.

"Thanks for breakfast, darling." Mom kisses Keanu on the cheek right in front of me and it's as though both Kate and I flinch at the same time. "I'll be in my office for a few hours, preparing for this week."

Keanu pulls her close for a moment, then lets her go. On her way out of the kitchen, Mom gives my shoulder a quick squeeze.

"Can I talk with you for a minute, Stella?" Nathan asks as soon as Mom has left the room.

"Um, sure."

"Do you want me to take these outside?" Kate points to her half-eaten plate of pancakes.

"No, since you're staying here too, we should all chat." Nathan leans his elbows on the island. "I just want to say I'll be keeping a low profile while Mary's away. I know we're all still getting used to this new living sitch." This guy actually uses the word 'sitch' to refer to living with my mom. "But it's important

70

to me that you don't see me as some kind of intruder or anything like that. I'll give you all the space you need." The problem with Keanu is he's actually super sweet. It would be so much easier to hate him if he were an asshole, but he's the opposite. "I have an urgent job over at Burbank Studios. Some high-flying director has decided he needs all-new sets by the end of the week. You know how it is." He fixes his gaze on me. I wish I did know how it is, because that would mean I spend all my time on film sets. "But I also want you to know that I'm here if either one of you needs me."

"Thanks, Nathan." I don't really know what else to say.

"I appreciate that." Kate flashes him a warm smile. "I really do."

"Kev and I are putting in a new wall in your bedroom today, so..." He drinks from his coffee, then puts two bowls of cut-up fruit in front of us. "Eat this. It's good for you." Here we go with the dad-vibes again. He can be my mother's boyfriend all he wants, but he'll never be my stepdad.

"I'll stop by later," Kate says.

"I'm going to get ready. Enjoy, ladies."

"Thanks," Kate and I say in unison. We wait until he's out of the kitchen to exchange a glance.

"Fuck, this guy."

"He's like a dream. It's like Mary won the man lottery." Kate shakes her head as though she can't believe it. "Handsome, good with his hands, and not a hint of toxic masculinity about him."

"He does make a fluffy pancake." I reach for the bowl of fruit Nathan prepared for us. "And the man sure knows how to cut up a mango."

CHAPTER 13
KATE

I'm still mortified about what happened last night, but bantering with Stella about Nathan helps blow off steam. I don't know whether to address the whole thing again or to just forget about it the way we agreed to.

"What are you doing today?" I try to sound as nonchalant as possible.

"Trying to keep my nerves at bay," Stella says. Fruit bowl in hand, she swivels her stool toward me. "Do we, um, need to talk? Does anything else need to be said?"

It's easy enough to decide to ignore that kiss, but it's much harder to actually do. But what other option do we—or I —have?

I shake my head. "I'd just like to apologize one last time. I'm so sorry. I don't know what came over me. It was totally uncalled for, and I hope it doesn't change too much between us." Because I need you, I don't add.

"Time will pass, and we'll totally forget about it, but, um, tell me this, Kate." Stella slants toward me. "What tipped you over the edge? I've been *racking* my brain over it..." She waggles her eyebrows. "And I can only conclude that my boobs mesmerized you to the point that you could no longer resist kissing me."

We both burst out laughing, bringing my tense muscles some much-needed relief. This is why I need her. Because this is what she does. Because she is the opposite of the person I always believed she was: someone who takes herself so seriously, she only ever sees herself.

An idea pops into my head. Once our laughter has subsided, I say, "You know what I like to do when I need a distraction before meeting a big new client?"

"You only have one sister-in-law to inadvertently kiss in the hot tub, so I guess it's not that."

"Okay, fine, you can tease me about that for as long as you like, and definitely until after your audition." I give her a mock stern look.

"Thank you so much, Kate." She clasps her hands to her chest.

"What I like to do is watch rom-coms, maybe even some Faye Fleming classics, but"—I'm so excited, I drum my fingers on the countertop—"I think we should go see your movie again this afternoon. Think about it." I fix my gaze on Stella. It's as easy as that. Just a few jokes and we're back to where we were before. "You'll get to see yourself in action and be reminded how good you are. And to be perfectly honest, I'd love to see that movie again under more relaxed circumstances." And with Stella right next to me this time, so I can witness her reaction to seeing herself.

"But you already think I'm so self-absorbed. Are you sure I should go see a movie I'm in?" Stella grins. "It's a great idea, actually. We can stop by the house on the way to the theatre."

"Forget about that. Kev and Nathan can manage without us." I sure hope Kevin will show up tonight, seeing as he'll be away most of next week. "You'll need to wear a hat and sunglasses when we go in, otherwise you might get recognized."

"Recognized?" Stella brings the back of her hand to her forehead. "*Moi?*"

"Hasn't that happened to you before?"

"Only after I did that DivaCup commercial and it was all really awkward." She snickers. "I haven't been out much since this movie's been released. Maybe I should put that to the test soon." She ostentatiously taps a fingertip against her chin. "Come to think of it, the only obvious result of me being in that movie is that my sister-in-law tried to kiss me, so."

I roll my eyes, because I can. She's going to let me have it, make me suffer for what I did, which is fine with me. It beats agonizing over it in silence and solitude.

———

The movie theatre is packed and, instinctively, I lean toward Stella, away from the stranger on the other side of me. Stella suggested getting a love seat for just the two of us, but I figured she was joking again.

Her kissing scene is coming up and restless anticipation courses through me. Whenever Stella's character isn't on screen, I try to sneak a peek at her. She's totally focused on the movie. I hope my suggestion works out and she can glean a bit of extra confidence from seeing herself at her very best.

On screen, Lana and Cleo lean in. Their lips touch and it's as though I can feel Lana kissing Cleo, or Cleo kissing Lana— Stella kissing Faye, and I'm Faye. Of course, I am. Only, Stella doesn't pull back. The kiss deepens instead of ending before it even began. They open their lips to each other and I'm no longer sure it's Stella I'm jealous of for kissing Faye.

"This is quite awkward, actually," Stella whispers in my ear, pulling me from my reverie. "Please, rest assured that I don't have my head that far up my own ass that I actually enjoy seeing myself kiss someone on screen. It's not really my thing."

I can only grunt in response. Lana and Cleo are still kissing in the movie and the chemistry between them is palpable. When will this film be available for streaming, so I can watch it whenever I want? But no, because seeing Stella and Faye kiss is what started all of this and I'm beginning to see that, perhaps, I'm the selfish one. I wanted to see this again. I wanted to see Stella kiss another woman in the way she couldn't kiss me.

"Are you okay?" I ask. "Do you want to leave?"

"No way. Then I'll be the homophobic bigot who left after seeing two women kiss on screen."

Someone in the row behind us rightfully shushes us.

Stella whispers a quick apology, then holds a finger to her lips. Those damned pillowy, kissable lips. But there's hope for me yet. My husband might spend the night with me tonight and might make me feel like a wife again. Like someone who is loved beyond her biological propensity to carry a child. I should be so lucky.

When the movie ends, the audience claps. If only they knew one of the stars is among them. Stella doesn't put her hat and sunglasses back on for our exit. We've barely shuffled out of our row before someone spots her.

"Oh my god!" the girl shouts. "It's Cleo Palmer."

"The one and only," Stella jokes. "But don't ask me to sing you a song, although I might be able to swing a duet."

She acts as though this is how she has always left a movie theatre—as a down-to-earth star willing to banter with anyone.

Stella takes the obligatory selfies with a few moviegoers, then, once we're finally outside, she finds my gaze. "That was fun. Thanks, Kate."

"How about a selfie?" I feel like I, too, need something to commemorate this weekend by.

"Just pretend I'm Faye," Stella says as she throws her arm around my shoulders, as though last night is a distant memory that she might one day remember but not any time soon.

"No need for that." I hold up my phone and snap a picture

of us. "You're Stella Flack. And you're going to kill it tomorrow."

CHAPTER 14
STELLA

"How was it?" I've barely gotten out of my car—barely parked it—when Kate bounds toward me.

"Really great. I think I did well, but yeah, you never know. They might be looking for something else entirely." It's hard not to get caught up in Kate's enthusiasm.

"My gut says the part is yours." She puts a hand on her belly. "Did they say when you would hear?"

"If it's a callback, it should be later today. My agent will let me know." I was on the phone with Damian all the way home, talking him through every detail. The man has a lot of clients, many with way more star quality than me, yet he wants this for me so much, his voice uncharacteristically wavered when we spoke earlier. "And when I say callback, I actually mean a chemistry test with Nora Levine." The mere thought of it is enough to make me break into a sweat again.

Kate ushers me into the house. "Mary and Kev left about an hour ago. They couldn't wait any longer without risking missing their flight."

"Mom texted me earlier. She'll call me once they've arrived in Washington." I pause to take a breath. "How was Kev? Did you get to spend some time with him?"

Kate waves off my question. "We can talk about Kevin all week long. Tell me every last detail of your audition first. Who was there? What did they say? How hard did you kill it?"

"For big-time parts like this they don't make you sit in a dingy waiting room for hours with dozens of other women who are a million times prettier than you, so that was a plus. It was all quite swanky, and no one was rude or made me feel as though I was replaceable."

"God, when you put it like that…"

"You kind of get used to it. Grow a thick skin. You have to. If you don't, you're a mess after every audition and it's too hard." I blow out some air, letting some tension escape from my body —although I won't be able to fully relax until I've heard from Damian. "That being said, if I don't get at least a callback for this one, I will be a mess, and there will be many pieces to pick up." I eye the pool through the window. "I might go for a swim. Just to burn off this restless energy." I flash Kate a grin. It's too easy to mess with her now. "Don't worry, I'll wear a bathing suit."

"You don't have to." She doesn't even flinch. She's gotten used to it already. "Just do you. Do what you would do if I wasn't here."

"Do you know when Nathan will be home?"

Kate shakes her head. "Not sure. Late, I think."

"Mom didn't think of that when she asked him to move in. I like to swim topless, but that's a no-go now because he can come home any time."

"How about you take off all the clothes you want and I'll keep watch? I'll guard your phone, as well. Keep an ear out for that all-important call."

Butterflies do somersaults in my stomach. It's not just about getting the part. My whole life would change if I nabbed a job like this one. I'd have steady work for the first time ever. I'd get to act all the time. Basically, all my dreams would come true.

"I'm going to take you up on that, thank you very much."

"My pleasure." Kate holds out her hand and I give her my phone, checking for the umpteenth time that I didn't accidentally put it on silent mode. "Let me be your personal assistant."

"Oh, I forgot." I take my phone back and scroll to the text I received earlier.

Break a leg, Stella. You've got this. Faye xo

"Oh my god." Kate's eyes go wide. "She remembered!"

"You did repeat it several times toward the end of the night."

"That might be so, but it got you this." Kate eyes my phone longingly, as though Faye herself is hidden in it somewhere. Then my phone lights up in my hand, its ring loud and piercing.

"Oh, fuck. This is it." Damian's name and picture flash brightly. "Oh, fuck. I'm actually afraid to pick up."

"Answer it. It's going to be good news. I know it."

I have no choice. I'm not letting this call go to voicemail.

"Hi, Damian." I make zero effort to sound casual.

"Stella. Hi." In the brief amount of time it takes to say those two words, the sound of his voice conveys all I need to know. "I'm so sorry. I was just on a long call with the casting director. They loved you. I swear to you, they really did, just not for this part. I'm really sorry."

"Oh," is all I can say, deflation washing over me. I've been looking forward to this day for weeks and this is what it amounts to—again. "Okay."

"But look, you're on the radar of many executives right now. These are not hollow words, Stella. This is not hollow agent speak. I'm going to get you the part you deserve. I promise you."

I have no more energy left to react. I put it all into gearing up for this audition.

"I know this is hard and you're very disappointed right now, Stella. You should be. It's their loss for not picking you. It really is. But this is only the beginning for you. We've been here before, you and me. And every time we get knocked down, we get up, and we make it a little farther. That's how it works. But don't forget, you're in a big movie and you're a scene stealer. Stella the-scene-stealer, that's what I'm gonna call you from now on."

"I'm going to go now, Damian. Thanks."

"Call me any time. You hear me?"

I hang up and even though I don't want to be the kind of person who cries for not getting a callback, my eyes fill with tears.

"Oh, Stella." Kate opens her arms, and I let myself fall into her embrace.

"Fuck. Fuck. Fuck," I say into her hair.

"Assholes," Kate replies. "Ignorant, stupid, blind assholes." She closes her arms around me and holds me tightly. "I can't believe these people."

I try to steady myself by taking a few more breaths, but every cell of my body is saturated with deep, paralyzing disappointment. Damian can talk sweet to me all he wants, and maybe some of the things he said are true, but once again, I'm not where I want to be. Once again, the bitter sting of rejection burrows its way through my body. I can't pretend this isn't happening. The worst part is there's absolutely nothing I can do about it.

"Hey." Nathan walks in. "Oh, no. Stella."

"She didn't get it," Kate says, while patting my hair.

"I'm so sorry," he says. What's he doing home already, anyway? Didn't he have some wood to cut for a set I'll never be on. In moments like these, just after another rejection call, it feels like I'll never set foot in a movie studio again.

I free myself from Kate's embrace.

"I figured I'd come home to either celebrate or commiserate with you." Nathan gives my upper arm an awkward squeeze.

"I thought you had an urgent job," Kate says.

"What's work when your family needs you." His voice is so matter-of-fact, it's almost like we're actually related.

"Can you tell that to my husband, please?" Kate snipes.

Nathan doesn't know what to say to that. Somehow, I appreciate that he's here. That I'm not alone. That I do have family here to catch the biggest force of the blow with.

"I guess we only have one option." Nathan walks to the liquor cabinet. "Shots." He produces a pristine bottle of tequila. "I've been saving this one for just the right occasion and this is it."

Not in a million years can I imagine Nathan doing this when Mom's here. I glance at Kate, find her gaze.

"Might as well," she says. "None of us are pregnant, anyway."

———

Too many tequila shots later, it doesn't hurt so much anymore, and I just have to ask.

Nathan has set himself up as our impromptu bartender at the patio kitchen, supplying us with fresh shots, lemon, salt, and a few snacks to soak up some of the alcohol.

"Can I ask you something, barkeep?" My words still come out pretty decently, I think, but I'm the worst judge of that. But I only have one purpose tonight: to get as blindly drunk as possible in order to forget that my big Hollywood break isn't happening yet. Kate and Nathan have had as many shots as I have. They're definitely not letting me drink alone, which I appreciate—even though I'm the only one who doesn't have to work tomorrow.

"Another?" Nathan's already reaching for the bottle.

"Nah. Let's take a break."

"I might go for a dip in the pool," Kate says.

"No, Kate, don't." I put my hand on her knee as though that can stop her.

"Why not?"

"You're wasted, and we don't have a lifeguard." I'm dead serious.

They both chuckle. "We don't need a lifeguard."

"Listen to me, Nathan." I am slurring my words now. "I know my mom is, like, exceptional and all that, but a guy like you, all buff and handsome and good with his hands like that… You could get any girl you wanted. Why are you with my mom?"

"Because Mary is the most amazing woman I've ever met," is all he says. I guess he doesn't have to explain himself to me. I just thought he might, given that we've had a few.

"Don't you want kids?" Kate chimes in.

Nathan juts out his bottom lip and shakes his head. "Nope."

"I'm never going to call you stepdad, okay? As long as we're clear on that." I try to look him in the eye, but my gaze keeps skittering away.

"Good, because I'm nobody's stepdad." He pours us another shot.

"What are you then?" I eagerly take the shot. "Apart from the guy getting me drunk."

"I'm your extraordinary mother's boyfriend." He slides the plate with lemon wedges in my direction. "And I'm here for you if you need me."

"Did Mom tell you to check up on me tonight? Is that why you're home?"

He shakes his head. "I just figured I should be here tonight. That's all."

"I'm sorry if I haven't always been so kind to you, Ke—"

Kate bumps her shoulder into mine.

"It's okay. I know you call me Keanu behind my back. I take it as nothing but a compliment."

"You should," Kate says. She's probably as wasted as I am.

We knock back our shots regardless.

"I'm going to have to call it a night. I need to get an early start tomorrow." Nathan slides the bottle our way. "But feel free to finish this."

———

"Look at me." I gaze at the bottle of tequila, which is almost empty. We certainly took Nathan up on his offer of emptying his fine bottle of booze. "I'm such a cliché." Although the sharp edges of everything I feel have been blunted, the many shots we've knocked back have caused me to descend deeper into a well of self-pity. "Totally wasted in my mother's backyard after another failed audition."

"I'm going to get us some water. Maybe some Advil as well." Kate looks at me but doesn't get up. "Maybe then this won't hurt so much in the morning."

"Call in sick." I chuckle, even though it's not really funny. "At least I don't have to do that because I don't even have a job and it doesn't look like I'll have one anytime soon."

"Fuck Hollywood. Fuck whoever decides who gets a part or not." Kate slides off the barstool she's been perched on for hours. She loses her balance and I somehow manage to grab hold of her arm. Maybe two unbalanced people can make for one balanced one. "I know you deserved that part, Stella. I know it in my heart of hearts."

I hold on to her wrist a little longer because she looks so unsteady—and I could use someone to hold on to as well.

"You know how I feel about you." Kate's eyes are watery as she continues. "I think you should get every part all the time." It's one of those nights when there are no more filters between what we think and what we say. It will help us laugh it all off in the morning, after which I can begin to heal.

"No impromptu lunches at Nora Levine's house for me. Sorry I won't get to take you there or invite you to the set."

"Have you texted Faye back?"

I shake my head. "I'm not going to text Faye Fleming that I

didn't get the part." It would have been so wonderful to be able to text Faye the good news. To have had a super-excited chat with my mother on the phone about the future and the good things it suddenly had in store for me. To have opened a bottle of champagne with Kate and Nathan to celebrate. To not feel like such a waste of space because some casting director decided my face is not right for the role.

"Okay. I get that." Kate slides her fingers down my wrist and takes my hand in hers. It feels good to have another human touch me so lovingly, so caringly. "But you know I think the world of you, Stella. I really do."

Really? I want to ask. Because I'm in two minds about quitting the acting biz. Of throwing in the towel after almost a decade of trying.

"I'll take another hug," I say, instead.

"You got it." Kate bridges the distance between us and gently folds her arms around me, as though I might break, as though my physical body has become as fragile as my state of mind.

I hold on to her, biting back a few more tears. As I inhale sharply to stave off another onslaught, the flowery smell of her hair hits me. She smells fantastic. Her body feels so good against mine, as though I belong in her arms. This is the best shoulder I've had to cry on for ages.

I take another breath, just to inhale more of her scent. My hand scoots up her back, to her magnificently soft hair. It's like silk gliding through my fingers. I could stay in Kate's embrace forever, or at least until I feel a bit better about myself. She doesn't move, which works out well for me.

She runs her fingertips over my back. Goose bumps break out on my arms. *Oh.*

"It's okay," Kate whispers. "It's all going to be okay."

I just lost a part I really wanted. But Kate has lost so much more. I wish I could say the same to her.

"I think the world of you too," I whisper.

"What was that?" Kate's fingertips travel from my shoulders along my upper arms.

Why is she making me feel like this? That's not a question my inebriated brain can answer. Not tonight.

I lift my gaze to her face, look her in the eyes. "I think the world of you too," I repeat. "I think you are absolutely amazing." I swallow hard. An impulse stirs in my gut. The last of my inhibitions was lowered five shots ago. All I want right now is to feel better about myself. To unclasp that cold, tight fist that settled in my belly when Damian called. Maybe Kate has the key to that. Maybe I'm seeing everything all wrong. I'm certain of nothing, yet I pull her to me again. I don't bury my face in her hair this time. My hands slide to her cheeks, my fingertips roam across her jawline.

Her gaze meets mine, but I can't read what hides in it. All I can do at this point is pull her so close that our lips almost touch.

"Fuck, Stella," she whispers, and as she does, our lips do touch. I feel how hers move against mine as she speaks the words. Her hands sneak up the back of my neck. Her breath is hot on me. We can still go back. We can laugh it off and pretend —again—that nothing happened. Nothing really has happened. Until now. Something's definitely happening now.

I slant forward. My lips land fully on hers. Is this a kiss or just two people standing very closely together? I tilt my head slightly, changing the angle of our lips on each other.

Kate dips forward. Her lips are soft and full on mine.

There's no more doubt about it.

This is a kiss.

CHAPTER 15
KATE

I open my lips to Stella. The tip of her tongue slips into my mouth. I respond in kind. Our tongues touch. Our lips open wider. Her hands are in my hair. I pull her close. Something awakens deep inside me. I can't name it, but I don't have to. I feel it. I push myself closer to her. Tighten the grip of my hands on the back of her head. I want her to know that I want this. That I want to kiss her—and maybe more.

But she pulls back. Gone is the divine sensation of her lips on mine.

"Um." She rakes her front teeth over her bottom lip, making her look even more sexy. "What's happening?" She scoffs, then shakes her head.

"Stella." I try to focus on her eyes. "Maybe what's happening is exactly what's s'posed to happen." I probably don't make any sense. No one would after downing a bottle of tequila.

"I'm drunk. I don't know what I'm doing any more," Stella says on a sigh. Instead of pushing me away, she pulls me closer, though. "Still. I want nothing more than to kiss you again. Is that okay?"

"Very okay." Because, in this moment, my blood saturated

with alcohol, all my defenses down, with nothing more to lose than I already have, I want nothing more than what Stella has just suggested. My lips ache for her touch.

She pulls me to her. She's still sitting on a barstool, her legs wide, me between them. I tower over her, look down upon her, on her lovely, sad face, into her gorgeous, teary eyes.

"Let's deal with tomorrow tomorrow," I say, then kiss her again. A real kiss this time, full of intention and desire. I cup her cheeks in my palms and kiss her again and again. Her tongue darts in and out of my mouth and it's so soft, her skin is so smooth against mine, her hands are so gentle on my back, already, I can't get enough of this.

This wouldn't be happening if we weren't drunk, but we are —and boy, do we have reason to be. I'm not a big believer in self-medicating, in drowning my feelings with booze, but tonight, that's how the cards have been dealt. And I'll be damned if it doesn't feel good to be able to do this, to act on my secret desire for Stella. To have her reciprocate. To have her kiss me back over and over, her lips, as well as her hands, growing more eager.

"We should probably go inside," I say, when we break for a decent breath of air.

Stella nods. "Let's go to the pool house." She slides off her stool and we tiptoe down the garden like two teenagers who've come home after curfew.

"I'll get us some wat—" I start to say, but Stella comes for me as soon as we've closed the door behind us. Maybe if there's too much room for thought, some space to actually think about this, she'd have to flee and never set foot in this pool house again.

I sink into her soft, lush embrace. Before I know it, Stella is hoisting up my top.

"Oh, fuck. I want you so much, Kate." She comes for me again, unlocking the clasp of my bra.

90

I find her ear. "I want you too," I whisper, so there's no mistaking my own intentions.

Stella's lips travel down my neck, to my collarbone. She lets my bra slide down my arms, then takes a step back.

"You're so fucking gorgeous," she says, her breath so ragged with desire, I can only believe what she says.

She swallows hard again, then resumes the path she was kissing down earlier. Her lips close around my nipple and it feels like someone has flipped a switch that's been stuck in the same position for years. When you're trying to have a baby, sex becomes something almost entirely functional; there's always the other purpose lurking at the back of your brain. Is it going to happen this time? What can I do to increase our chances of getting pregnant? This is the opposite of that. This is sex for the sake of sex—the only purpose of our actions to make each other and ourselves feel good.

She clamps my nipple between her teeth, and I feel it all the way in my core. Stella's playful and gentle, although, when she looks up at me, she seems dead serious. Like my pleasure is a big deal to her. I'm happy to open myself up to her like this tonight. I'm happy to be whoever she needs me to be. Because ever since I saw her kiss Faye Fleming, I've wanted to be on the receiving end of her kiss. I didn't know I wanted *this*. Probably because I wasn't allowed to. Because I know damn well this shouldn't be happening, but the fact it is makes it all the more delicious. It makes me feel Stella's hands on me a thousand times more, makes me crave her tongue on my skin with a desire I could never have imagined.

Her finger hooks under the waistband of my jeans. Oh fuck. We're getting down to business. I'm letting the booze blur the very last of my boundaries. I'm not too far gone to actually realize that.

I should take a moment to check in with myself, to ask myself if I really want this, but Stella's finger dips lower and then there's no longer any need to ask myself anything at all.

My body speaks for me. My desire does all the talking. I'll deal with whatever comes next tomorrow.

Stella unbuttons my jeans and slides them down my legs. I've already seen her naked from the waist up, and I can't wait to see that again. We fumble with her clothes until her upper body is naked and her near-perfect breasts are bared. As a designer, and as a human most of all, I know that perfection doesn't exist, but if there was an award for most near-perfect breasts in the universe, of all the breasts I've ever seen, Stella would win all the prizes.

Reverently, I cup her breast in my palm and close my lips around her nipple. Between my legs, I go wet like a river. The more I let my tongue skate along Stella's nipple, the more my own arousal grows. To feel her perfectly shaped breasts in my hands, with those tiny, tight knots of nipples that beg to be taken into my mouth, is one of the more divine sensations I've experienced in my life.

Stella moans low in her throat and the guttural, raw sound of her desire connects with the desire deep within me. I'm more alive than I've been in many months, years even. It's because I'm drunk and there's nothing standing in the way, most definitely not rational thought, and I need this so much. I need to feel untethered from common sense for a while, just for tonight, in Stella's arms. I need to let out all the darkness that comes with such smashed hope, and I haven't found a better way yet. Maybe this is the way. An extraordinary communal experience with someone I care deeply about. Because Stella and I are both victims of our current circumstances, of life throwing us a curveball, and we found each other, as improbable as it might be, in that wasteland where grief and disappointment fester, in the hinterland of what our dreams used to be—mine of babies; hers of her big break. And it's not for me to compare my dreams to Stella's, to attach a weight to them. Because the Stella I saw after her agent's call today was every bit as devastated as I felt after each phone call from our fertility specialist. Sometimes, two people can only find each other at the point where they've hit rock bottom, if only for a day, or an hour—or a night.

We tumble onto the bed wearing only our panties. I still can't get enough of Stella's breasts, but her lips are competing for my attention, because Stella's kisses are equally stunning. Her lips are immeasurably soft as they find mine, again and again. Her knee presses between my legs, and she now kisses a path away from my mouth. When she reaches my ear, she tugs at my lobe for an instant, then says, "I want to make you come so badly." It's more a moan, a begged plea, than a statement. As though it's the only thing that can make her feel whole again. I'm more than happy to oblige.

"Please," I say. "Yes." Of course I say yes. I've been saying yes to Stella since I moved into this pool house. To different parts of her. From casual conversation, to going to the premiere, to walking into Faye Fleming's house. To her cooking me dinner. To jumping into the hot tub with her. To taking her to the movies just so she could feel better about herself. To opening myself up to her the way I haven't been able to do to anyone else in so long. I genuinely believed we were becoming the best of friends, but maybe we're becoming something else instead.

Stella's fingertips dip inside my panties.

Instinctively, I spread my legs for her.

I watch her face as her fingers dive deeper, as they meet my wetness. Stella's eyes widen, as though she's astounded at my arousal for her. I guess I don't have to repeat how much I want her—how much I want her to make me come.

"You're so hot," she says, as a fingertip slides through my wetness. To my disappointment, her finger retreats. But it's only so that she can lower my panties. She glides them slowly along my legs, until I'm totally naked on the bed in front of her.

My clit pulses like a second heart. My breath is ragged in my chest. Stella kisses me again while her fingertips draw patterns on my inner thigh. Until her finger is back where I want it, stealing through my wetness, taking my arousal to ever higher levels. She circles my clit, and a groan escapes my throat. She catches it with her mouth and kisses me deeply while her finger keeps circling.

When she breaks from our kiss, she looks me in the eye and, as she does, slides a finger inside me.

It's so intimate and reckless and unexpected but extraordinary all at the same time. Stella's finger is inside me. It shouldn't be. It shouldn't be anywhere near me. What's most astounding, perhaps even terrifying, is how much I want her finger there. How much I want her to move it inside me. How much I want her.

Stella moves her finger. Long, slow strokes drive inside me. I try to keep my gaze on her, but all I want to do is pull her near, close my eyes, and lose myself completely in this sensation. She spreads me wider. Adds another finger—adding to my plea-sure. She fucks me. It's the only way I can think of it. Stella's fucking me. And I'm loving every single second of it.

Her fingers are delicate and subtle inside me, igniting brand-new sensations within me. She amps my pleasure all the way up to that divine edge, that point of no return, when the climax starts announcing itself deep inside my muscles. But then, she stops thrusting.

"I need more of you," she whispers into my hair, then with-draws her fingers altogether. She shuffles to the foot of the bed, then takes position between my legs. Next thing I know, her lips are where her finger was earlier. Her tongue flicks along my clit and every synapse in my brain catches fire. Stella's tongue on me there makes me forget all about what her fingers were doing to me earlier.

I delve my hands into her hair as my muscles tense up, as the arousal in my body is amped up and up. Stella licks me, and I might be beyond tipsy, yet I know I will never forget the moment her tongue touched down between my legs. As it lapped against my wetness and made me feel like this, like anything is still possible in my life. That no matter how hard the past years have been, the best is yet to come. I can be whomever I want to be—including a mother.

Right now, though, I'm a woman coming at another woman's tongue. A wave of pleasure rolls through me, followed instantly by another. I clasp my thighs against the sides of Stella's head, wanting to keep her tethered to me there forever, because this sensation, this ultra-satisfying climax, is not something I want to let go of any time soon.

"Are you okay?" Stella asks from between my legs.

"Yes," I gasp, then set her free and pull her up so she can be close to me again, but in another way.

"I don't, um, really know what to say." Stella chews on her bottom lip. "I—"

"Don't say anything." Tonight, we don't need words. I press my lips to hers and kiss her again.

CHAPTER 16
STELLA

Even though I'm still drunk, my brain is not a blissful, conflict-free zone. I know I shouldn't be here, that we shouldn't be doing this. I'm curious to get Kate's take on this, although I'm glad that she has chosen to kiss my doubts away instead. For now, it's so much easier.

She kisses me more, deeper, longer. She kisses me until everything else melts away again. Until we're just two bodies writhing together, coaxing pleasure from each other. Kate pushes me onto my back. She lies on top of me, one leg pressed between mine. I'm so wet for her, for this. For us. And there is a tiny space, a mere fraction of a second, where I'm aware I can still make the decision to stop this, to not let it go any further. That not getting a callback is not an excuse for doing this. But that's where the million shots come into play. That's where the self-pity and utter selfishness bubble to the surface. The moment passes, and I'm all Kate's again. I'm aroused but also curious. As far as I know, although I certainly don't know everything about Kate, she has never been in bed with a woman. If it's another one of my many flaws that I find that arousing, then tack it on to the long list, because utterly flawed I am. Although strangely, right now, I feel anything but.

The Hollywood execs that I wanted to like me might not, but it's obvious Kate does. She was here for me when I fell apart. She's going there with me. We're in this together.

She kisses and licks her way to my breasts, where she stops. She studies my chest as though it's the centerpiece of the Louvre or something—like it's the Mona Lisa of chests and all she can do is stare at it in wonder.

She runs a fingertip from my collarbone over the middle of my breast to my nipple. She does it so slowly, so teasingly, that I gasp for air. To have such self-control in this moment. I can only be in awe of that. Light as a feather, she circles my nipple with her fingertip.

"You're so beautiful, Stella," she whispers as she brushes her hair away from her face with her other hand. She lowers her mouth to my nipple and flicks her tongue against it. First-time gentleness is so ridiculously arousing. To experience all the delights of her discovery along with her, makes lust flare up in my belly even more.

But if this is Kate's first time, she quickly gets over that hesitation. She sucks my nipple into her mouth, her tongue caressing it. Her hand skates down, her fingertips edging along the soaked panel of my panties. The last barrier to what I want to happen. I can't wait to slide them along my legs and toss them into the darkness of the room. To remove the last hurdle, because while I can't completely shut off the part of my brain that knows this is wrong, other parts of me are very much in charge. In Hollywood, I may remain a nobody for a while longer, maybe forever—one of many who tried and tried but didn't have that extra bit of luck to propel them into the big time—but here, I'm *someone*. I'm the one who made Kate come with my tongue. I'm the one who's been making her feel better about herself. I've been a good friend to her, and our sudden closeness just happened, because of circumstance and proximity, and this is the result. If it's unnatural, it most certainly doesn't feel that way right now.

Kate can't seem to get enough of my breasts. She cups them in her hands and plays with my nipples as if there's no tomorrow—probably because there isn't. This is it. But, as she said earlier, let's deal with tomorrow tomorrow.

I run my fingers through her impossibly soft hair. It seems to pull her from the trance my breasts have put her in. She gazes up at me, paints on an unexpected devilish grin—that does nothing to quench my desire for her—then kisses her way down. She plants kiss after delicious kiss on my lower belly, along the waistband of my panties, on my inner thighs when she spreads my legs.

I can't believe this is happening. What does this make me? No, I can't think about that. This is the result of pure chemistry. Of the alcohol in my blood doing what it always does. Taking away my common sense. Erasing any sign of good judgment, of being sensible. And Kate is so hot and kind and, argh, her tongue skates along the panel of my panties now. I want to push them down so badly but I also want to let her do this at her own pace. I don't want to rush her or push her into anything she doesn't want to do. But she wants this. She said so herself.

She hooks a fingertip underneath my panties, exposing me to the air. A groan escapes me. I'm so hot for her. I'm so ready to erase the last painful memories of this wretched day—and I'm going to need Kate's tongue to help me with that. Because when I left the audition, I had the gut feeling that I had done well, that things had gone my way. That this might really be it. I wasn't so cocky as to think I'd bagged the part—ultimately, that was always going to be out of my control—but I was confident in my performance. It left me with a premonition that fate was on my side. But I was wrong, and that hurts.

Finally, Kate slides my underwear off my legs. I spread for her. She gazes at me there. I might be pretty far gone, but I'm still aware enough to check in with her. For many reasons, this may be too much for her—a bridge too far. What we're doing might be wrong in so many ways, but at least we're doing it together. We're both in it one hundred percent. Before anything else happens, I need to know if that's still the case.

"Kate," I whisper. "Are you okay? Don't feel as if you have to—"

"Oh fuck, Stella." Her gaze finds mine. "I want to so much. I want you."

The lust in my flesh skyrockets. My clit pulses wildly. To have her say these words to me while my legs are spread wide for her is one of the most arousing moments of my life.

Kate crawls over me and maneuvers herself between my legs. The throbbing in my clit ignites into the next level. I have trouble catching my breath. My body's on fire, waiting for her to do something about it. Is this just the effect of pent-up lust mixed with too much booze? This insane way in which I want her? This isn't just any woman. This is Kate, whom I've known for a decade. This isn't a stranger I picked up in a bar—which isn't my thing, anyway. This is someone I care deeply about. That must be it. No matter how you look at this, it's a mess, and the only way out of that mess, out of everything coursing through me right now, is for Kate to give me the climax of climaxes. The orgasm that's going to make things right again.

Kate folds at the waist, bows toward me, her hair fanning out over my belly, and then her tongue is on my clit. Instantly, I lose my mind completely, because I feel it all. Everything I'm not supposed to feel blends in with everything I do feel. All the conflict, all the disappointment, all the love, and all the shame. It makes for a powerful cocktail that enflames the lust raging in my bones, as though all my poor clit ever wanted was for Kate to lick it the way she's doing now. But I swear that the thought of this never before crossed my mind, not before tonight. Yet, if that's the case, why does this suddenly feel so right? Like only Kate's tongue can take me there from now on. Like right here, between my legs, in this bed with me, is where she belongs. Like her place in my life is not what I thought it was. Like she belongs with me and not with my—

Kate sucks my clit between her lips and I'm coming already. I'm so revved up, so ready to go, so turned on that her lips on me for only a few moments is all I need.

Maybe I love her in entirely different ways than I ever thought I could or should. Maybe I'll hate myself forever for allowing myself to feel like this, like something divine is traveling through me at high speed, like butterflies are dancing underneath my skin, like a great wrong is finally being righted, but damn it, I haven't felt like this in a very long time.

I screw my eyes shut because it's all a bit much. This climax is not some magical reset button. It's the opposite. The day I've had comes crashing down on me again, but then there's Kate—again—gathering me in her arms.

"Are you okay?" she asks, with such obvious kindness in her voice, while she wraps her arms around me and pushes her warm body against mine. Maybe this is what I need most of all. For someone to hug me like she's hugging me right now. Some intimate skin-on-skin contact. Although I already got so much more than that.

My chin bumps against her shoulder as I nod. "I'm fine," I whisper, because in that moment, in her arms, I am.

CHAPTER 17
KATE

It's still dark when I wake up. The air around me is stale. I'm hot. I throw off the covers. My hand touches something as I do. I turn to my left, the too sudden movement igniting a painful throb at the base of my skull. *Oh no.* All of last night's events come flooding back, because my hand just bumped into Stella's hip. Stella, who is sleeping in my bed in her mother's pool house. Oh, fuck. Another arrow of pain burrows its way through my skull. Instant punishment. As good as it all felt last night, that's how awful, how unseemly, how utterly horrible it is this morning.

My mouth is dry. I reach for the glass of water I usually keep by my bed, but it's not there. I've been sleeping at the house and most of my stuff is in the guest room. There are bottles of water in the fridge and it's all I can think of right now. Water. A shower. Some miracle to make last night not have happened.

I try to be careful as I get out of bed because I don't want to wake Stella. I don't want to have that conversation now, deep in the throes of a horrible hangover. I need some more sleep first, and a strong painkiller—possibly something to erase my memory.

I down a bottle of water and open another. My cosmetic bag

with medication isn't here either. Nothing's here anymore. There's only Stella in the bed, breathing gently, seemingly oblivious, with the covers thrown off her chest.

Despite being bone tired, I can't possibly get back into bed with her. I can't willingly lie down next to her again. What the hell did we do? I can only hope Nathan didn't see anything, that he was wiped out by the shots he had with us and fell into a deep sleep. Because no one can ever know about this.

There's a couch at the other end of the room. I sink into that, but it's too short for me to find a comfortable position. Maybe I should just wake Stella and ask her to go to her room. I don't know what to do. I was going to become a mother, not the kind of person who does this. Maybe I should go to Iowa for a while, stay with my parents. Go back to my roots. Find myself again. Because the person in bed with Stella last night, that wasn't me. That person couldn't be further removed from who I really am.

But before I can do anything, before I can take action to undo what happened, I'm going to have to sit here and suffer for a few hours. I can't face going to the house, although if I were to bump into Nathan I could make it sound entirely plausible that Stella and I were so wasted we didn't make it to our bedrooms and crashed in the pool house. No one would question a simple explanation like that. Maybe I should just go, but my limbs are so heavy, and my head hurts so much, I don't want to move a muscle. I'm so tired, my eyes drift shut and, despite my uncomfortable position, I nod off.

When I wake up again, my neck as sore as my head, it's light outside, and Stella's gone. I check my watch. I have some time before work. But I have no choice, I need to go to the house. Nathan said he had an early start so he might already—mercifully—be gone. Hopefully, Stella decided to sleep it off in her room. I need liters of coffee and some strong pain meds. I need to shower for a very long time. And at some point, I'm going to have to talk to Stella. But I can only imagine that she'll want to keep this our secret as much as I do.

I make my way over to the house. All evidence of our transgression has been removed from the garden. No dirty glasses. No empty bottle of tequila. Did Nathan clean up before he left for work? Or did Stella? The kitchen's empty but someone's made coffee. I walk to the front of the house to check if Nathan's car is gone. It is. I allow myself a small sigh of relief. He probably made coffee before he left.

I tiptoe into the kitchen, my robe pulled tightly around me, and pour myself a cup of coffee. The mere thought of breakfast repulses me. I only consider calling in sick to work for a brief moment, because what else am I going to do? Hang out here all day? Or maybe I should go by the house, remind myself of what I have, of what my life was like and what it can become again. Maybe start thinking of the new decor, of the wallpaper I want for our bedroom and the type of faucets we should have in our bathroom. In between the avalanche of shame washing over me, memories of last night flare up. Like a part of my brain, maybe my subconscious, wants me to know how much I enjoyed that. But joy should not be part of this equation. I did something despicable. Unforgivable. Disrespectful. Shame is the only possible response to that.

I hear stumbling upstairs. Stella must be up. Here we go. I brace myself for a conversation I don't want to have because the need for it should simply not exist.

"Oh, great," Stella says. "Coffee. Thank goodness." She walks right past me, her gaze focused on the coffee maker. "We sure knocked them back, didn't we?"

"Stella." I can barely say her name.

She pours herself a cup of coffee, then walks to the other end of the kitchen island, as far away from me as possible.

"I've thought about it and, um," she says. "I don't think we should talk about it or acknowledge it or make it more real than it was. We were drunk and we made a mistake. That's all I have to say about it."

Denial. That's one way to go about it.

"Did you see Nathan? Did he say anything?"

Stella shakes her head. "I heard him leave a while ago. I left the pool house around six. You were asleep in the couch, and I didn't want to wake you."

Relieved that Nathan is probably none the wiser about what happened after he went to bed, I push a little. "We can't just ignore what happened."

"Maybe not, but… what else are we going to do? Relish in how fucking good it felt? I don't think so, Kate." Her tone is snappy, even though she just alluded to how it good it felt. Maybe one is the result of the other.

"I don't know." I wrap my fingers around the mug I'm holding tightly, as though it can offer me some much-needed support. The coffee's helping a little with that queasy feeling in my gut, but my head's still pounding, and last night still happened. "You're right. We were totally off our faces. Like, um, yeah… It was a huge mistake."

"No doubt." Stella puts her mug down and rests her forehead on her fingers. "Nathan and his fucking tequila."

We can always blame Nathan. He'll never know, which makes him an even easier scapegoat.

"So… that's it? We'll never talk about it ever again?"

Stella looks up. She tries to find my gaze, but she can't look at me. I understand. I find it hard to look at her as well. "We can't even think about it anymore. We can't undo it, but we sure as hell can pretend it didn't happen."

Like we did with that kiss, I think. Am I the one who made this all happen? Did I instigate it? Should I move to a hotel? Book an Airbnb for a few weeks? But that would only raise suspicion.

"How do you see things evolving… on a practical level," I ask. "I'm going to be here for a while. Is that going to be a problem?"

"Pretending it didn't happen doesn't equal erasing you from my life, Kate." Stella pushes out an exasperated sigh. "You're married to my brother." Her voice breaks a little. "Oh, fuck. What the fuck did we do?"

Even though I find it hard to look at her, I have to stop myself from walking over to her and taking her into my arms. But I can't tell her everything's going to be just fine. Although everything will just have to find a way to be just that.

"No more tequila," I say.

Stella scoffs. She gazes into her mug. "We should probably stay out of each other's way for a bit. As much as we can. I want you to feel comfortable here."

"I'm not going to live here forever, and I want you to be at ease in your own home. I'll move back into the pool house, at least." I'm not sure I can ever sleep in that bed again, though— at the scene of our crime.

"You don't have to do that. Let's just keep things how they were, but just… not spend as much time together. You do your thing. I'll do mine. We'll take some time to process. I was heart-broken last night, but I'll get over that soon enough."

"Okay." I nod my agreement. "I need to get ready for work."

"How's the head?"

"I hope Skye isn't bringing Thiago to the office today."

"Lots of water, and there should be Advil in the guest bath-room." Stella shoots me a lopsided grin. "I'll be out tonight. Dinner at Hayley's."

"I'll see you when I see you then." I walk to the door but even though I know I need to forget about what happened as quickly as possible, and various pain signals in my body are acute reminders of what we did last night, part of me finds it hard to walk away from Stella. Because she has been my only source of real comfort. She's the only one who has been able to make me feel better about myself. Yet, I walk away from her because I have no other choice.

CHAPTER 18
STELLA

I sit at the kitchen island for a long time after Kate has gone up to shower—to wash away the last remnants of our scandalous behavior. I meant everything I just said to her. We were drunk and vulnerable and hurting. We can plead extenuating circumstances. We need to forget it happened as soon as possible. All of that is indisputably true. But what's also true is that it did happen. And underneath the first layer of reasons why, if I scratch that surface only a little bit, another layer hides. But those reasons should remain hidden. I know that much. And I'm sure it was an entirely different experience for Kate than it was for me. In our own ways, we both needed to be held, to be loved, and it turned physical. But when push comes to shove, I'm single and gay. Kate is straight and married to my brother.

I can't imagine what might happen if he ever finds out. I don't want to be responsible for breaking my brother's heart, and tearing our family apart in the process. Hence, I stop scratching at the surface, and I bury whatever it is I might feel for Kate somewhere deep inside myself, where it will wither and die.

She's setting me up on a blind date. Maybe this Elena will blow my socks off. Maybe I'll feel that spark that probably

HARPER BLISS

doesn't even exist—although, if anything, last night was a brutal reminder that it does—with her.

My phone buzzes with a text message from Nathan.

Hope you're ok. That bottle was nearly empty this morning. Drink plenty of fluids. See you tonight.

Fuck you, Nathan, and your fucking bottle of tequila. But what happened isn't Nathan's fault. He didn't push Kate into my arms. The only thing I can hope for is that he didn't see anything. We started kissing in the garden and, you never know, he might have just been looking out of the window at that exact point in time. It's unlikely, but that doesn't mean it can't have happened—look at all the other things that happened last night. I text him back to obtain just a sliver of peace of mind—not that I'm entitled to that, although I'm not a catholic and I don't believe we should suffer too much for our sins.

Ouch! Hope we didn't keep you awake.

My heart races as I wait for him to reply. If he did see something, we're in big trouble. I don't know him well enough to predict his reaction. He texts back a few seconds later.

I was out like a light. Shall I pick up dinner on my way home tonight?

Relief washes over me. Thank goodness. It can remain our secret. Nathan and I text back and forth a bit more and I inform him I won't be home for dinner, and I don't know what Kate is up to. What will she do? Just her and Nathan here tonight without Mom as a buffer. Maybe she'll want to be out of the house as well. Maybe she'll talk to a friend—speaking of, we didn't discuss if talking to our best friends about this is something we can do. Or whether this is the sort of thing that no other living soul can ever possibly know about. I suspect the latter. I'm not an expert at keeping secrets—that was more Toni's specialty. I can't believe I've stooped to her level. Because I might be single, but Kevin is my brother, my only sibling, the guy who went out of his way to look out for me after our father died.

I decide I don't even need to ask Kate. I will take what happened between us to my grave and no one will ever know about it except the two of us. I'm not telling anyone. Time will do its thing, like it did after Toni and I broke up, and I will forget. Maybe I'll go to another audition and maybe I'll get that amazing part one day. Maybe I should call my agent for a meeting, to come up with a new strategy to finally land me something decent. I played Faye Fleming's age-inappropriate lover in a Hollywood blockbuster, for crying out loud. Doesn't that count for anything in this town? I'm convinced that if I'd gotten the part in Nora Levine's new show, I would never have ended up in bed with my sister-in-law.

"I'm going to work." Kate pops into the kitchen. She looks like a different person. Her wet hair's been pulled into a ponytail, and I don't know what magic she applied, but she almost looks fresh-faced—maybe we can use some of that magic to erase last night.

"Just so you know, Nathan didn't see anything. We were just texting, and he was out like a light, apparently."

"Thank fuck," Kate says on a sigh of relief.

"You should let him know if you'll be here for dinner tonight."

"Oh. Okay. Sure." She shuffles her weight around as though she's going to say something else, but doesn't. Then she disappears. I wait to get up until I've heard her car pull out of the driveway. To breathe. To try and feel like myself again and no longer like the person who slept with her sister-in-law. It's as though, now that I'm alone in the house, and I can finally take that breath, after holding it for way too long, I can allow some of the memories we made last night to come back to me. My hangover might be vicious, but it's not merciful; it doesn't include a blackout or even a hint of memory loss. I remember everything in perfect detail. I remember how Kate told me she wanted me. How I checked in with her, and she, again, said how much she wanted me. I also remember how she kissed me in the hot tub last Saturday night. It's hard to forget, even more so because I have to. The lust that bloomed in my chest when she traced her fingertip over my nipple. That very first moment our lips touched in what was almost but not quite a kiss, until it was. Until we opened our lips and so much more to each other.

I make a mental note to have that long overdue chat with my brother and tell him that he needs to be there for his wife. If not, he might very well lose her. Not to me, of course, but—

Thank goodness my train of thought is interrupted by Damian calling.

"Just checking in with my favorite client. Did you get some sleep?" he asks.

If only he knew what I got instead of sleep. "They haven't called you back to say they made the biggest mistake of their lives, have they?"

"Not yet, but it's early days." Damian plays along. "Can I take you to lunch? We can talk about the future instead of rehashing the past."

"I'd love that," I say to him, and also a little bit to myself.

CHAPTER 19
KATE

"Here you go, sweetie." Skye brings me another coffee. "I've said it before and I'll say it again. You should take the rest of the day off. Laze around by Mary's pool. You're already staying in the pool house, so you might as well."

The thought of the pool house, of doing anything at all by Mary's pool, makes me feel queasy again. I shake my head. I don't want to go to the house and the truth is I have nowhere else to go. I don't have a home anymore—not for a while, anyway. I don't have a place to retreat to, somewhere I can hide out until everything blows over. It sounded perfectly reasonable when Kevin suggested we stay at his mother's for a while. Mary's house is huge and she's often away. But I hadn't taken Stella's presence into account. How silly of me to ignore her like that, but that, too, is entirely logical because it's basically what I've been doing since I met her. Until now.

"What's the point of being your own boss if you can't take a sickie when you're hungover?" Skye's probably fed up with having to watch my tired, defeated face all day long.

"I have no house," I say, sounding very sorry for myself.

"You're hardly homeless. You know what I would give to stay at Mary Flack's house even for one night?"

I wish I could swap places with Skye. She can take my room at Mary's, or the pool house, and I'll stay with Roland and the kids. Not tonight, though. Even though the painkillers are doing their job, everything about me still feels tender, like an exposed nerve that might cause me the greatest possible pain at the slightest wrong move.

"You're very welcome to stay. She and Kev are out of town until Thursday and there's plenty of room."

Skye chews the inside of her cheek. She probably doesn't want to say to me, in the sorry state I'm in, that she has to go home after work and be a mother.

"I might take you up on that," she says, but I know she won't. Roland's a stay-at-home dad and come seven o'clock, he's in dire need of a break. "How's the house coming along?"

"Far from finished."

"Maybe you should just hire some guys and get it done. I know Kevin wants to do all the work himself as some sort of menial therapy, but is that even realistic?"

I shake my head to both her questions. We can't hire help, and it's not realistic for Kevin to do all that work by himself in a timely fashion. Maybe I should put my foot down. I have a say in this marriage, too, and we need to talk.

"What can I do to help?" Skye is one of the sweetest people I know. I should have turned to her instead of Stella. Oh, Stella. I'll never get that image of her breasts out of my head. I hope that, come tomorrow, I'll be stronger. So much for dealing with things the day after they happen. Who knows how many days it will take me to get over one single night?

"Bring me a new head." *And a new brain that makes better decisions.*

"The best I can do is more coffee and painkillers." She puts a hand on my shoulder. "What did Nathan put in those shots, anyway? Have you seen him? Did he look as worse for wear as you do?"

"Trust me, it wasn't Nathan."

"All that because Spoiled Stella didn't get the part." Skye has only met Stella in person briefly a few times. Most of what she knows about her is through me, and I haven't always been the kindest about Kevin's supposedly spoiled little sister.

"Don't call her that, please."

"Are we no longer doing that? You should have said."

There's so much I haven't said—yet so much I've done that can never be spoken of.

"She's actually not that spoiled, and you should have seen her when she got home. She was devastated, and Mary wasn't there so…"

"You and Nathan drank yourselves silly with her. I get it."

"It's not like I was suddenly over everything going on in my life. Sometimes, you need to blow off some steam, especially when your husband's ignoring you under the guise of reno-vating your house." As if that's an excuse for anything.

"You're preaching to the choir, sister. This weekend, we're dumping all the kids with my parents, and Roland and I are off to Napa, thank you very much."

That's the first I've heard of this trip, or have I not been listening? It can't be that impromptu because it's impossible to be spontaneous when you have four children.

"That sounds like heaven."

"And don't worry. The tubes are tied. We won't be making another bambino, you can be sure of that." Skye freezes for an instant, then says, "Sorry. Was that insensitive?"

"No. It's fine. You don't have to watch what you say around me. You have four kids, and I don't have any. That's just how it is. Please, say whatever you want. Just be the Skye you've always been. That's the person I need around me."

"That person's not doing much for your complexion. Are you sure this is just a hangover?"

I looked presentable enough in the mirror before I left the house this morning, but it was just a temporary mask, a facade that is quickly crumbling.

"I wish it were just a hangover," I blurt out, because I can't hold it in any longer. "Things… happened. Things that should never have happened."

"What do you mean?" Skye sits down. "What sort of things?"

I shake my head. "Things that can never be said out loud."

"You can talk to me about anything, sweetie."

"Not about this." I press my fingers against my throbbing temples. I need to confess. I need to tell someone in the hope it will make me feel a teeny tiny bit better, that sharing this burden of my own making with my best friend will make it a fraction more bearable. "I—I cheated on Kevin."

I don't know how Skye reacts because I can't look at her. I can only focus on the stain on my desk that has been there forever.

"But… who with? You were with Nathan and Stella all night, weren't you?" She gasps. "Oh my god. Don't tell me you slept with Nathan."

I shake my head again.

"It wouldn't be entirely inconceivable. He's very gorgeous and all that, but I thought he was totally in love with Mary?" Skye's mind can't even go there. She can't even fathom that I would have slept with Stella.

"Not with Nathan." I screw my eyes shut, hoping that it will all go away.

"Did you go out after? Where did you go?"

"Skye." I huff out some air. "I slept with Stella." There. I said it. It's out there. I don't feel any better, on the contrary, I feel worse.

"What? No. You're kidding, right?" She attempts a chuckle but it's a very hesitant one. Of course she doesn't want this to be true. I wish it weren't true. "Kate, please, tell me that you're pulling some sick joke on me."

"I'm not." I swallow hard, but I can't fight the tears any longer. "I slept with Kevin's sister."

"Oh, no." Shocked silence fills the room. "That's bad," Skye says after a few moments. "That's really bad, Kate."

"I know. It's the absolute worst."

"But, I mean, you were both totally wasted and depressed and… was it, like, a comfort sort of thing?"

I nod because that's exactly what it was.

"Hot damn. No wonder you look like death warmed up."

"There's no excuse for what we did, despite having our reasons. It doesn't even matter why we did it. The only thing that matters is that it happened and it really shouldn't have and now we have to find a way to deal with that."

"Never, ever tell Kevin, sweetie." Skye's voice is high-pitched. "I'm all for moderate honesty. It works wonders in a marriage."

"I wouldn't dream of telling Kevin. You're the only one who knows, and you can't tell anyone. Not even Roland."

"Don't worry. I wasn't thinking about telling Roland. Aside from the fact that Stella's Kevin's sister, well, she's also a woman, obviously. What's up with that?"

"I don't know." I finally cast a quick glance at Skye's face. "I don't know anything anymore." I puff up my cheeks and let the air out slowly. "Or no, that's not true. I very much know what I want. I want my husband back. I want my house back. And I want a god damn baby." Tears rain down my cheeks. "Instead, I ended up with this mess."

Skye gets up and curls an arm around my shoulders. "You can have all those things, honey. You can make it happen."

I wipe some wetness from my cheeks, but the waterworks keep churning. "That's the thing. I'm really not sure that I can."

CHAPTER 20
STELLA

I t's after eleven when I get home, but I hear voices in the garden. Both Nathan and Kate are still up. Thank god there isn't any tequila to be seen, only a few empty bottles of water and the remnants of a meal.

"Hey, Stella. I take it you've eaten?" Nathan, obviously none the wiser, asks.

"Yeah." I send a lightning quick smile in Kate's direction. "I think I'll go straight to bed. I just wanted to say goodnight."

"Sure. Sleep it off." His phone starts buzzing. "Oh, sorry. That'll be Mary," he says matter-of-factly. He picks up and walks deeper into the garden.

"Hey." Kate looks like the exact depiction of how I feel inside. Deflated. Confused. Ashamed. Exhausted. "Are you okay?"

"I had lunch with my agent today, so that's something." My gaze is drawn to the barstool I sat on last night, when it all kicked off.

"Um." Kate looks behind her, perhaps to check that Nathan is far enough away. "Look, I'm sorry, but I told Skye. I had to tell someone. I was going to pieces."

"You told someone?" Inadvertently, I sink into the chair next to her. "Fuck."

"It's okay. I trust Skye with my life. She's not going to tell anyone."

"I sure hope not." I understand the impulse to talk about it, to process with another person. Earlier, over dinner with Hayley, there were a few times when I considered telling her, but, in my view, it's too unseemly. Too out there. Simply too unbelievable. Kate must feel differently about that. But we're very different people.

"I thought you should know," Kate says.

"Okay." Before I can think of anything else to say, Nathan's walking back toward us.

"I'll tell her," he says into his phone before he ends the conversation. "Your mom's going to call you in—" Before he can finish his sentence, my phone buzzes. My mother is the last person I want to talk to right now, but I pick up anyway.

"Hi, darling. How are you holding up?"

I need to be away from Kate in order to talk to my mom. I walk away from the table but everywhere, there are reminders of what we did. The hot tub. The pool house.

Mom tells me about their pitch and then the conversation goes in a way that I can only ask, "How's Kevin?"

"Honestly, I think he's happy to be away for a few days. This is his design we're pitching and if we get it, at least he'll be able to take pride in that. How's Kate?"

The question was to be expected, yet it still knocks me sideways, as though my mother asked me how my night with Kate was instead of inquiring about Kate's general well-being. "I think she misses Kevin," I say, even though, right now, I don't know how Kate is doing. As far as I can tell, she's a mess, just like me.

"Before we come home, I'm going to talk to him about the house and how it's getting out of hand." Mom sighs. "He's only gone and redrawn the plan again. He needs someone to tell him to stop."

I tell her about lunch with Damian while I wonder whether Nathan told her about the bottle of tequila he shared with us, but I don't want to talk about that. We ring off and I linger by the pool for a while. My gaze drifts to the pool house and my brain, not for the first time today, is flooded by what happened there last night. Wrong as it might have been, it was also amazing. I take a deep breath. Today was difficult, what with the cold hard glare of the morning light illuminating what happened in the darkness of the night, but tomorrow is another day, and it can only be better than this one.

When I get back to the patio, Nathan's cleaning up.

"I'm not allowed to help," Kate says.

"Maybe we'll get used to having him around." I hesitate to sit again.

"He's obviously trying to get into our good books."

"We should probably do something for him."

"I think the best we can do for him is accept him," Kate says. "How's Mary?"

"Good. Have you spoken to Kev?"

"Briefly before dinner, but... I couldn't. I couldn't talk to him. It's—" She puts a hand on her belly. "It made me feel sick to my stomach." She blinks slowly. "I can't believe I did that to him, Stella. I never once thought I'd be that kind of person, and look at me now."

Poor Kate. All she wanted was to feel better and now she feels infinitely worse.

"You're not just that person. There's context."

Nathan walks back out so we fall silent.

"I'm going to hit the hay. Be good, ladies." He shoots us a wink—as though he knows something, although that's just paranoia on my side—and disappears inside the house.

"I should go to bed, too. I'm beat." Kate suppresses a yawn.

121

HARPER BLISS

I turn to her. She has purple-tinged circles underneath her eyes and looks as though she could fall asleep just sitting here. "I know what we did is bad on so many levels, but cut yourself some slack, okay? We're humans and humans fuck up. We do things we shouldn't, and we hurt the people we love. It's all part of the deal."

"That's very philosophical of you."

"I just hate seeing you like this."

"I need a good night's sleep. That's all," Kate says.

"Go." I nod at the house. "Sleep."

"If only things could be different tomorrow."

"Things might not be, but you'll be. You'll have slept well, and you'll be able to see things differently."

"Thanks, Stella." Her gaze lingers on me. She shoots me something between a lazy grin and a crooked smile. "Sleep well." Before she walks inside, she gives my shoulder a quick squeeze, and I feel it in every fiber of my being.

CHAPTER 21
KATE

"I fucking killed it, babe," Kevin says while undoing the top button of his shirt. "Nailed it like a fucking carpenter. Ha, a bit like Nathan would, actually." He pulls me close. It's like a different man got off that plane from Washington. "How was it being here alone with him? Without Mom around?"

"He's such a sweetheart, really." Because I can't look my husband in the eye, I put my head against his chest.

"A sweetheart, huh?" My head bops up and down as he chuckles.

"Just a really good guy."

"And Stella agrees with that?" The mention of Stella's name makes me want to disappear altogether.

"I believe she does."

"Maybe Mom and I should go away more often." He kisses my forehead.

"It sure seems to have done *you* the world of good." I wriggle myself free from his embrace.

"I never needed a win so badly. To feel like I'm actually still good at something."

"Congratulations, babe."

"Hey." He pulls me to him again. "I know I've been absent

and a bit of an asshole in general, but that's going to change. I promise."

"What about the house?" I need to get out of here—I need to leave the scene of our crime.

"I can't just undo what I've already done. I need to see it through and that's going to take the time it takes. Do you mind staying here a while longer?"

"Your family's lovely and Nathan's cool, but we need a place of our own, Kev. Can't we rent somewhere short-term?"

"Really?" He eyes me curiously. "Is it Stella? Did she do something? Was she rude to you?"

"It's not your family. It's us. How can we regain any sort of closeness while living here? How can we make the decisions we need to make about our future, about what we want, without the necessary privacy?"

Kevin knits his eyebrows together. "Are you sure nothing happened while we were away?" He sits down on the foot of the bed. "I noticed some tension between you and Stella earlier. I have a sixth sense when it comes to her. I often know some-thing's up before she even suspects."

"Why aren't you listening to me? I said it has nothing to do with your family. We—you and I—need a space of our own."

"And we will have the most magnificent one, I promise." He juts out his bottom lip and pulls his face into a sad puppy dog impression.

"Kev, I'm serious. I can't stay here much longer."

"Okay. Sure. If you want somewhere more private, we can look for something short-term. But I honestly thought it would be better for you to stay here than be home alone all the time."

"I don't intend to be home alone all the time. Either you get some people to help you or you take time off work so you can finish what you started."

"But isn't the whole point of renting a place of our own that I can take my time while you don't have to stay here?" He scratches his five-o-clock shadow.

Argh. Men. Why can't he just get it? But, of course, he doesn't get it. Although, some parts of it, he really should get.

"You know what?" Frustration fizzes inside me. "Maybe I should just rent one of the apartments above the office. You stay here with your precious family, or sleep at the house, and I'll stay there."

"Babe, what are you talking about?"

I don't know. This is unbearable. Being here with him, in Mary's house, is excruciating. Having this conversation, which I've wanted to have for so long, is suddenly so devastating, the only way I see it continuing is by me blowing the whole thing up—because the guilt I'm carrying for what I did with Stella is too suffocating.

"I am deeply unhappy, Kev. Nothing is going the way I want it to go and I can't just go and knock some walls down in a house and rebuild them to make myself feel better. I have to deal with my shit and it very much feels like I have to deal with it on my own, because you're never here, and certainly not when I need you most." *When I'm kissing your sister in the hot tub. When I do unspeakable things with her in the pool house.*

"I get it. I do, but that doesn't mean we have to live apart."

"At least then I wouldn't be waiting for you to get home."

"I told you. Things are going to be different from now on." He rises and walks toward me, arms spread out. "Let's get a place of our own for a while. Anything you want, it's yours."

Apart from the things I really want, I think. I let him fold his arms around me. Even though I'm standing very close to him, I've rarely felt so separate from my husband. Because of what I've done and the shame it stirs in me, added to all that came before and the distance that had already been created between us.

For the first time since I met him, for the first time since our fertility journey crashed and burned, I consider that maybe Kevin and I are not meant to be together forever. This lovely, talented, gorgeous man that I married. He certainly deserves better than me.

"I'll start looking tomorrow." I'm well acquainted with the LA rental market. Either we'll have to pay inflated Airbnb prices for a decent short-term rental or live somewhere I wouldn't wish on my worst enemy. And all the while, we could be living in Mary Flack's fabulous mansion with too many rooms. I know it sounds ludicrous, but how can I stay here, with Stella lurking behind every corner?

"Whatever you want, babe." Kevin kisses the crown of my head. "It's so good to see you." He tightens his embrace, but that's not a place I can comfortably stay either. Being alone in this room with him is already so nerve-racking, as though I might betray myself any second, and he'll be able to read it off my face. I can't stay in this room and I can't escape it. It's the perfect analogy of how I feel inside. Physically as well as mentally, there's nowhere for me to go. Because of my actions, I'm stuck in this purgatory of my own making.

I shuffle out of his embrace again.

"I need some air."

"Sure." His eyes are heavy lidded. "I need some sleep. God, I need to sleep for about a week."

"Sleep in tomorrow. Mary will understand."

"You know what?" He flops onto the bed. "I think she would. Nathan has had a calming effect on her. She's more chill now. And I did land us a huge project." He scrunches up his lips. "Pity about Stella not getting that part she wanted so much. How was she? Crushed?"

I can only nod.

"I heard some whispers about too much booze," he says.

"That's right." I paint on the worst kind of smile you can give your spouse: a fake one. "Which is why I barely remember anything." *If only*.

"It would have been nice for the family to celebrate together."

"Yeah." I head to the door. "I'm just going outside for a bit."

"I'll be asleep when you return." He blows me a kiss. "Love you, babe."

"Love you too," I say, as I walk away from him. Even when we got the worst news, I never experienced that gut-wrenching feeling of not being able to stay in the same room as my husband, my partner in crime, the man who knows everything about me.

Guilt coursing through me, I skulk through the hallways of Mary's house, hoping everyone has gone to bed. I make out voices in the garden. Stella and Mary are still up. Mary has her arm around her daughter's shoulders. She's probably comforting her. Once a mommy's girl, always a mommy's girl. Maybe I should take that trip to Iowa now, but Skye and I have a big project starting next week—a B-lister who just crossed over onto the A-list and wants to upgrade the inside of their house according to their new status.

I look at Stella and Mary through the kitchen windows and I can't stop a tear from rolling down my cheek again, because something inside me, maybe my deepest, truest intuition, is telling me that this family will never be the same again—and it's all because of me.

CHAPTER 22
STELLA

I t's almost eleven and I'm still in bed. I'm about to text my trainer to cancel this afternoon's session because I simply can't be bothered to work on my body today, when my phone rings. It's Damian. Maybe he has an audition for me or, who knows, maybe Faye Fleming worked her magic and I've been requested to promote 'our' movie, although it doesn't really feel like our movie at all. Cleo and Lana might still be together, but in the span of Lana's long life, Cleo has only been recent history, and the biopic is mostly about everything that came before she met Cleo. But still, you never know.

"Morning, sunshine," I say, trying to sound much more upbeat than I feel.

"Morning? It's almost lunch time, Stella. Anyway, never mind, I have huge news."

I sit up in bed and throw the covers off. When I haven't just been to an audition, a call from my agent is always a hopeful experience.

"Apparently," he pauses. "Nora Levine didn't vibe with any of the actors that were selected for the callback and she knew the person who played Cleo Palmer in *Like No One Else* had also auditioned. She's a huge fan of both The Lady Kings and The Other Women. Anyway—"

My pulse is picking up speed. I jump out of bed.

"Nora Levine wants to meet you for a chemistry test. She asked for you specifically. She loved you in *Like No One Else* and she was appalled that you hadn't been requested for callbacks."

"No fucking way." Tears of pure joy well in my eyes.

"Are you available this afternoon?"

"Yes. Of course." Even if I had the busiest calendar in the universe, I'd clear it for a callback with Nora Levine.

"Okay. Great. I'm going to send you all the details as soon as we hang up. Do you need a pep talk along with that? Do we need to meet for lunch? Anything you need, Stella. I'm here."

"No, I'll be fine." Hot damn. I won't just be meeting Nora Levine this afternoon, I'll be acting alongside her. "I'm ready. Although I can't really prepare to have chemistry with another person."

"Sure you can. Just think of the latest object of your affection," Damian says. It's hard to tell whether he's being serious or not.

"The character I'm auditioning for doesn't have a romantic relationship with Nora's character." At least not in the portions of the script I got to read.

"Not yet, but you never know these days. These things can go in a different direction at any time."

"What are you saying?"

"Nothing. Nothing at all." Is my agent just as hyped about this as I am? It would be a big win for him too. "Just be your fabulous self, Stella, and ignore everything I've just said."

"I'll try." We end the conversation and I pinch myself. Nora Levine asked for me specifically—for the actor who played Cleo Palmer. I'll be fucking damned.

Before I do anything else, I call my mom to give her the good news. I message Hayley next. Then, I need to stop myself from texting Kate. I want to share this news with her so badly, but all the rules have changed, and it's no longer appropriate.

After I've showered and decided what to wear, it's as though my hands get the better of me, and I text Kate without considering any consequences because this is huge news and she's been there for me every step of the way. She simply needs to know. I've barely sent the text, when she calls.

"Oh my god, Stella," she yells into my ear. She must be operating on pure instinct, from that place where we were so in tune with each other before everything changed, and it feels so good to bask in her enthusiasm. "I can't believe this. Or no, I can actually believe it and it's so amazing. You're going to knock Nora Levine's socks off. There's no other way." This is the Kate from before that wretched bottle of tequila—the woman who turned out to be irresistible to me. I think about what Damian said earlier—about conjuring the object of my affection when I run lines with Nora. I shouldn't even admit this to myself, but beyond what's logical and acceptable, I know that person for me right now is Kate. "Thanks for letting me know, Stella. I'm so, so happy for you. I'll be rooting for you all afternoon."

"I'll let you know how it goes."

"Please, do." The enthusiasm in Kate's voice has made way for something else. The guilt has probably caught up with her again. "Um, yeah—"

"Everything cool?" I ask.

"I'd like to talk to you about something. Later. Tonight, after your callback. Or whenever suits you."

"Okay. Sure. I'll probably be out tonight, though."

"Is Mary making a big fuss?"

"She wanted to change her plans with Nathan and take me to some fancy restaurant, but I told her not to. It's amazing that I get to do this, especially after Monday's disappointment, but let's not act as though I've got the part already. This is nowhere near in the bag yet." Nerves are starting to get the better of me.

And the clock is ticking. I need to be downtown in an hour. I'd best get going.

"That sounds like Mary, but you're right. One step at a time. We will all be there with you in spirit, rooting for you."

"Thanks. I have to go now. See you later."

Maybe this is how it will be from now on. Maybe, bar a few hiccups, Kate and I can move past this and become friends again, or at the very least friendly in-laws. But I have no time to think about all that now. I have Nora Levine to impress.

———

"It was the best audition of my life." I'm still so pumped when I get home, I can't stop talking. "Nora and I just… clicked. At least when we were acting. When she's not, she's a bit… distant, I guess. I mean, she tries, but you can tell it doesn't come that natural to her, all that small talk and chitchat while waiting. But yeah, it felt really great, Mom." I'm blabbering to my mother in her room while she's getting ready to go out to dinner with Nathan and some friends. "Then again, I also felt great last time, so I don't really have anything to go on." Nora might have liked me and having her attached to the project clearly gives her sway, but she's not the boss. She's not the one who makes the ultimate decision. Just like always, my fate is in the hands of some faceless Hollywood producer.

"God, what are we going to do with you this weekend, darling?"

"I don't know. I'll be totally nuts by Monday."

"Maybe you should go to the cabin? Go hiking all day to wear out your body. Be in nature."

"Go to Topanga by myself while I wait for news? I don't think so."

"I'd go with you." She stops applying makeup. "But the Lippmanns will never forgive me if I don't go to their fiftieth anniversary bash. It's been planned forever. I'm sorry, darling.

Why don't you and Kate go? She looks like she could use the distraction."

Instinctively, I scoff. "No. I'm not going away this weekend." And certainly not with Kate. "I'm going out tonight." Who knows, maybe I'll find that elusive spark again. Kate and I have barely talked and she hasn't said anything about that possible blind date—it's all a bit too awkward now, I suppose.

"Ready?" Nathan appears in the door frame. He gives me a thumbs-up again. "Take it as a sign of my faith in you that I won't be replacing that bottle of tequila any time soon. This time around, you won't have to drown your sorrows because there won't be any to drown."

"Where are you going tonight?" Mom turns to me, ignoring Nathan's comment about our bender. It's possible that she doesn't approve—that it reminds her a little too much that her boyfriend is so much younger than her.

"I'm meeting Hayley and the gang later."

"Okay, darling." Because she doesn't want to ruin her lipstick, my mother doesn't press her lips all the way to my cheek as she kisses me goodbye.

———

"Are you dreaming of Nora Levine already?" Hayley says. "I had expected you to be ecstatic, but you're more absentminded than anything."

"I can't possibly dream of Nora Levine." The more I drink, the more my mind is drifting to somewhere it's not allowed to. "It's too soon and I don't want to jinx it. It may still never happen. This is Hollywood. Anything's possible, but also not."

Hayley nods. She's been through the many downs and the occasional up of my career throughout the years. She knows how soul-crushing it can be.

"You can still dream of Faye Fleming, though," Melissa,

Hayley's still-quite-new girlfriend, says. "We've been to see that movie twice already."

"We have to go see it together, Stella," Hayley says. "How come we haven't done that yet?"

I shrug. I was too busy seeing the movie with Kate and… "Let's go this weekend." Although, as the night progresses, the prospect of a weekend out of town, away from the ever-presence of showbiz that is hard to escape in this city, is starting to appeal to me. Maybe I should ask Hayley and Melissa to go with me. That could be fun.

"Oh, we can't this weekend," Melissa says. "My parents are coming to town. I'm formally introducing them to Hayley."

"Oh my god. That's great."

"I need you on standby in case I have to make an impromptu escape," Hayley jokes.

"I might go to Topanga, actually. Just… get away from everything for a few days."

"You'll go stir crazy out there on your own," Hayley says.

Not as stir crazy as waiting at the house with only Kate as company most of the time. "I'll see. I'll sleep on it."

"But first." Melissa holds up her glass. "We drink to it."

And that we do, although, in the back of my mind, all throughout the evening, I can't help but wonder what Kate wants to talk to me about.

CHAPTER 23
KATE

Mary's house is completely empty when I arrive home from drinks with a client. Kevin called me earlier to say —surprise, surprise—he's sleeping at our house so he would be fully prepared for tomorrow, when Nathan's coming over to help him again. He made it sound as though this was a good thing—as though he was granting me my wish of not doing everything by himself. While I'm sure Nathan's a great help, it's not what I meant. But part of me is happy that he's not here tonight. That it's just me.

I sink into one of the chairs by the pool and my eye is drawn to the pool house. Unlike what I said to Kevin, I haven't started looking at rentals yet and, right now, I'm glad I haven't. To have this gorgeous place to myself is a luxury. And maybe I shouldn't run away from what I'm facing. Maybe Stella and I should learn to deal with what we did sooner rather than later. It has already become easier, although I haven't seen much of her since.

When I received her text this morning, I had to call. I had to hear her voice, had to share some of her happiness. She messaged me again after the audition to tell me it went better than she could have hoped for and that we could talk tomorrow. As soon as I read it, I wanted to call her again, hear her voice, ride that wave with her, but I stopped myself, because I have to draw the line somewhere.

I venture into the kitchen, which is all glossy marble and swanky cabinets, and compare it to what we could get in a short-term rental, shallow as that may be. It wouldn't matter to Kevin because he lives on take-out dinners these days, he's worse than his sister when it comes to that. My thoughts seem to have a way of always circling back to Stella. But I have to accept that it might be like that for a while. That it's okay. That time will pass and Kevin will finish our house and then I'll finally get to work my decorating magic. We'll move back in and make the decisions we can't yet make now. Our life together can be wonderful again. I have to believe that although I don't have much to hold onto.

I open the fridge to find something to eat but nothing excites me. I might as well order take-out myself. I flip through the offerings on my phone and order sushi from a place that comes highly recommended by Stella.

Stella. Stella. Stella. Maybe it isn't a good idea to stay here after all. Yes, I like nice things and all the luxuries Mary's house has to offer, but I also like my privacy, although it's not privacy I'm after as much as peace of mind. Stella lives here so everything makes me think of her. Her jacket in the hallway. Her car in the driveway. Even ordering food. Not to mention the tornado of memories in my head.

The truth is I have no clue what to do. How could I possibly know? I've never been in a situation like this before. Clearly, I can't trust my gut either. Stella's the one who's been cheated on before. Maybe I should ask her opinion, but that doesn't strike me as the best idea either.

I go back outside to wait for the food to arrive, trying my utmost not to think of Stella while I do.

———

"You ordered sushi, milady." I nearly jump out of my chair. I've been keeping an ear out for the doorbell but, instead, Stella walks into the garden carrying a paper bag. "Sorry. I didn't mean to scare you. The delivery guy arrived at the same time as I did." She grins at me. "Don't worry, I tipped him generously."

"Thanks." I take the bag from her, even though a constricting feeling in my stomach has instantly killed my appetite. "You're home early."

"Yeah. Hayley and Melissa left early because of a thing tomorrow and I figured I'd head home as well." She shoots me a smile. "You said you wanted to talk, and I might go away for the weekend, so."

"Oh." I go inside to fetch some cutlery and we both end up at the kitchen island.

"We can talk now, if you want," Stella says.

"Sure. Have you eaten? Do you want some of this?" Without waiting for her reply, I distribute the rolls onto two separate plates and push one in her direction. "Congratulations again on getting that callback, by the way. How was Nora Levine?"

"Kate." Stella reaches out her arm, but then thinks better off it. "Take a breath. Eat some food. Everything will be okay." A sparkle lights up in her eyes. "But Nora is amazing. She has this really intense energy. Unlike anything I've encountered before. This laser-like focus. Or maybe she was trying to psych me out, or testing me in some way, I don't know. Although a touch distant, she was very nice and not full of herself at all."

"Sounds like a wonderful potential co-worker."

Stella pushes some air through her nostrils. "We'll see." She accepts the chopsticks I hand her and dips a roll in the soy sauce. "What did you want to talk about?"

"Did you say you're going away this weekend?" It's as though I need to get reacquainted with her presence before I can talk about what I want to talk about—adapt to who we are to each other now, which is something quite undefinable.

"Just to the cabin in Topanga for some nature bathing."

How the Flacks refer to their gorgeous three-bedroom house in Topanga Canyon as 'the cabin' says a lot about how they live their lives.

"Sounds like a good idea."

"Just get away for a few days. Clear my head."

I'm not sure I feel relieved or sad at the prospect of Stella not being here the rest of the weekend. I should be relieved; I should be ecstatic. I'm not, though.

"Yesterday, I was talking to Kev about us, um, maybe renting somewhere while he finishes the house."

Stella nods. "Because of me?"

I push my plate away. The sushi looks delicious but it's no match for the knot in my stomach.

"Yeah, I mean, not because of you. More because of me. I don't know. It's hard to… to think straight, I guess."

"Interesting choice of words." Stella chuckles.

It's so much easier to have a laugh with her than to hold onto all those recriminations against myself. As well as Stella and I having to find a way to live with what we did, I'm also going to have to forgive myself.

"You know what I mean."

"It's good to see you smile, Kate. It feels like it's been ages."

"I need some more time to get over… you know." What it has done, more than anything, is take my mind off all the things I had to get over before I ended up in bed with Stella.

"I know." She puts her chopsticks down. "It's different for you, but I do get it. He's my brother and I so don't want to hurt him. It's the last thing I ever want to do if I can help it."

"Wouldn't it be easier for you as well if Kevin and I didn't live here?"

"Kevin might as well not live here and as far as you're concerned, Kate, I'm not going to be the person who asks you to move out. For starters, this isn't my house, nor is it my place to do so. And, well, you and I, we're going to be in each other's lives forever, so we might as well get past the hard bit now. Bite that bullet instead of avoiding it. But I understand if it's too hard for you." She arches up her eyebrows. "You could stay at the cabin if you needed privacy. It's all yours after the weekend. Or as soon as you want. I don't have to go."

"Kevin's not going to like that. It's too far from his office and our house."

"I love my brother very much, but Kevin doesn't get a say in this. This is your decision. Whatever you need to do to feel better."

"Before we moved in here, we considered the cabin, but we ruled it out because of the commute and LA traffic. Not just Kev. During rush hour, I'd lose at least an hour to and from work."

"Sure. Either way, take your time to think about what you want to do. I won't be here this weekend, so."

"Time, I have… I just—" I stop myself before I say something I shouldn't.

"What?" Stella cocks her head. She looks much more appetizing than that plate of sushi. A few strands of hair have come loose and fallen across her cheeks and that twinkle in her bright blue eyes is hard to resist. No wonder Nora Levine wanted her for a callback.

"Nothing." I try to wave it all off.

"Tell me. Please." I don't think Stella's trying to be seductive. This is just how she is—charming and curious, especially if it's about her.

"I—I kind of miss you. Spending time with you has been so much fun and it really helped me… look forward. Now we can't do that anymore and I miss it."

"Just for a little while." Stella's voice has dropped in volume. "Until things cool off."

I want to ask her so badly what she means by that, but I think I know, and it's not a good idea to steer the conversation that way.

"Maybe we can do something next week. Have lunch or something. Go hiking. I don't know. Just to see how it feels."

"I'd like that." I try to keep my voice steady. I thought I knew what it felt like to so desperately want the one thing you can't have, but it seems I haven't explored all gradations of that harrowing experience just yet.

CHAPTER 24
STELLA

I've just come back from a glorious hike up the mountain—there's nothing like putting one foot in front of the other while surrounded by lush greenery everywhere you look. I'm sitting on the deck overlooking the valley, drinking water, when I hear a car approach. It's so quiet out here in the woods, that you can hear it coming a mile away. I check my phone for any missed messages. Maybe Hayley had to make that escape—and where better to escape to than here?

I go to the driveway to see who has decided to surprise me. I shouldn't be thinking it, let alone wanting it, but I hope it's Kate. Because I miss her, too. Through a cloud of dust, the bright red color of Kate's Prius emerges. My heart pounds in my chest. What the hell is she doing here?

She gets out of the driver's seat, then walks to the trunk and produces two paper bags.

"I brought you some food. I didn't know if you'd taken enough."

"You brought me food?"

"Yes, and I should really put some of it in the fridge pronto. Give me a hand, will you?" She thrusts one of the bags into my arms.

We silently occupy ourselves stowing away the groceries. She's brought a weird mix of things. Apples and protein bars I get, but flour and sun-dried tomatoes? Unless she has come here specifically to cook me a gourmet meal from scratch.

I grab us both a bottle of water and then I ask, "I'm just dying to know, Kate. What are you really doing here?"

She inhales deeply, then turns to the view. She leans her elbows on the railing and takes in the breadth of the valley. "I forgot how gorgeous it is here." She opens the bottle and takes a few quick sips. "And I'm afraid I engaged in some deeply irrational thinking."

I try very hard not to show the glee I'm feeling on my face. Even though I'm an actor, it's hard, because acting isn't about hiding how you feel, it's about channeling your emotions the right way. There's a big difference.

"Nathan and Kev are at the house. Mary's doing whatever Mary does on a Saturday."

"Drawing," I say. "She's obsessed."

Kate nods. "And I thought…" Her gaze skitters away. "Well, you and I need to work on finding a new normal between us. To act like regular sisters-in-law again and what better place to practice than out here? There's no social pressure to act a certain way because we're alone. It's the ultimate testing environment."

"I hate to state the obvious." I didn't necessarily come here to be away from Kate, although I'm sure my subconscious would have something to say about that if it could. "But your plan is a little flawed." Kate looks like the quintessential LA woman on a weekend getaway with her long, flowery dress and understated makeup. The only aspect of her that doesn't match her otherwise country-chic vibes is the ashen pallor of her skin.

"I know. Oh, I know, Stella. I'm so sorry for barging in here. I should have called, but how could I possibly explain this insanity over the phone?"

She's right about one thing. This is madness. It's like putting the creamiest, freshest saucer of milk in front of a cat and telling the poor thing not to touch it because it's not normal. First of all, the cat doesn't understand that, and second, it would take said cat all of three seconds to lap the whole thing up because that's all it wants to do and who's going to stop it?

"Well, you're here now. We might as well try." Us being out here, not quite in the middle of nowhere but far enough removed from our ordinary life, feels more like I've been given a free pass to do what I want—not what I should. And my brain might not want to admit it, not all the time anyway, but my body knows damn well what it wants. Her.

"Okay. What shall we do?" Kate claps her palms together like an over-enthusiastic teacher.

"I'm going to take a shower. I just got back from a hike, an activity I greatly recommend for, um, clearing your head."

"It's been ages since Kev and I made the effort to come here, what with all the trying to make a baby." She nods at the house behind us. "I'm going to walk around. See what parts of the decor could do with an upgrade."

"You do that." I need a cold shower. I hurry to the bathroom, wondering how the hell this happened.

———

The sun has almost set, and Kate has lit a fire on the deck. She's keeping a close watch over it, even though it's not necessary—if I remember correctly, she's the one who advised Mom to buy this particular kind of firepit because it's so low-maintenance.

"Maybe I *should* move here. Work remotely. This place is fucking magical," she says, when she finally relaxes a bit. It's been a tense affair since she arrived, both of us trying to pretend that we're nothing but the most ordinary sisters-in-law. "Unfortunately, my job is not very work-from-home friendly."

"Neither is mine, although I feel like I work from home all

the time, waiting for my agent to call and reading manuscripts for parts I'll never get."

"Have you ever thought about quitting? Trying your hand at a different career?" She twirls her glass of red wine between her hands. Beforehand, we set a firm limit on one bottle between us for the night. Neither one of us has finished the first glass, so afraid of what might happen if we take a proper sip.

"Almost every day, but it's what I want to do," I say.

"Indulge me." Her head resting against the high back of the Adirondack chair, she turns to me. "What would you be if you weren't an actor?"

"Just like most other people in this town, I have a screenplay I've been tinkering with for the better part of ten years."

"Really? I didn't know that."

"There's a lot you don't know, Kate."

"Such as?" Her lips curl into a smile.

"Up to a few weeks ago, we never really talked about anything else but the occasional family stuff."

"True. So what's it about? Your screenplay?"

"It's this completely off-the-wall sci-fi caper set in a world where the patriarchy never existed, but as it turns out, the matriarchy ended up destroying the planet as well, but not before discovering there's another world out there where we can survive."

"I'd love to read it some time."

"You don't have to say that. It's just a hobby. It's not meant to be anything other than a means to engage my frequently overactive imagination."

"Still. I'd love to read it." She exhales deeply. She blinks slowly. "I'm not going to lie, Stella. Part of me wishes I could just stay here with you forever. Or at least for more than another day. Maybe a week. Or a few months." She puts down her glass and reaches out her hand. "Simply being with you makes me feel... lighter."

I gaze at her outstretched hand. I swallow hard. I shouldn't take it, but I already know I will. Like an out-of-body experience, I watch myself reach toward her. The touch of her fingers against mine is like an electric shock. All the emotions I've kept at bay since Monday unleash at once. I run my fingers up her arm.

"I get the feeling I'm about to fail at something spectacularly again," Kate says. With her hand still in mine, she pushes herself out of the chair. Still seated, it's as though I'm worshipping at her feet. I might as well be. I get up, too.

"I can't say no, Stella," she says. "Try as I might, I can't. Please, say no for both of us."

"Say no to what? I didn't ask you anything." My hand is glued to her wrist. I slide it down and interlace my fingers with hers.

"I shouldn't have come here, but I couldn't stay away. It's like…" With her other hand, she grabs a fistful of my shirt. "I need you or something. More than I need anything or anyone else."

"Even stone-cold sober?" There's a hitch in my voice.

"Especially stone-cold sober," she repeats.

It's wholly unfair to leave it up to me to stop this now. Because I may not need her, but I want her. And just like Kate, I want her even more now that I'm sober. Now that I can't hide behind the excuse of intoxication. Now that all extenuating circumstances have evaporated. She came here for me, that much was clear the minute she got out of her car, all flustered and full of bullshit excuses.

"I can't say no either." It's like her words from earlier echo back to us from the depths of the canyon, but this time, it's me saying them. "Don't ask me to."

"I'm not asking you anything." Just as our conversation is like an echo, like something coming back to us again and again, Kate pulling me closer has happened before. But unlike an echo, the need with which she pulls me to her doesn't diminish with time. It only intensifies.

The tips of our noses touch. "I still want you," she whispers. "Maybe we can have—" I stop her from speaking by pressing my lips to hers. No more promises, I want to say. Neither one of us can promise the other anything at all.

CHAPTER 25
KATE

The ways in which I managed to fool myself astound me once again. I got in my car and I drove all the way here, pretending it could solve exactly what we're doing right now. Because Stella's kissing me and of course I open my mouth to hers. Of course, I let her tongue in. I could cry, that's how much I want her, although I'd probably be crying for a million other reasons. But that's the thing. None of those reasons matter when Stella takes me outside of myself. When she presses her lips to mine, when our tongues and our fingers intertwine. I slip my hand under her shirt. Her skin is so soft and warm and everything I want.

Maybe we can have one more night, I wanted to say. Perhaps Stella decided to kiss my words away because how can they not sound hollow? How can they not be a reminder of all the reasons we shouldn't be doing this? We *are* doing it and words are utterly inadequate.

"Let's go inside," Stella breathes into my ear.

I nod eagerly and follow her. She drags me into her room. There's no need to close the door behind us. No one can see us here. No one knows what we're doing.

Fully clothed, we tumble onto the bed. Stella's hungry for me. She slides her hand from my cheek into my hair and pushes me onto my back. She gazes into my eyes and pauses. Is she having second thoughts? I hope not, but I need to give her the time to think through whatever she's processing; to push away all the things we need to let go in order to do this.

She sucks her bottom lip between her teeth and continues to stare at me. Her face is so close that her breath caresses my cheek. She looks as though she might say something, but doesn't. As though she has inwardly convinced herself of something, she slowly bridges the last of the distance between us and kisses me so gently, I should barely feel it, yet I feel it everywhere. My entire skin is lit on fire again, making me feel like the woman I was before everything went downhill. A woman full of hopes and dreams and desire. A woman I'd barely recognize if I saw her walking down the street these days. Because the long, arduous process of trying to have a baby and having absolutely nothing to show for it in the end has hollowed me out from the inside. It has chipped away at what Kevin and I used to have, at our love and respect for each other. To ride that roller coaster of hope and disappointment time and time again is eviscerating. Maybe it's no longer possible for us to find each other again underneath the ruins of what happened.

It's not an excuse for what I'm doing now, but it is a reason. An explanation. And sometimes, an explanation is all you need. Because what Stella has to give, I want to only take more and more of. Being with her makes me feel alive again, like I matter again, like I'm important to someone—and because of that, despite the fact that I'm betraying my husband, I can see myself in a different light. There might be other ways for me to change how I feel about myself, to dig myself out of that hole of desperation, but this is what I've got. This is what has presented itself. And it's surely selfish of me, and reckless, and maybe even cruel, but I need to feel this. I need to be here. My body knew this better than my brain; that's why, on automatic pilot, it drove me here—into Stella's arms.

I can't speak to Stella's motivations. She can't pull the disappointment or the drunk card any longer. Maybe she's just really into me. It's the only conclusion I can draw by how she kisses me. Her tongue against mine is soft but full of intention. Her fingers steal across the side of my neck. The way she kisses me, so full of obvious desire and raw lust, is easy to mistake for a loving kiss. Because that's the other thing with Stella. She's not a stranger. We might not have been close, but a foundation was there. Or maybe there's another reason why we were never close before. Maybe if we had been, this would have happened sooner.

The dress I'm wearing is twisted around my body, constricting my movements. I tug at her top to make my own intentions known. We have all night, even all day tomorrow—perhaps we can even tack on an extra night—yet I want us naked as soon as possible. It's only been a few days, yet it feels like weeks. And this time, everything is different. This is not a drunken mistake. This is two consenting adults actively and enthusiastically choosing to do this no matter the consequences—and there are many.

We fumble with our clothes. I need to get off the bed to get this dress off. Stella keeps her gaze trained on me, watching me like a hawk. Before I get a chance to unhook my bra, she pulls me to her. I guess she wants to do that particular job herself.

All the while, we don't speak a word. There's no other sound but the rustle of the wind in the trees outside and the sound our skin makes when we move across the sheets. When our lips touch. When my breath quickens.

I sit on my knees on the bed across from her. Her hand slides along the back of my head and she pulls me close. She kisses me and I kiss her back. And I can try to push away thoughts of my marriage as much as I want, but something inside of me knows that it's crumbling as we do this. That it can never be the same again. That some things can't be repaired—or undone. Me doing this with Stella equals me saying no to my marriage.

Stella's hands move onto my back and find the clasp of my bra. She undoes it and without breaking from our kiss, slips her hand underneath the cups. Her thumbs caress my nipples and she might as well be caressing my clit, that's how ravenous I am for her. While I can explain why I'm doing this, it's harder to explain my sudden attraction to her. But maybe I don't need to explain it. Maybe it can just be there for me to enjoy, at least for now. Because there's no denying it's there. There's no denying I want this every bit as much as she does.

While I moan into her mouth, I try to unhook her bra, my clit throbbing wildly with the anticipation of seeing her magnificent breasts again. All this kissing must be impacting my dexterity, because I fail at my task. Stella lets go of my breasts and gives me a hand. She slants her body away from me and, gaze firmly pinned on me, sends me the sweetest, kindest smile, and that's a reason right there. An explanation for why I like her so much and I enjoy her company to the extent that things have heated up between us well beyond friendship. She's not the spoiled brat I always believed her to be. She's kind and considerate as well as insanely hot and talented.

Stella tosses her bra behind her, and I take the opportunity to get rid of my own. Instantly, I'm engulfed with a need to suck her perfect nipples into my mouth. To flick my tongue along those gorgeous, tiny buds. But she doesn't let me. For days, I wished I remembered nothing from our first night, yet now I'm glad I remember everything. It allows me to notice the difference in her behavior tonight. There's a different edge to how she goes about things, in how she catches my wrists and moves them away from her body so she can push me down. Our first night was bathed in first-time curiosity and exhilaration, but in our second one, I get the feeling I see more of Stella, of what she's really like. I very much like what I see.

She pushes me down and has no qualms removing my

panties as soon as I'm on my back. She doesn't need tequila to lower her inhibitions, not now we've come this far already. She lowers her body onto mine, our breasts touching, her elbows above my shoulders. She buries her hands in my hair again and gazes down at me. I look into her blue eyes, into her sweet and sexy face. I wish I could look inside her head, find out what she's thinking, what's going through her mind right now. But I don't need telepathic abilities to know that this isn't just sex for Stella either. It's so much more than that for both of us.

She looks at me a few moments longer, as though wanting to etch every detail of my face into her memory. I do the same with her. That freckle to the left of her nose that I only first noticed when I saw her on the big screen. The fullness of her upper lip compared to her lower one. The impossible blue of her eyes that can sometimes go cloudy, like a typical LA smog day. I may not know her very well, yet I feel like I've known her all along. That, somehow, this was inevitable. That she's been put on my path for a reason. Maybe she was the Flack I was supposed to marry all along. But no. My mind can't go there. Not now. I need to trick myself into believing that this is, in its own way, a beautiful thing we're doing for a while longer. I need the joy that the next few hours will bring me. I need it to undo some of the sadness that has accumulated inside me.

It's intimate to peer into each other's eyes like this. It's the opposite of drunkenly groping at each other. It's like saying a thousand times yes without using words.

It almost feels like love.

When she finally kisses me, her lips are even softer than before. And I'm ready to give myself to her again. To surrender and give up the part of myself where too much pain has crept into my muscles, tensed up my flesh.

We kiss for what seems like hours. There are no time constraints. Coming here, away from everything and everyone, is the best gift I've given myself in a very long time. It's the most radical act of self-care. It's not as if I have children to take into consideration, to stop me from only thinking about myself.

She slips off me and her hands roam across my body, leaving nothing but acute arousal in their wake. The way she cups my breasts betrays her own need. How her tongue flicks against my nipple tells me all I need to know. Stella's in this as deep as I am.

She maneuvers herself between my legs. I let my knees fall apart for her; I let her see all of me. She runs a featherlight fingertip over me, careful not to brush against my clit—I may spontaneously combust. I'm so ready for orgasm number one because, in my bones, I know there are many more to come tonight. Maybe, come tomorrow, I'll be so spent, all this foolishness will have miraculously been expelled from me, and I can pick up my life again where I left it. Fat chance of that.

Stella's strokes intensify. The touch of her finger heavier on me, more insistent. It slides through my wetness again and again, to the point where I'm already losing my breath every time she brushes against my clit. Then, she lifts her finger to her lips and sucks it deep into her mouth and, even though she's no longer touching me, I'm close to coming right there and then just at the sight of that. Yet another image that will be etched into my brain forever.

She returns her hand to my sex and tips her body toward me. She spreads my lower lips, while her tongue skirts along my clit. My hyper-aroused state is no match for this particular combination of Stella's dexterity and tongue skills. More than anything, my body wants to give itself up to her. I need her to make me feel like this. It may be a sick and selfish and depraved feeling, but she's the only one who can make me feel like this. She's the only one who can take away some of the pain while replacing it with a strange combination of hope and an entirely different kind of agony—one that is, at the very least, more bearable than the pain I've been living with for too long.

A life free of hurt is an illusion, I know that much. And if there's going to be pain, I need Stella to override the most acute, the most devastating part of it, every once in a while.

When I scream out Stella's name, pain has nothing to do with my heart-wrenching cry. It's born from pure relief, from pent-up emotions being freed—finally—from the cage I've been keeping them in too long.

CHAPTER 26
STELLA

When I look into Kate's eyes, it's like looking at a different person. Or at least a different version of her. Maybe a version I've created for myself, or for this bubble we find ourselves in, that I can project some of my feelings on.

"Stella, Stella, Stella," she whispers. The first words we've spoken since we agreed to go inside. "What the hell have you done to me?"

"Me?" I can't possibly let this slide. "*You* drove here to see me."

Kate nods. "I know." I can also see the conflict in her eyes. Unlike before, when I looked at her for long seconds, at her beautiful face with its button nose and deep-brown eyes, I can see it all. Without lust clouding my vision, I can see what we're doing and the kind of person that makes me—that makes us. I know what it's like to be cheated on and I wish that kind of betrayal on no one, least of all my own brother. Doing this once under the influence is, if not excusable, at least understandable. Doing it again, saying yes to each other while having use of our full faculties, is not okay on any level.

"Why is it like this?" Kate asks. "What is it about you?"

I swallow hard. I haven't had real feelings, the kind that run so deep there's no other choice but to pursue them, for anyone in years—not since Toni. It simply can't be that the first woman I'm going to fall for is my sister-in-law. Then again, if I really wanted to protect myself, and my family, I shouldn't be sleeping with her.

"It doesn't matter what it is, Kate."

"Hey." She runs a fingernail over my back. "Can we agree that for the next twenty-four hours, we pretend it's just us? That there are no negative consequences to what we're doing?"

"All this pretending," I say. "We fool ourselves when we're together and we fool everyone else the rest of the time. It's no way to live."

"You're right. It's not." Her hands sneak into my hair. She twirls a strand of it around her finger.

After Toni left me for Sheena, it took me months, years even, to realize that they didn't cheat on me with the sole purpose of hurting me—that was just a by-product. They did it because they couldn't help themselves. Because they fell in love, no matter how badly that might hurt me. And I had to ask myself the question: would I deny two people I care about the best experience of their life—the magnificence of a great love—for the sake of my own heart? My own ego?

Toni and Sheena are still together. Maybe they were meant to be together, and I was the mere conduit to making them see that. But I can't possibly think about my own brother in that way. Nor is it my place to judge Kevin and Kate's marriage.

"But I'll take the twenty-four hours," I say.

Kate nods and curls her lips into a soft smile.

"After that, this stops or… I don't know. But I'm not having an affair with you behind my brother's back. I can't do that. It will kill us all." Never mind that I'm already doing it—that the damage has already been done. Once, twice, or dozens of times doesn't make a single difference. Cheating is cheating.

"Deal." Kate tugs me near. "Come here," she says. Her fingers run down my belly and stroke the sensitive skin there, before slipping inside my panties. I want her so much, I already know that twenty-four hours won't be enough, will never be enough, but they will have to do, nonetheless.

————

I wake up with Kate's lips around my nipple. My body's stiff from all the things we did all night, my head fuzzy from not getting enough sleep, and my heart aches for all the reasons we have to stop now. We have to start another bout of pretending: that this never happened. That we're just sisters-in-law who only care an appropriate amount about each other.

Kate's tongue slides along my nipple and an arrow of arousal burrows itself all the way through my body.

"Oh," I moan and she looks up at me.

She lets my nipple fall from her lips, but keeps her hand firmly clasped around my breast. "Morning."

"What time is it?"

"It's early, but I didn't want to waste any more of our remaining twenty-four hours on sleep."

"Come here." I pull her up until our lips are level. This couldn't be further removed from when I woke up with the most heinous hangover in my mother's pool house to find Kate asleep in a crooked position in the couch, my head full of instant regret, and my body not knowing what to do with itself. I look into her dark eyes and I could cry for what I'm about to lose, but I've lost before. I lost someone I loved and compared to that, this should be easy. I kiss her and a door inside me opens farther, a door that, strangely, only Kate seemed to have the key to all along. A door I'm going to have to find a way to close again, to lock firmly, and keep all these unbidden, unsavory feelings behind.

It's the way she lightly groans into my mouth when we kiss. And how her fingertips are soft against the skin of my neck. How her rock-hard nipples press into my side. How her warm body makes me feel like I've come home after a long and challenging journey. It's as though all the reasons we shouldn't be doing this cancel each other out and somehow converge into one big reason why we should—because we can't not do it. Not this morning when, even though guilt gnaws at me and shame's lurking not too far behind, I can just pull her to me and kiss her as though she's mine.

It's so easy, so seductive, to fool myself into believing this is a real thing, something viable, a relationship worth the name. And I know it's none of those things and that my feelings for Kate are amplified by the lure of the forbidden and confused because of who we are to each other, conflated by what we've been through. But still. There's nowhere else I'd rather be than here with her. The morning light is streaming through the windows. Kate's body feels perfect in my arms, as though it's the only place she belongs. Her tongue is soft against mine. Her hand travels lower and that, too, is exactly where it should be. I become wet for her instantly, like she has the key to the floodgates inside me as well as the key to all those feelings I shouldn't be having. To wake up like this is like waking up in heaven. The day stretches before us, and it may take some effort but we can block out the real world for a few more hours.

Her fingers find my wetness and, for a split second, her kiss stalls. Maybe she's astounded by how much I want her, but only momentarily so, because our kiss deepens again, as she slips her fingers inside me.

This is how every Sunday should be, I think, because I also still have all that hope running through me that I might actually get that part next to Nora Levine. Everything's still possible. I have so many highs to ride and Kate's fingers are divine inside me—

"Stella?" I'm so far gone it takes me a while to realize it's not Kate saying my name. Her fingers have stopped all motion. Her body is stiff and still next to mine. A knock on the door. "Stella? Are you up?"

158

My heart skips a few beats. Oh fuck. Oh no. "Mom?"

"Yes, darling."

"Don't come in," I shout, but it's too late. My mother appears in the doorframe. Kate's fingers brusquely slide out of me. We are both naked, barely covered. She's all over me. There's no way to spin this.

"Wha—I—" Mom's gaze sweeps the bed, then skitters from me to Kate as she puts two and two together. She turns and flees the room.

"Fuck!" Kate steals the sheet and wraps it around her body, leaving me completely exposed.

"What the hell is she doing here?" Why didn't we hear her arrive? Where was the crunch of the tires on the gravel? But, of course, we didn't hear. We were too lost in each other.

"Oh, Jesus. Please tell me this isn't happening." The sheet still wrapped around her, Kate paces the room.

I try to take a few breaths. I try to remind myself that this isn't the worst that can happen. It could have been Kevin. Oh, damn. Is Nathan with her?

"I'm going to talk to her." I find my clothes and quickly put them on. "I'll try to come up with something."

I find my mother on the porch, where it all started again last night, her face as pale as her knuckles gripping the railing of the deck.

"Mom, um, what are you doing here?"

She holds up her hand and inhales sharply. "Tell me I didn't just see that. Please, Stella, tell me there's a perfectly good explanation for what I walked in on."

"There is—I mean, we just…" But there's no more use in pretending now. My mother isn't blind—nor is she stupid. "We just shared the bed," I say, sounding the least convincing I've ever sounded in my life.

"Stella, what is… What is going on here? Am I going mad?"

"It's not a thing, Mom. It's nothing." My heart breaks a little as I say the words.

"Promise me you will never tell your brother about this."

"No. Of course not."

"Mary. Hi." Kate walks onto the deck fully dressed. "Um, I'm so sorry."

Mom looks at Kate as though a ghost just walked out of the house.

"What are you even doing here, Mom? Didn't you have the Lippmanns' party last night?"

"Yes, but that shouldn't stop me from surprising my daughter and daughter-in-law with a lovely breakfast, should it? I thought we could eat together and then go on a hike, just the three of us."

"Why didn't you call?" I know it's ridiculous to make it sound as though this is all her fault, but I don't have many options.

"Because I wanted to surprise you. I picked up all your favorites from Bread & Butter. I figured both of you could do with a pick-me-up. I'm your mother, that's what I do." She gives us both a very motherly once-over. My mom has never been strict or overbearing in any way, but now I'm quaking in my boots. Because there's a big difference between being caught with your hand in the cookie jar and sharing a bed with your sister-in-law. Mom puffs out some air.

"Mary, it's all my fault. I came here. Stella didn't invite me. It's, um, all me."

I shake my head. "That's not true." I can't let Kate take all the blame.

"It doesn't matter whose fault it is or who started it." Mom's voice is sharp, like when she's talking to a supplier whose delivery's going to be late. "How long has this been going on?"

"Not long," Kate and I blurt out at the same time. I try to look at her, to tell her I've got this. I know how to talk to my mom. But I can barely look at her. Aside from finding out about Toni and Sheena, this is the most embarrassing moment of my life.

"Just this week," Kate says. "Neither one of us wants to hurt Kevin. It's not what it might look like to you, Mary. We're not having some sort of sordid affair."

"Could have fooled me." Mom sinks into a chair. She gazes into the trees while drumming her fingertips on her knees before looking at us again. "Can you promise me." She pins her gaze on me. "Me. Your mother, Stella." She brings a hand to her chest. "That this ends now. That it doesn't go any further. I will not have my family destroyed because of... because... I don't know what to call it. But I won't let you do that to your brother. He has suffered enough."

If I could shrink, I would have just lost inches from my height. There's nothing like a stern lecture from your mother to see the grave, unmistakable, silly error of your ways.

"I don't want to hurt Kev. I never—" I say, but Kate puts her hand on my arm, making me shut up.

"This is my fault. My mistake. I started it," Kate says. "I was hurting. I was in so much pain and Kevin wasn't there. Stella was."

"That's hardly an—" Mom starts saying, but Kate silences her as well.

"I know that's not an excuse for cheating on my husband. Nothing is. We didn't do this to hurt Kevin. It just... sort of happened, like things do sometimes. And I let it go too far. But you have my word, Mary. This ends now. There isn't really even anything to end. It was just some... mindless fun, really."

Mindless fun? The relief I felt at Kate sticking up for me is quickly replaced by sheer deflation. But this was only ever going to be a lose-lose situation. Something that felt good for a short while, only to make way for a world of hurt after.

I nod to support Kate's words. It had to end either way. To have it end like this is painful, but maybe it's for the best. Maybe we need Mom's watchful eye on us to stop us from doing it again. The added shame might make it easier as well.

"Thank god," Mom says. "For a second there, I thought you

were going to tell me you were in love with each other." She scoffs. "That would have been… unthinkable."

"We're not," Kate is quick to say. "I love Kevin."

Tears sting behind my eyes. Less than twenty minutes ago, Kate's fingers were buried deep inside me, and here she is telling my mother how much she loves my brother.

CHAPTER 27
KATE

I wish the wooden deck below my chair would open wide and swallow me whole. I wish I could disappear and leave this mess behind, start over fresh elsewhere, because this is too humiliating. To be caught in bed by my mother-in-law, cheating on her precious son, with his sister, must be the absolute low point of my life. Yet, it's not. That happened after the second time I got pregnant, after I had lived with an unbearable blend of hope and fear in my veins for five long weeks, and the doctor told me that, once again, it wasn't going to happen. That I should, perhaps, start to accept that becoming a mother, that Kevin and I becoming parents, might not be on the cards for me. That moment, that certain death of all hope, was much worse than this. Of course it was. But this is hardly pleasant. To have Mary look at me as though she's considering taking me out with the trash is mortifying. Not only did I cheat on her son; I did it with her daughter. And she has every right to look at me the way she's doing, with nothing but disgust in her eyes—as if I'm the great destroyer of her precious family. Which I might very well be. Because how can I go back now? How can I sit at her dinner table with Kevin to my left and Stella to my right, and Mary's knowing glare on me? It's no longer an option.

Mary says a swift goodbye and Stella makes a thousand solemn promises to follow her home immediately. Mary barely throws me a glance before she disappears.

I rub my forehead and try to swallow the bile that has accumulated at the back of my throat.

"I'm so sorry. I had no idea." Stella sits in the chair that is the furthest removed from me. "Fuck."

"About what I said... About it just being some mindless fun."

"It's fine. You said what you had to say. I get it. Besides, it's not because it feels like something else, like it can be more than that, that it can actually be that, if you know what I'm saying."

I nod, because I know exactly what she's saying.

"I'm just really sorry that my mom had to see us like that." She blows some air through her nostrils. "But maybe it was the shock we sorely needed, because otherwise... I don't know."

"What are you saying?"

"Nothing." Stella shakes her head.

"I don't suppose we should finish what we started," I joke.

"Oh, Jesus Christ. I don't know if I'll ever be able to have sex again. That is not how you want your mother to see you and, well, with you." She chuckles. "You have to laugh, really. Otherwise, all I'd do is cry."

I rise and walk over to her. I open my arms. "One last hug."

Stella's glance is full of trepidation. "Mom might have turned around. Felt the need to check up on us."

"She won't be able to sneak up on us a second time. Besides, it's just a hug."

Stella pushes herself up and walks into my embrace. I hold her close. I let my hand ride up into her hair. I let her know that whatever it is she might be feeling, it's probably not too far off from what I'm feeling as well.

"What are you going to do?" she asks. "Are you coming back to the house?"

I shake my head. I don't want to let her go—I don't want to

let go of the one person who makes me feel good about myself. But I have to. I let my arms fall away until we're just two people standing very close to each other.

"I think I might stay here for a while. Regroup. Come back to my senses."

"I'll deal with Mom. Try not to worry about her too much."

I reach for her hand. "I might not come to the house for a little while. Let things cool off. But keep me in the loop about the part. I want to know, okay?"

"You'll be the first person I call, I promise." She curls her fingers tightly around mine.

"Thank you." For everything, I think. For making me feel like a woman again, a human with other needs than the over-powering one to have a child, to have a family, to let only that come first.

"I'd best get going. I think she might time me."

"This is LA. You can always blame traffic." Or blame me. Blame me for everything. Blame me for this. I look deep into her eyes and, one last time, lean in to kiss her.

———

There's nothing like a solo hike up and down the canyon to settle your thoughts. To really listen to yourself—look deep inside—and face all the mistakes you've made, and how to possibly find some sort of redemption for them.

By the time I see the house loom in the distance, my tank top drenched in sweat, my feet sore, and my mind exhausted from all the processing. I know I can't just go back to pretending everything's normal. Because things were hardly normal before I threw myself into Stella's arms.

As a couple, Kevin and I have some things to come to terms with. But instead of talking to each other, working our way through it, we withdrew, each in our own way. Maybe this is just a bottomless valley in this journey of ups and downs we're on together, that every marriage goes through. Or maybe it's the end, and the end can be the beginning of something new. I can't predict the future, but I can talk to my husband—although I have no desire to confess my indiscretion with his sister. I just want to talk to him, find out what he's feeling, because apart from the fact that he's hurting, that he's nursing a painful, festering wound, I don't know anything. God knows what he's thinking when he bashes in another wall.

Before I hit the shower, I text him to tell him—it's neither a suggestion, nor a question—to meet me at the cabin tonight, and to bring some stuff from the house because I'll be staying here a while.

CHAPTER 28
STELLA

"Come here, darling."

I hadn't expected my mother to receive me with open arms, but, then again, when hasn't she? In my almost twenty-nine years, she has never once made me feel like a failure—when you go from audition to audition and never get the part, she had many opportunities for this. My mother, just like my brother, has always believed in me. If there were times when she didn't, and there must have been plenty, she never let it show.

"I'm going to make us some coffee, and then I'd like you to tell me what's going on with you," she says.

I'm suddenly starving—I was up most of the night burning a ton of calories—and wonder what she has done with the food she brought for Kate and me, but I ignore my hunger because I suspect the conversation I'm about to have won't leave much opportunity for munching on breakfast goodies.

I settle at the kitchen island the way I have done a gazillion times.

"Where's Nathan?" I ask, while I watch her push a few buttons on the fancy coffee maker she can't live without.

"He got up at the crack of dawn to help your brother. Kevin

may have infected him with whatever renovation bug he caught. Suddenly, Nathan's six a.m. presence at Kev's house was a given. Hence my impromptu trek to Topanga." She presents me with a state-of-the-art cappuccino. "Here you go, darling." She makes quick work of fixing her own hot beverage, then comes to sit next to me at the island. "Now, tell me. Not the details, I don't want to know those, but, just… what's going on? This isn't like you."

"Nothing, really," I say on a sigh. "I had a hell of a week, and Kate was there for me and… with all the stuff she and Kev have been going through." I take a quick sip. "And then there was this bottle of tequila and suddenly we didn't know what we were doing anymore."

"But she's Kate. You've known her forever. And, well, she's straight. Isn't she?"

"That's not for me to say." She was anything but straight in bed with me last night, but I can't reveal that to my mother. "All I know is that we've never been close. She never thought much of me, and it never bothered me. Frankly, I probably had my head too far up my own ass to care about what Kate thought. But, suddenly, we found ourselves in this house, spending all this time together, and… something clicked." It's the best way I have to explain it. "After that drunken night, we felt awful, obviously. The morning after was dreadful because we knew what we'd done, and we very much knew that it shouldn't have happened. It was easy enough to write it off as a silly, drunken mistake. But now… I'm not so sure."

"What do you mean?" There's pure panic in her voice.

"I don't really know. I went to the cabin to relax, to distract myself until I heard about the part and, truth be told, also to be away from Kate and then… she turns up out of the blue. I didn't invite her. She didn't tell me she was coming. She was just… there with some lame-ass excuse and…"

"It happened again?" Mom asks.

I nod.

"Was there a bottle of tequila involved again?" Mom very much sounds as though she knows the answer to that already. She's my mother and I live with her. She knows what I look like hungover.

"I wish there were."

"So… what happened?" Mom insists.

"I don't know."

"God, what a mess." My mother isn't the type to let her head hang low. She gazes straight ahead, focuses, as though, just because she walked in on us, this is now her problem to solve. And Mary Flack hasn't encountered many problems in her life that she can't solve.

"Kate's going to stay at the cabin for a while."

"Probably a good idea. Obviously, after all that has happened with her and Kevin, I don't want to kick her out. I care about her, but you and Kev are my kids. My flesh and blood. And she's…"

"Please, Mom, don't blame Kate."

"Kevin's not innocent in this either." She peers into her cup of coffee. "I tried talking to him while we were in Washington, but I couldn't get through to him. It's like he's using all the bricks from the walls he's tearing down in his house to build a wall around his heart. It must be hard for Kate. He's been so absent, so distant, she might as well be going through this whole thing alone." She turns to look at me. I can feel her eyes fixing on me, but I don't have it in me to return her piercing gaze. How can I? "What about you, Stella? I get that you were feeling blue, but… to do something like that. That's not the person I know you to be."

I try to hide behind my cup, but it's much too small to cover up all my embarrassment and shame, and all the other things I'm feeling but most certainly can't admit to. "I wish I knew," I whisper, my throat closing up because of the emotions I'm trying to push down. I really like her, I want to say, but that's another thing that can't be said out loud. "I'm so sorry," I say instead. "I must have lost my mind for a minute there."

"We all do things we shouldn't, but… you have to promise me, again, that it ends now."

"I promise. You have my word."

"And Kevin can never know."

"He won't." I'm certainly not going to tell him, and I don't think Kate has any plans in that direction.

"Kev and Kate might not make it." Mom's voice breaks. "Kev has been hurting so much, and that's not how a mother wants to see her child. I was glad they decided to move here for a while, so I could keep an eye on things, but I've barely seen Kevin outside of work."

"How is he at the office?"

"If you saw him at work, you'd think everything's just fine. That he's happy as a clam and his marriage is going swimmingly."

"Maybe they'll find a way." The words barely make it past the lump in my throat. Of course, I can't wish for my brother's marriage to break down, but I can't wholly wish it to survive either—and I know what an awful person that makes me.

"Either way, they'll have to fix things on their own," Mom says. "We can't get involved."

"Hey," I say, because I need a change of topic. "You know what I've learned the past week?"

"What's that, darling?" My mother sounds as wistful as a woman whose children are giving her a massive headache would.

"Nathan's a really good guy."

"About time," Mom says. "I don't just go falling in love with anyone. You should know that about me."

Neither do I, I think, but I sure hope that's not what my mother's thinking right now.

CHAPTER 29
KATE

Despite only a few hours of sleep, the drama of Mary walking in on us, and an exhausting hike, I can't find an inkling of peace. I may have found a glimpse of clarity, but it means nothing as long as I haven't faced my husband. As long as some harsh truths haven't been spoken between us.

To my surprise, Kevin texted me around three to say he was on his way already. Maybe he wants to catch the sunset over the canyon together, or maybe someone told him to get his ass over here as quickly as possible.

I wish I could talk to Stella, not only to find out what's what, but just to hear her voice. To know she's all right. And to find out how upset Mary is about the whole thing.

Kevin arrives unshowered, his clothes full of dust and with dark patches of dirt across his face. It's not as though I've suddenly stopped loving him. What Kevin and I have can't just be destroyed in a matter of days, but I do know that if what he's giving me right now is all he can give me for the foreseeable future, then I need to protect myself. I need to put myself first—although, I guess, I've already done plenty of that.

While he's in the shower, I pour us each a large glass of wine. Stella and I didn't even finish the bottle we allotted for last night. Oh, Stella. If she wasn't Kevin's sister, I'm beginning to think I'd choose her and all the things she does have to offer. The kindness. The excitement. The breathtaking climaxes. The easy companionship. The deep connection that we forged in such a short amount of time. The delicious chemistry.

I wait for Kevin in the same chair I sat in last night, when I glanced at Stella and knew what was going to happen. Why I had driven over here in a mad rush in the first place. Why I had allowed my naive, stupid brain to trick me like that. Because I wanted to be with her in this idyllic place, just Stella and me between the trees, our naked bodies—

"I almost forgot how gorgeous this place is." Kevin freshly showered in just a T-shirt and a pair of jeans is a sight for sore eyes. All the work he's been doing—in all the time he hasn't been spending with me—has bulked his muscles, his biceps bulge as though he has just returned from the gym. If I remember right, he's building one in the basement of our house.

But my desire for him is not physical—at least not sexual. I want to be in the same place as him, but I can't possibly think of sleeping with him. Not after last night. But that's not why he's here. He leans over my chair and kisses the top of my head. "And I almost forgot how gorgeous my wife is." You'd think a sweet talker like him would be better at expressing his feelings. He's never been the kind of man who shares his emotions freely and it's never bothered me before, but, right now, I need more than I'm getting. The problem is that, because of what happened with Stella, I no longer feel in a position to ask anything from him.

He squeezes my shoulder before sinking into the chair next to me with a big, manly sigh. He must be exhausted. Time off has become non-existent for him.

"It's called active recovery, babe," he said, the first time I expressed my worry that he was working himself toward a certain burnout. And that was me told.

He updates me about the house, about the bathroom he has

relocated from one end of the first floor to the other and the new wall he and Nathan finished before he drove here. It makes me wonder whether it will even still feel like my house once I go back—if I ever go back.

"We need to talk about some things," I say, after a short silence.

"I know." He doesn't look at me but keeps his gaze on the treetops in the distance. "I've been thinking. Maybe we should adopt."

This is what he's leading with? I can't help but scoff. "Kev, um, that's not what we need to talk about first."

"It's not? I know adoption can be a long road as well, but it won't be as hard as... what we've been through. I'm convinced we can do it."

"I never see you. We might as well not live together anymore." We might as well not be together anymore. "And you want to talk about adoption?"

"You don't?" He turns to me with a look on his face so perplexed I almost feel sorry for him.

"Maybe. At some point in the future, but I think we need to talk about our marriage first."

"What about our marriage?"

"It's no longer a marriage if we stop seeing each other and communicating with each other."

"I told you I needed some time to myself, to put myself together again after the whole IVF thing. I have feelings too, and that's how I've decided to deal with them. Why is it so hard for you to give me the time and space I need?"

"What about what I need? Because I need to see you, Kev. If I don't, if things continue like this then..."

"Then what?"

"I don't know. I guess, then... I'm not sure we still have a future together."

"Don't be silly, babe." He grins at me as though I just told a lame joke.

"I tried to have this conversation with you a few days ago, but you were too tired to listen."

"I did listen. You said you wanted to move out of Mom's house for privacy reasons. I agreed, and now you're staying here. Admittedly, it's a bit far from everything, but if it's what you want, that's fine with me."

How can he be so utterly clueless? Or have I not made myself abundantly clear?

"What does it even matter where I'm staying? You sleep at our house most nights, anyway."

"I'm here now."

"When's the house going to be finished?"

"A few weeks."

"Maybe… until then…" It's hard to say this, but maybe not as excruciating as I had imagined it was going to be. "We should take a break."

"What do you mean? What does that mean?"

"We shouldn't see each other. I'll stay here. You stay with your family or at our house." Nothing much will change, but maybe the semantics of it can make him see I'm serious.

"Is that what you want?" His breath hitches in his throat. "A break from me? From us?"

"No, it's not what I want, but it seems to be all I can get."

"For the record, that's not what I want. All I want is some more time, and yes, that means time alone, because that's how I process. I know you don't like it, but I can't change myself. Not now."

"You'll have time. You'll have all the time and space you need without having to take me into account even for one single minute."

"It's not because we're not in the same space that I'm not thinking about you. You're constantly on my mind."

"I need a break, Kev." It's the best I can do. It's all I can tell him. "I need to know what it feels like to…" To what? This part,

I didn't think through. I guess because I was hoping it wouldn't have come to this. "I just need to be alone."

"But," Kevin says. "You are alone."

"Exactly." A tear runs down my cheek. "But at least then, I'll be alone by choice, not because you don't want to spend any time with me."

"Don't you get it?" His voice breaks. "It's too hard for me to spend time with you right now. It reminds me of the children we can't have, of all the things I can't give you, of..." He hides his face in his hands.

"Oh, Kev." I rush to him and put my arms around him. I want to say I'm sorry, but I would be apologizing for the wrong thing, for the thing he should never know about. How can I expect him to be open and honest with me about his feelings when I'm keeping this huge secret? It's also beginning to dawn on me that what Stella and I did wasn't simply sleeping together, wasn't just giving into a physical urge for each other, but much more than that. "I know it's hard." I let all the tears I've been keeping at bay stream down my cheeks as well. I let them fall into his hair while I hold him as he cries. While all the things we could have had flash through my mind, as well as all the things I no longer want.

"You can't leave me now," he says after he's regrouped. He holds my hand in his tightly. "You just... can't."

"But, Kev, most of the time, it feels like you've already left me."

"I haven't left. I'm just working on putting myself together again so I can be strong for the next leg of our journey."

"I wish I could say the same."

"You've always been strong, babe. You're the strongest person I know. Physically and mentally. What your body has been put through, I can't even imagine. I—"

I can't look my husband in the eye and have him call me strong. Not after what I did. "I'm not as strong as you think."

"Ditto."

"What are we going to do?" I settle in his lap to avoid having to look him in the eye.

"Just let time heal some of our wounds, I guess. What else can we do?"

Inside me, a war rages. It's tempting to stay here, wrapped in his arms, and pretend we can do that, pretend everything will be all right, because there's a tiny chance it will be. But my conscience is far from clear, and I may be the kind of person who cheats on her husband, but I'm not the type who can hide it, who can play this part of the hurt, dutiful wife. I can't tell him—I can't destroy him like that—but I also can't simply stay with him.

"Kev," I say into his hair.

"Hm." He wraps his arms around me a little tighter.

"I'm so sorry, but I'm the one who needs a break. For my own selfish reasons. I need to be by myself for a while. I need… some time and space as well."

His arms slacken around me. "But what does that even mean? Going on a break? We're married. You want to date other men for a while or what?"

"No. Absolutely not," I say on a sigh, utterly convinced I'm telling the truth—and maybe it's about time. "You just said it hurts you too much right now to be with me and it hurts me too much that you're pulling away. Let's just… name it instead of staying in this limbo, the two of us in pain but unable to come together in the way we need to."

He shakes his head. "That sounds more like the beginning of the end to me than any kind of solution."

"It's not the end."

He huffs out some air and pushes me off him.

"I don't get why it needs to be named. It sounds to me like, I don't know, you need permission for something." He fixes his gaze on me. "Is there someone else?"

"No, Kev." I hate lying like this, but I can't possibly tell him either. "Of course not."

"I'd understand." His voice breaks again and it's the most devastating sound. "I've not been a good husband. I haven't been there for you, but we did say through good times and through bad."

"I haven't exactly been an exemplary wife either, but... can you please just give me this, even if you don't understand why I need it?"

"Yes. If that's what you need right now, I can give that to you, but... for me, nothing changes. I need you to know that."

What am I even doing? What if Kevin's right, and I am just doing this to get permission—permission to sleep with his sister again? I can't maneuver or scheme my way out of this, but nor can I accept him into my bed again just like that.

"Maybe I don't really understand it either, but I know I need it." My own lies are starting to exhaust me. What I need is time away from him, from everyone, to come to terms with what I did, so he never has to know. But I can't tell him that either.

"Okay, fine. Whatever you need, then." Just like that, he gets up. "I'd better head back."

On automatic pilot, I start to say that he doesn't have to go, although he does. His presence is a reminder of everything I've done wrong. And I know it's devious to use his own guilt against him for my own reasons, but I have no choice, because the only other option is to tell him the truth, and I won't do that.

CHAPTER 30
STELLA

M om, Nathan and I are having dinner outside when Kevin walks into the garden. Instantly, my stomach ties itself in knots and my throat closes up. Am I seeing that right? Has my brother been crying?

"Hey, darling." Mom pulls out a chair for him. "Nathan said you were going to the cabin."

I want to get out of here so badly. I want to run away from the direct consequence of my actions—but I can't. The time to face the music was always going to come.

"Turns out Kate wants a break." He hasn't thrown me any particularly nasty looks. He must not know why. Wait. What? They're on a break?

"Really?" Mom puts a hand on his shoulder. "Are things going that badly?" She throws a nasty look my way.

"Apparently." He lifts his hands in desperation.

"I'm sorry, man," Nathan says.

"It's just a break," I say, but I can't bear the sound of my own voice. I can't be the one comforting my brother about this.

"What the fuck is a break, anyway?" The look he throws mom is so desperate, so vulnerable, it breaks my heart into a million pieces. "Are we separated now? Do I need to find a divorce lawyer?"

"Maybe it's just what it says on the tin, darling. Maybe Kate needs a bit of breathing room. Some time to sort through everything that's going on in her head."

"It's all my fault," Kevin says. "I've completely neglected her. The past few weeks, months even, she might as well not even have existed. I didn't want her in my life and of course she's going to know that. I pushed her away more and more, so what do I expect?"

"There are always two people in a marriage," Mom says. "Besides, it's not about whose fault it is."

It's my fault, a voice inside me screams. Mine and Kate's. But I prefer to believe my mother. Maybe it's not about whose fault it is—that thought is much easier to cling to, anyway, now that I still can.

"Did she say anything else?" Mom asks.

Kevin shakes his head. He's already said more words than we're used to from him. He's already let us see how hurt he is. Knowing my brother, he's about to put a stop to that.

"Do you want me to talk to her?" Mom asks.

"No, Mom. I know you mean well, but I'll deal with it. It's my marriage, my mess. Poor Kate. I really hurt her by pulling away as I did. But I just… didn't know what else to do. I might have hurt her more, might have damaged our marriage more if we'd spent more time together. I don't know." He buries his face in his hands and starts sobbing. My heart breaks a little more.

Maybe, I think, no one's really to blame for any of this. Maybe this is just how life can be. But no, Kevin and Kate's marriage might have been on the rocks before that bottle of tequila, but that certainly didn't give me the right to swoop in and sleep with his wife.

"Oh, fuck." He pushes his palms against his eyes. "I think I'll go to bed."

"Do you want a drink?" Nathan asks. "I replaced that bottle of tequila."

"What bottle of tequila?" Kevin doesn't know anything about his wife's life anymore, although it's probably for the best that he doesn't know about this.

"The one Kate and Stella murdered a few days ago." Nathan's really none the wiser either.

Mom squirms in her seat.

"Sure," Kevin says. "I'll take whatever you can give me."

Nathan gets up.

"How about a day off tomorrow instead?" Mom says.

"How about you have a drink with me and raise a glass to the possible end of my marriage?" Kevin replies. "How about you, Stella? You're in, right?"

I could do with a drink, so it's with real gusto that I agree, although drinking tequila with my brother is the last thing I should be doing.

"I don't want to be the mom here," Mom says, "but is tequila really the best way to deal with this?"

"But you are the mom, Mom. You're a great mom. So, have a drink with your son, please?"

"Maybe just the one."

Nathan returns with the same accoutrements as earlier this week. The very reason we have to turn to tequila again.

He prepares lemon wedges and salt, then pours us all shots. Mom only sips from hers, but the three of us knock them back as though there's no tomorrow.

I won't let myself go the way I did last time, not only for fear of what I might say under the influence—clearly my actions can't be trusted—but because I'm expecting a very important call tomorrow.

"I told her I'd been thinking about adoption, but instead, Kate wants a break from our marriage, which means from me." Kevin holds out his glass for Nathan to refill.

Mom shoots Nathan a look, but he pours the shot, anyway.

HARPER BLISS

"Bro, go easy," I say, now that I still can.

"You're right." He knocks back the shot regardless. "This doesn't solve anything, but… I love her. She's the best woman I know. I can't lose her. I won't."

"Kate loves you too, man," Nathan says.

"I'm going to let you guys finish this." Mom gets up and gives Kevin a hug from behind. "I'm sorry, darling. I'm here for you, but I refuse to drink myself silly. Please, take the day off tomorrow."

Kevin grabs hold of Mom's shoulder for an instant and the gesture touches me deeply.

"Stella, can you give me a hand with something inside, please?" Mom asks.

"Come back soon," Kevin says. "This bottle isn't going to drink itself."

I follow my mother inside. She walks me into the pantry where she's sure Kevin and Nathan can't hear us. She doesn't say anything, just heaves a big sigh.

"I'm sorry. I didn't know they were going to go on a break. I didn't know Kate wanted that."

"Clearly, she did." She points in the direction of the garden. "That's your brother out there, Stella. Drinking his sorrows away."

"I know, but what can I do about that now?"

"Nothing, I guess." She leans against the door. "What happened to this family? And here I was thinking Nathan moving in was going to cause friction—"

"I'm sorry, Mom." How many more times can I say I'm sorry? And what about Kate? Does anyone care about how she's feeling right now, all alone out there in the canyon? Because I sure do. "I never wanted this. It was never my intention. I hope you know that."

"Come here." She opens her arms to me. "Come on." She sounds as though she won't take no for an answer, and I could use a hug much more than another shot of tequila.

182

I step into her soft embrace and, as she puts her arms around me, try not to cry as some of the tension releases from my body.

"Hey," she whispers. "No one died. We're all still alive and in good health. We both know that's all that really matters in the end."

It's not exactly the most uplifting mom-speech, but I get that's the best she can do right now.

"Go be with your brother." She lets go of me. "He needs you."

He's not the only one. "Sure." Before I go back out there, I sneak up to my room to text Kate. When I'm holding my phone, punching in some meaningless words, I change my mind and call her instead.

It takes a while before she picks up, leading me to believe I'm the last person she wants to talk to, but then she does.

"Hey," I say. "I just needed to know you're okay. Kevin's home. He told us about the break."

"Fuck, Stella. What have I done?"

I don't think I'm supposed to answer that, so I just wait.

"How's Kev?" she asks.

"Downing a bottle of tequila with Nathan."

"Oh no," Kate says.

Imagine if those two ended up in bed together, I think. What kind of hell would break loose then? It's preposterous to think about, but Kate and I did end up in bed together, and that's just as preposterous, even though, at times, it doesn't feel that way at all.

"I'm probably not the person you want to talk to, but I'm here if you were to, um, need me," I say, which I probably shouldn't, but I can't help myself.

"Thanks, I—I mean, it was the only way, Stella. Pretending you and I didn't sleep together is one thing, but... I have no choice but to lie to him when we're together and I can't do it. I've debased myself enough already. Taking a break is the only way this is bearable for me, even though it hurts him. And me."

183

"I get it." I blow out some air.

"How is it for you?"

"Agony, especially because Mom knows."

"I can imagine. I'm sorry. I'd invite you to the cabin but that's the worst idea ever."

"Yeah," I say. "We'll just have to find a way through. All of us. See what waits for us on the other side."

"Meanwhile, I'm keeping my fingers crossed for you."

"Thanks. I appreciate it. I'd better go."

"I hope your hangover is mild tomorrow. Bye, Stella."

I sink onto my bed. I don't want to go back out there and drink with Kevin and Nathan. Maybe they can just do some male bonding. It doesn't feel right in any way but, then again, that can be said about a lot of things I've done recently.

There's a knock at the door. "Yes?"

My mother opens the door and just looks at my phone in my hand as though it's the most incriminating piece of evidence.

"Someone needs to look out for Kate." I don't mean to sound so defensive, but I do.

"Perhaps, but not you, Stella. Let it go, I beg you. For the sake of this family, let her go."

"Okay. Goodnight."

At least she takes the hint and leaves. What does she even mean by let it go? Of course I'm letting it go. I've let it go already. Tequila it is, then. At least I won't be ending up in the pool house tonight.

CHAPTER 31
KATE

"Oh! My! God! Good grief. Mary knows? And you and Kev are on a break?" Skye waves her hands about as though she has no clue what to do with them. "I go out of town for a weekend and all of this happens?" She clicks her tongue. "And worst of all, you slept with Stella again? What were you thinking?"

"I was thinking that… I just really wanted to see Stella." I can tell myself I didn't drive to Topanga to sleep with Stella again, but I will always know it's not true. "Then I saw her and I felt… something. I felt good. For once in this wretched time in my life, I felt good. I felt seen and wanted. I felt cared for. I felt fucking loved for once."

"Oh, no, Kate. No way. You're not bringing the L word into this. Lust, sure. Confusion, yeah. And of course you wanted to feel good for a few minutes, but what you feel for Stella is not love."

"How would you know what I feel?"

"I don't, yet I still know it's not love, and you want to know how I know that?" She puts her hands on her hips. "Because it's not possible. She's family. You don't fall in love with your family, Kate. You just don't. That's the end of it."

"And what if I am? What if I am in love with Stella?"

Skye rolls her eyes at me. "Then fall out of love with her, for crying out loud."

"How?"

"By not sleeping with her again, for starters. By taking your husband back and no longer being on a break."

"It's not that easy."

"No, I imagine it's not, but you can do a hard thing. We all do hard things all the time."

"I've done my fair share of the hard stuff. I want something easy for once."

"And you think falling in love with your sister-in-law is going to be easier than denying your feelings for her? Are you willing to ruin that family? To do that to Kevin? And what about Stella? She still lives with her mother. You think she's the kind of girl who's going to give up her family for you?"

"No, of course not."

"I know I'm being harsh, but someone needs to snap you out of this. I figured Mary would have set you straight, but the poor woman was probably too much in shock."

"I'm not sure I can ever face her again. For her to see me like that…"

"Exactly," Skye says. "It's mortifying and it should be more than plenty to snap you out of this." She exhales slowly and comes to sit next to me. "We all know what it's like to have butterflies in our stomachs. To sleep with someone new and have them rock our world. I understand the allure of that, the delightful distraction it offers from real life, but that's just the point. It's not real life. You and Stella can never be a thing in real life, not without some big ass consequences."

"Yeah." I know she's right. Of course I do. "But just so you know, Kevin and I aren't just on a break because of Stella. I'm not even sure what we're doing anymore."

"You both just need time, although not too much. Eventually, sooner rather than later, you're going to need a plan to find your way back to each other."

I try to shake off some of my most acute emotions. We have work to do. Our clients will be here soon to approve the final plans we drew up. The buzzer rings, startling us both. They're early.

"Let's do this." Skye shoots up. "Are you ready?"

"As I'll ever be," I say as Skye walks to the intercom to buzz them in. She does a double take when she looks at the video feed. "Either the Saldanas have morphed into an elegant middle-aged woman or that's Mary Flack at the door."

"What?" My heart's ready to explode out of my chest.

"Should I let her in?"

"I'll go out. Talk to her there. Are you good for when the Saldanas arrive?"

"Don't worry. I'll deal with them."

"I owe you one."

Skye waves me off. Heart thudding furiously, I head out of the building to face Kevin and Stella's mother.

"Is there someplace we can talk in private?" she asks, not bothering with courtesies.

"Is Kevin all right?" My heart might suddenly stop now.

"Just hungover, I imagine." Mary looks as though she hasn't had a proper night's sleep in a while. "I'd just like to have a word with you. I need to say a few things. It will only take a couple of minutes."

I walk her to the back of the building, where Skye and I drink coffee on our breaks. We sit down on the bench.

"I'm not sure I can trust Stella when it comes to this," Mary launches into her speech without preamble. "So I'm asking you, Kate. Don't do this. Don't leave Kevin for Stella. It will destroy him and our family."

"I'm not leaving Kevin for Stella." What does she mean when she says she can't trust Stella? "That's just... unimaginable."

"Okay. Good. It was, um, horrific to have Kevin come home like that last night. He was devastated, Kate. He knows he's not innocent in this. No one is. He blames himself, really. If things don't work out between the two of you it would be awful, of course. That's an outcome no one wants, but these things happen. Couples grow apart because they can't get past certain events. But, for the love of god, don't let the reason for your break be Stella. That's unacceptable. As their mother, who loves them both to death, I'm begging you, don't do that. Don't drive that kind of wedge into my family."

"No, Mary. Of course not." Good thing she wasn't a fly on the wall for the conversation Skye and I were just having.

"I worry that Stella may have some untoward feelings for you and maybe it's too big of an ask after all you've been through, but you're going to have to be the strong one here, Kate. You're going to have to dissuade her of any misguided notions she might have about this."

Stella has feelings for me? My mind can only focus on that. I nod anyway.

"Can you give me your word?"

My word? My word is worth nothing. "Look, Mary, Stella and I are both adults. We both know... what it is we need to know. We both love Kevin, so. We will do what's right."

"Good." Mary shakes her head. "I so hope she gets that part so she can have something else to focus on, something tangible."

A pang of something—Pain? Guilt? Jealousy?—runs through me at the prospect of Stella moving on, effortlessly replacing thoughts of me with thoughts of her possible new job.

"I hope so too."

"Okay. I'll let you get back to work." She rises. "Take care, Kate," she says, as though we'll never see each other again.

I let my head fall against the brick wall behind me. Both Skye and Mary couldn't be more right. But Stella has feelings for me, and I might as well admit to myself, really let myself feel it, that I have feelings for her too. But there's no room for elation at this discovery of reciprocity. We can never be together. I know what to do. My first task on a long list of many is to have another chat with Skye.

CHAPTER 32
STELLA

Kevin's rummaging around in the pool house when I go out to the garden. If only he knew what happened there. If we left any clues at all, I'm sure Kate erased them forever.

I carry my phone with me everywhere, hoping for a call from Damian. As long as I don't hear anything, the news can still be good, but I'm also dying to know what Nora Levine thought of me.

"Hey, Stella," Kevin yells. "Can you give me a hand, please?"

I enter the pool house. All the furniture has been pulled away from the walls. He points at the bed—the scene of our first crime—and says, "That is one heavy bed. Can you help me move it over there?"

"What are you doing?"

"I thought I'd repaint, now that I'm here."

"Seriously?" He and Nathan sat outside with that bottle of tequila long after I went up to my room, unable to sleep but equally unable to knock back any more shots with my brother. Kevin doesn't seem to be suffering too hard from a hangover. Maybe after imbibing too much, he simply drank a bottle of water and slept it off—instead of ending up in bed with someone he shouldn't. "What about your own house?"

"What's the point of renovating the house if Kate doesn't want to live there with me anymore?"

"Are you sure that's what's going on here?"

"I just… need to do something. I can't sit around doing nothing. It drives me completely insane."

"These walls don't need painting. Go to the office if you want to work."

"I can't deal with people today." He pushes his fingertips against the wall as though assessing whether to knock it down or not.

"Fair enough, but I really don't think you should take on yet another project."

He exhales loudly, then leans with his back against the wall —I guess it's still deemed strong enough. "You know what I was thinking last night? When I was drunk out of my skull?"

"No." I stand next to him, my back against the wall as well.

"That if Kate doesn't want to be with me anymore, maybe I'll find another woman who can have kids with me." He scoffs. "Can you believe that? Can you believe how vile and awful that thought is?"

"You were drunk. We all think and do things we shouldn't when we've had a few too many."

"Maybe that's why she wants to go on a break. Maybe she wants another man who can make a baby with her because her and me together simply doesn't work on that front."

"But it works on all other fronts," I say. "You've been married ten years, Kev. You don't just throw that away." It's not only my brother that I'm trying to convince.

"I'm not so sure of that."

"I'm not moving that bed with you, just so you know."

"Whatever." He shrugs. "She'd hate me for repainting without consulting her, anyway. Paint colors are Kate's domain."

"Do you want to do something? Go to a movie? Go for a hike? Have a swim?"

"Sorry, Stella. I've been so caught up in my own shit, I forgot about your audition. You must be beside yourself waiting for news."

"They probably haven't decided yet. They may take weeks. I don't know."

"Yeah." He overlooks the room. "Help me put this stuff back?"

"Sure." I cast one last glance at the bed, at the couch Kate was sleeping on when I woke up in the middle of the night, my head sore and my soul ripped to shreds.

I'm arranging the chairs under the table when my phone rings. It's not Damian. Unknown number. I pick up because when you're an unemployed actor, you always do.

"Stella Flack speaking." I sure hope it's not Kate calling me from a number that's not in my phone—not with Kevin only a few feet from me.

"Hi, Stella. This is Nora Levine. I wanted to give you the good news myself."

I'm already jumping up and down with excitement. Kevin stops what he's doing and rushes toward me.

"It looks like we'll be getting to know each other a lot better, because you got the part. It's yours if you want it. There was a really great vibe between us, don't you think?"

"Um, yeah. Oh, my god. Thank you so much."

"My pleasure. I really look forward to working with you. Let's get together soon, okay?"

"Yes. Definitely."

"Okay. Bye, Stella." With that, Nora abruptly ends the call.

"Was that what I think it was?" It's so good to see a genuine smile on my brother's face.

"Oh, my god, Kev. I got it. I'm going to be Nora Levine's co-star in an awesome TV show." I stare at my phone in disbelief.

"That's so amazing." Kevin throws his arms around me for a bear hug. "Finally, some good news. I'm so happy for you."

My phone starts ringing again. This time, it is my agent.

"It's Damian. I have to take this," I whisper against my brother's shoulder.

He lets go of me and crashes into the couch, as though he too has been waiting for the news and getting it has released all the tension from his muscles.

I chat with Damian, our elation growing as the conversation progresses.

"You did this, Stella," he says. "And you're going to kill it."

When we hang up, I crash next to Kevin in the couch.

"My sister's going to be on TV." He smirks at me. "Does that mean you're going to be even more insufferable than usual?"

I play-punch him in the biceps. "I've never been insufferable," I reply while thinking that, at the very least I'll stop sleeping with his wife. I do text Kate the good news, though.

CHAPTER 33
KATE

I glance at the text on my phone screen. I wish I could share with Stella how ecstatic I am for her. But I can't. Of course, I can't. At least now, as Mary wished, Stella will have something to focus her attention on. But I also intend to take myself out of the equation. Under the guise of celebratory drinks, I ask her to meet me at a bar around the corner from my office. I need to see her one last time and, for obvious reasons, it needs to be in a public place.

When she arrives, it hurts to see her walk toward me. To see that smile on her face that lights up the entire room while knowing she might never smile at me like that again.

I do allow myself a hug. "Congratulations," I whisper in Stella's ear as I hold her close.

"Thanks." She studies my face. "I was a bit surprised to get this invite."

"Your mother came to see me today."

"Oh, no." Stella puts the menu away. "I'm so sorry. What did she say? I can hazard a guess, but... Oh god, was she doing her micro-managing mother-in-law act?"

A server stops by, and we order a glass of wine—definitely not a bottle.

"She's worried and she has every right to be."

"Yes, but still. I can't imagine it's fun to get that kind of visit from your husband's mother."

"It wasn't meant to be fun. But this isn't really about Mary. I've made a decision and I wanted to tell you in person." It's the only way I see out of this.

"Okay." Stella's smile dims considerably.

"I'm going away for a while. I'm going home to Iowa. Spend some time with my own family."

"Oh. Okay." The light in this place is low and not very good at illuminating people's faces. It's hard to gauge Stella's reaction —not that it still matters at this point. "How long?"

"As long as it takes for me to feel like I can come back. I'll work remotely as best I can, but Skye's going to have to cover for me, maybe hire someone new."

"Does Kevin know?"

I shake my head. "Not yet. I needed to talk to you first, Stella, because… I think we should tell him the truth."

The light might be weak, but there's enough of it for me to see Stella's eyebrows shoot all the way up her forehead. "Tell him? About us? Have you lost your mind?"

"No, on the contrary. How can I ever go back to him with that lie festering between us? I can't do that. I'm not that person."

"You can't tell him and then leave for Iowa for an undetermined period of time. What about me?"

Stella's right. I can't leave her to deal with the massive fallout of this on her own. "I don't have to tell him everything. I don't have to tell him I have feelings for you, although he might put two and two together. Let's not forget that Mary knows, and these things have a tendency to come out at some point. That's why I figure complete honesty is the best policy."

"Oh, no. I disagree. A lot."

Our wine arrives, which gives me the opportunity to take a much-needed breath.

"Why can't you just go away without saying anything? Think about your life and whatever else you need to, and only then decide whether to tell him about your… indiscretion."

If only it was just that. "It's not just the sex. I need to be honest about all of it. What I feel for you."

Stella pauses and briefly looks me in the eye. "You have feelings for me?"

I can only nod. "All the more reason for me to leave."

"Fuck." Stella stares into her glass. "Those feelings are very mutual, you know, in case you were wondering," she mumbles into her wine, but I can hear her loud and clear.

"We have no choice, Stella." It takes all the willpower I have to not put my hand on hers. "We can't act on our feelings. We can't do that to Kevin."

"Agreed, so please don't tell him. This is not a decision you can make on your own. My life will be impacted by it as well."

"I won't tell him it's you, but I have to tell him something."

"Why? You have plenty of reasons to go away, to take a break from your marriage. Why add insult to injury?"

"Because I'm sick of lying to my husband."

"That may be so, but you'll only hurt him even more. And me. And Mom. Everyone, only so you can get some relief." Stella pins her gaze on me. "Sometimes it's kinder not to tell someone the truth, especially someone you love."

"Do you really believe that? After what Toni did to you?"

"Toni didn't sleep with my brother. She slept with my best friend and Sheena has not been my friend since. Of course she had to tell me. I needed to know, but there are some things you can't come back from."

"Maybe you can when it's family."

"Sheena was like my family. I wanted to marry Toni. Now, I never see them anymore and I miss them, because they were my two best friends in the world, and then suddenly, I didn't have a girlfriend and I didn't have a best friend anymore either."

"But either way, Stella, they had to tell you."

"Yes, but the circumstances couldn't be more different. They fell in love. Toni was leaving me for her." Stella shakes her head, sadness in her glance. "I don't wish that kind of pain on anyone. Most certainly not on my brother."

"So, even though you've been cheated on, been lied to by the people you loved the most, you still don't think we should tell Kevin?"

"No, because you and I are not a thing, Kate. You're not leaving Kevin for me. We're not having an affair. We were together for two nights. It's…. What did you call it? Some mindless fun. Certainly nothing to break my brother's heart over and have him hate me for the rest of my life."

I reach for her hand. She doesn't pull away. "It was anything but mindless fun. I miss you. I miss walking out of the pool house and seeing you there. Making plans with you. Doing things with you, even if it was just hanging out, just chitchatting in the kitchen. I miss how simply being with you makes me feel."

"Yeah. Well." Stella takes a deep breath. "As I just said, as we both know, as my mother begged us, you and I can't be together, so."

"I know." I release her hand although I'd like to hang on to it a good while longer. "That's why I have to get out of LA."

"Please, Kate. Don't tell him. I'm asking you. Me." She brings her hand to her chest. "Please."

"I won't tell him it's you. You have my word, but that's the only promise I can make."

"When are you leaving?" Stella says on a sigh.

"As soon as I've talked to Kevin and sorted things out with Skye."

"Will you be in touch?"

"No. I can't be, not with you. I hope you understand."

"I get it."

"You have so much to look forward to, Stella. Your life's

about to change. You will meet so many great people and, who knows, maybe you'll meet someone who makes you feel the spark." I definitely don't want to be around when that happens.

"You made me feel the spark." She grabs my hand now. "Just so you know."

"I know."

"I need to get out of here. Is that all right?"

"I'll walk you out." I can't just let her walk away. I quickly pay the check and follow Stella outside. It's another mild Los Angeles evening and I slip my fingers through hers on automatic pilot. As though it's a gesture I've performed all my life.

"Say hi to Nora Levine for me."

"I'm surprised you haven't asked for an introduction yet." Stella steps closer. "Also, I've been meaning to ask." She grins at me. "Are you still gay for Faye?"

I burst into a chuckle. "Only for you." One final time, I press my lips against hers, and kiss her in the blue-dark of the night.

CHAPTER 34
STELLA

"Who the hell can it be?" Kevin twists his beer bottle between his fingers. "Kate may claim it doesn't matter. That there's no reason for me to know, but not knowing is driving me mad."

It's been like this for days. Kevin going nuts while, ironically, spending a lot more time at Mom's house than when Kate was living here. While I'm relieved Kate didn't tell him it's me she has feelings for, this is becoming equally unbearable. A few more days, and I might start seeing sense in telling him the absolute truth. For now, I can only hope it blows over. That he gets over the fact that his wife has feelings for 'someone else'. As far as I know, Kate didn't tell Kevin that she actually slept with this mysterious other person who is also me. That would probably drive him all the way up the wall.

"You were chummy with Kate before she left." Kevin pins his gaze on me. "She didn't tell you?"

I wish I could escape to Iowa as well. Maybe I should make something happen for myself. Look into the possibility of doing some promotion with Faye for our movie. Getting this part has given my professional confidence a massive boost. Damian might be able to arrange something for me—I've suddenly become one of his top clients. Production on the Nora Levine project doesn't start for another few months. What am I going to do with myself until then? Not listen to my brother complain about his estranged wife, that's for sure.

"No," I lie, and I'm beginning to understand why Kate couldn't bear to lie to him any longer. It's excruciating to have to do it over and over again to someone that you love with all your heart.

All of a sudden, an image of Toni pops into my head, but I push it away. It's not the first time memories of Toni and Sheena —of the good times—have crept up on me, but I've always been able to quash them as soon as they appear. Things are a little different these days; what I did with Kate has made me a touch more sympathetic to what they did to me.

"What's with you?" Kev says. "I thought you'd be over the moon, but you've been surprisingly crabby all week."

I miss her too, I think. "I'm worried about you guys." At least that's not a lie. "And I've been thinking about maybe getting in touch with Sheena." Always a good idea to move the conversation away from Kate.

"Sheena? Okay." He doesn't dismiss my idea immediately although Kevin has been just as furious with her as I've been for the past few years. "Can I tell you something?"

"Um, yeah." My heart starts thumping, because that's the other part of not telling the truth. You never know if the deceived person will put two and two together on their own. If they'll get a sudden flash of clarity and everything just reveals itself to them.

"I ran into Toni and Sheena a couple of months ago. They asked about you. I told them about the Lana Lynch movie."

"You saw them? Where?"

"In the street. A few blocks from the office. They were having coffee."

"How, um, were they?"

"Fine, I guess. It was all a bit awkward, but, I mean, what

they did was bad and how they treated you was awful, but they're good people at their core, otherwise they wouldn't have been so important to you for such a long time." He clears his throat. "What I'm trying to say is that I'm pretty sure they'd love to hear from you. You're in a good place right now. Why not see what happens when you get in touch?"

"Maybe." That's the fatherly part in him rearing its head. "I'll do that."

"Wasn't Kate going to set you up with someone, by the way? Skye's niece or someone?" He scratches his five o'clock shadow. "Did she fail to see that through as well?"

There's no way I can possibly go on a blind date arranged by Kate. "It fell through."

"Why? Are you saying this other woman wasn't interested in meeting Stella Flack? My one and only sister? Maybe I should talk to Skye." He narrows his eyes. "Hm, maybe I should meet up with her. She might know more about this mystery dude my wife has a crush on."

I don't know Skye well enough to be certain she can keep a secret, because I do know she knows about us. I have to assume she has Kate's best interests at heart.

"Maybe you should just let it go, Kev."

"Let it go? That my wife is *interested* in someone else?" He slams down his beer bottle. "I really don't think so."

I wouldn't be able to let it go either. In fact, I know very well, in my heart of hearts, that one of the main reasons I've barely dated since Toni, is fear of it happening again. Of falling in love with someone, putting my trust in them, only to have them leave me for someone else again. I don't need years of therapy to figure that out. Not dating has just been easier than putting myself out there again. To love someone who loves someone else is one of the most devastating experiences. Because there's nothing you can do but wallow in the power-lessness of it all. You can't make someone love you. They either do or they don't. It's just a massive pity that the first woman I do have feelings for after all this time is the one woman I can't be with.

"You know what?" I may understand how Kevin feels, but I can't sit here with him while he's in so much pain about his marriage falling apart—which I'm partially responsible for— any longer. That's even more mortifying than having the woman you love run off with your best friend. "I'll text Sheena now."

"Go for it." Kevin gets up. "I'm making dinner tonight."

While I search for Sheena's number, which I'll have to unblock first, I watch Kevin saunter into the house. Maybe he's just grieving, and he really believes that working on his house is pointless now that he and Kate are on a break, but I can't shake the feeling that he's relieved about something as well. He's even making dinner.

———

I'm meeting Sheena for coffee without Toni. There are limits to what my poor heart can take and in my hierarchy of hurt, Toni ranks higher, although it's practically neck-and-neck with those two.

"Oh, my god. Stella!" She gets up when she sees me. "I'd love a hug, but I understand if it's out of the question."

I hug her because it feels damn good to have someone throw their arms around me who isn't Kate, who fled to Iowa and whom I haven't heard from since we said goodbye—since that final kiss outside the bar.

"I was so glad you got in touch." She swallows hard. "I'm so very sorry." She brushes away the beginning of a tear.

How can I still be angry with her? Not only has time done its job of healing the most painful part of the wound she and Toni inflicted on me, but I now know what it feels like to betray a loved one. At least I know it's not a purely black-and-white situation.

"I saw you in *Like No One Else*. When you kissed Lana Lynch I didn't know what to do with myself. It was out of this world to see that. You were awesome, like you were born to play Cleo Palmer."

"Thanks." Everything about being here with Sheena reminds me of Kate. She flipped out when she saw my character kiss Faye's character in that movie. That's probably when it all started. "It was an amazing experience. And Faye's so nice, like you can't believe. She's Faye Fleming. She doesn't have to be nice to me, yet she was nothing but." I'm babbling, trying to chatter my guilt away. Maybe I'm not here to restore my former bond with my best friend. Maybe I'm only here looking for some sort of twisted absolution and she's the only one who can give it to me. "How have you been, Sheena?"

"Good. Better now that I'm seeing you." The thing with Sheena starting an affair with my girlfriend was that I never, not for one split second, believed she had that in her. She was always the best person I knew. Always full of kindness and endless patience and just sheer goodness. Now, I know that maybe everyone's capable of betraying the people that they love the most.

"How's Toni?" I can hardly pretend she doesn't exist.

"She's good." Sheena reaches for her ring finger and fiddles with a ring, drawing my attention to the small diamond it holds. "Please don't think it was easy for us. It wasn't, but we had each other, while you…"

"I didn't even have my best friend." I lean over the table. "Is that what I think it is?" I point at the ring on her finger.

"Yes," she says on a sigh, as though this is a bad thing. "We're getting married."

Although it's the most common action people take after they've been together a few years, the news still stumps me. "Wow. Congratulations."

"Thank you." She tilts her head. "How about you, Stella? Are you seeing someone?"

"Me? No."

"For real? After that movie? Surely women are throwing themselves at you by the dozen wherever you go."

"No, they really aren't." Only Kate did. "Can I ask you a potentially difficult question?"

"Of course. Ask me anything, Stella. Anything you want." Her gaze softens. "I've missed you so much. Maybe it's not my place to say, but fuck, I miss you. Just sitting here with you… despite all that has happened, something about it just feels right, because it's you. Because I've known you forever and you're so familiar to me."

Maybe I'm carrying too much guilt, or still too much residual hurt, to feel the same way. "I've missed you too," I say, because I have missed some parts of being friends with her. "But I'd just like to know how… you and Toni… how you learned to deal with the guilt? How you got over what you did to me?"

She inhales deeply. "The thing is that it didn't feel as though we were doing anything to you. We fell in love, and it was hurtful to you in so many ways, all of them inexcusable, because we should have waited." She brushes away another tear. "I regret many things, but that I regret the most. That we carried on behind your back as though you were just anyone. Not that it's ever the right thing to do, but you were my best friend. But in the end, we couldn't stop how we felt. We tried, but… either way, Toni couldn't stay with you and…"

"Then she might as well have ended up with you."

"To put it bluntly." She closes her eyes briefly. "Many mistakes were made. Too many."

"And now you're getting married." What they did no longer hurts me, although I might never be able to forgive them. Or does one require the other? Can I not forgive them because, on some level, it does still hurt me?

Sheena nods.

"In hindsight, was it really never an option for you to break things off with Toni? Because of me?"

"There are always options and, in hindsight, that's what I should have done."

"But then what?"

"In that case, I think Toni would have broken up with you and maybe, after an appropriate amount of time, we would have gotten together again. Or not. It's impossible to say. Things should not have gone down the way they did. I will always be sorry for that, but, I don't know, it's like part of me knows that I was always going to end up with Toni. I'm sorry if that sounds harsh, but that's the only way I can explain it to myself. That she's *the one,* and I knew. I felt it in my bones, and it made me do things I would never otherwise have done to a friend. At least I never thought I would. It's not an excuse. There are no excuses, but sometimes, life is just painful like that, and you have to lose someone… for love."

Once again, I'm stumped. I truly don't know what to say to that.

"I will never be so foolish to ask for your forgiveness, Stella. I don't deserve it, because I was your best friend and I should have had your back. I should have nipped it all in the bud when I still could, but I wasn't strong enough. I chose Toni and myself over you and I'll have to live with that for the rest of my life, but, um…"

"It was worth it," I say.

"How can I say otherwise? Things might not have worked out between Toni and me and then I would have lost it all too, but that's not how it went. We're a good couple. I know how much you loved her and maybe if we—"

"Please, Sheena, stop. I know I asked, but I'm not sure I can take any more of this."

"Oh god. I'm sorry."

"No, look, I get it. I do. It's an impossible situation to be in

and you chose yourself and, frankly, why shouldn't you have?"
It's not like I'm your sibling.

"It's not as clean cut as that, Stella. It wasn't a coldhearted, spur-of-the-moment decision. It was a long and arduous process and something we still struggle with to this day. We bumped into your brother not so long ago and that set us off again... We may have found this great love, but what we did to you will always come between us in one way or another. But maybe that's not so unlike most relationships. That's how I've learned to live with it. There's always something. That kind of purity is an illusion."

Good for you, is my first thought, but I can no longer, in good faith, be so callous with my thoughts. I lost that right when I kissed Kate for the first time.

CHAPTER 35
KATE

I've been here for almost two weeks, and it's as though my mother still can't believe I'm home. Or maybe she doesn't really know what to do with her only daughter's prolonged presence. I don't know what to do with myself either, so I've decided to do not much at all. To try and find some sort of peace deep inside me, hoping it will guide me to whatever my next step will be, although there are only two options: go back to Kevin, or not.

What has proven hardest of all, especially now that I spend so much more time on my phone, is not texting Stella. Not knowing how she's doing. Trying not to think about our night together. Technically, we had two nights together, and the first paved the way for the second, but the second night is the one that counts. The one that keeps coming back to me because I suspect—I'm afraid—that during that gorgeous night out there in Topanga Canyon, I might have fallen in love with my sister-in-law.

I can take a plane and travel hundreds of miles to put some much needed distance between us, but my heart doesn't care about that. Not if all the yearning it does for her is anything to go by.

I join my mother on the front porch. It's a habit I've taken up since the first day I got here. After dinner, we sit in two adjoining chairs and drink one glass—never more than that—of wine.

There's not much to see in the street beyond the front yard. The occasional car drives past but that's it. It's not silent, but it's peaceful—like in Topanga.

Every time I've sat next to her, my mother has tried to pry more information out of me. She's not the live-and-let-live type. She likes to know things and me coming home for an extended visit—with no leaving date confirmed—is cause for much speculation.

I've told her about the six rounds of failed IVF; the two failed pregnancies, and the one possibly failed marriage, although not in those words.

"So you're separated but you're not leaving him?" she asked on the first night. Every following night, she's come up with a way to ask the question in an alternative manner. Do you still love him? Does he still love you? Is there someone else? Can you live with the two of you not having any children?

None of those questions have been easy to answer, and most of my replies have consisted of the same three words: I don't know.

"Look at this, Kate." Mom shows me the magazine she's been reading. "I know you never really got along with Kevin's sister, but she's in this big movie with Faye Fleming."

The one topic I've avoided since arriving is Stella, because I'm afraid of what I might say.

"Yeah. We all went to the premiere together." A dubious kind of warmth spreads through me at the memory. "Stella even took me to a party at Faye Fleming's house."

"She did?" Mom puts the magazine away with a decisive gesture—as though I've also failed as her daughter by not telling her about that as soon as it happened. "You met Faye Fleming?"

"And Ida Burton." As amazing as that night was, it pales in comparison to everything that happened to Stella and me afterward.

"What were they like? Why didn't you tell me about this? I know you live in LA, in Hollywood, and that your sister-in-law is an actor, but that's about the extent of it. I'm your mother, Kate."

"Stella, she, um..." I take a sip of wine. I find myself wholly unable to discuss Stella in this situation. "We get along better now."

"Sounds like it." My mother's piercing gaze burns my cheek, but I'm afraid to look at her. I stare straight ahead, at the nothingness I came here to find.

"None of that's a big deal, Mom. Faye and Ida are two women just like us."

"Goodness, darling, you must be more depressed than I thought if you can't even get excited about something like that anymore."

"Depressed? I'm not depressed." Just relentlessly confused.

"Could have fooled me. You may not tell me a lot about your life anymore, but you came here for a reason. I'm still your mother, and I can still sense certain things." She pauses. "You don't have to, but you can talk to me. Isn't that why you're here?"

"Maybe." I wish I could talk to my mom, but she's only going to tell me the same thing Skye and Mary—and Stella for that matter—told me.

"If you no longer see a future for you and Kevin, that's okay. Most marriages don't last. It's a small miracle if a marriage does last these days."

"You and dad have lasted for over forty years."

"Not without a lot of give and take." She huffs out some air. "And at times, it has been a small miracle."

That's the first I've heard of that, but I haven't lived here for two decades. I haven't come to visit as often as I should have. I try to make it at least once a year for Christmas or Thanksgiving, but it's always too short, and there are always other family members around.

"Is there something you want to tell me, Mom?" I do look in her direction now.

"No. It's all water under the bridge now."

"But… do you think that you should have split up at a certain point? Do you regret not doing so?"

Mom shakes her head. "I regret many things, but that's how life is." She sends me a small smile. "Except for having you, darling. I've never regretted that for one single second." She leans her elbows on her knees. "I'm really sorry that you and Kevin can't conceive. I know how much you want it and yours wouldn't be the first marriage to break under that kind of strain, nor would it be the last."

"It's not like I suddenly stopped loving him, but—" I pause to take another sip. "We haven't had fun in such a long time. I think we lost our sense of humor somewhere around IVF round number three. That was a long time ago."

My mom remains uncharacteristically silent, so I continue.

"All the treatments and doctor's offices were dreadful enough, but what's been most excruciating has been going home after and despite having all this common ground, and this huge joint wish for a child, despite all the love we have for each other, we weren't able to find each other, like a wire in our connection broke and nothing can fix it." I drain my glass of wine. As though she knows that tonight we will need more than one glass, Mom gets up and walks back out with the bottle. She refills both our glasses.

"Do you know how Kevin feels about all this?" she asks.

"He pretty much told me it's very hard for him to be around me. That it's too painful." To repeat my husband's words doesn't hurt me the way I expect—and I know why. I've found my very own special, immoral kind of protection. I've gone and developed feelings for his sister to cushion the blow.

"As your mother, that's really hard to hear."

"For a few years now, our marriage has not been going the way I've wanted it to. Or is that a foolish thing to say? Am I too controlling?"

"You've been disappointed time after time, Kate. No wonder you feel like that."

"He's not been there for me, and I've not been there for him. I tried, but it was too hard. And now… Oh god, Mom." I look into the distance. "I'm not sure I can go back to him because… there's someone else."

I don't have to see her face to register her sharp intake of breath. "What did you say, darling? There's someone else?"

"I think I may have feelings for someone else, although how can I be sure with the state I'm in? The state of my marriage?" Maybe if I can be abstract about the person, my mother can help me find some clarity.

"I think that, um, when you have feelings for someone, you always know. Whether you act on them is another matter, of course." She squirms around in her seat. "Have you? Acted on your feelings?"

"It doesn't matter." That is the biggest lie of all and I'm so sick of lying. It's one of the reasons I came here, so I would no longer have to lie to the people I love.

"It's hard not to take that as a yes, darling." Mom's voice is barely a whisper. "Have you been unfaithful to your husband?"

Unfaithful? What does that word even mean? What does a wedding vow mean when fifty percent of marriages end in divorce?

"I've been in so much pain, Mom. I've been so lonely. I've felt so utterly alone and then…" I can hardly say 'she was there', but I can't say 'he' either.

"This other person came along and took away some of your pain?" she says.

"Yes. Exactly that. They—*She*." I can't be coy about this any longer. "It's a woman, Mom." I turn to look at her, just so she knows I'm not ashamed of that part, although I am about many others.

"You have feelings for another woman?" Her voice has a surprising lightness. "A friend of yours?" She smiles at me. "Someone you've confided in and have grown close to, I suppose. Don't worry about that too much. It's only normal for you to project all the feelings you can't express to your husband on the most available person to you. It's good that it's another woman, because it means it's not serious."

My turn to do a double-take. "What do you mean?"

"Well, as far as I know, you're not gay, so how can it possibly be serious?"

"It is serious and maybe I am gay. Or bi."

"Maybe just for now, Kate, but surely you're not... Really. Not after all this time with Kevin. I mean, what would have happened if you had gotten pregnant? You'd simply have continued being straight."

Maybe my mother wasn't the best person to have this conversation with. But she's my mother and she needs to know. I must have wanted her to know, otherwise I wouldn't have gone through the awkwardness of telling her, of having her react this way.

"I get that this is surprising for you. Unexpected. But I'm not straight, I can tell you that."

"Okay. Okay." Mom holds up her hands. "I'm sorry. You're right. It was unexpected and I shouldn't have reacted in that way. I'm well aware, but... I need some time to process."

"No, I know, Mom. It's fine. I didn't mean to spring this on you, but the fact she's a woman is not the issue here."

"No, I guess not. You're right." She takes a few big gulps of air. "So what are you saying? You want to leave Kevin for this woman?"

I shake my head. "That would be quite impossible."

"Why?"

"Because…" After I say her name, my mom may never look at me in the same way again. Her opinion of me might be forever changed—and not for the better. "It's Stella, Mom. I'm in love with Stella."

"Kevin's little sister?" Her voice has gone all high-pitched.

I can only nod.

"You've been having an affair with Kevin's sister?"

It sounds awful when said out loud like that, and it is awful in many ways but, in some other ways, being with Stella has given me so much. It has returned a vital part of me to myself.

"Not an affair," I say, weakly, in my equally weak defense.

"Oh, darling," Mom exclaims. "Did she… try it on with you?"

"No." If anything, I tried it on with her, but saying that now is not a good idea. "I was so lost and she was there. We became friends. Close friends and then… more. And I know it sounds terrible, but, to me, here"—I bring a dramatic hand to my chest —"it's been anything but. She's just… like a dream. Actually, yeah, that's the best way to describe it. Like the most delicious dream you have just before waking up, but then you do wake up, and you realize none of it was real and all you want to do is go back to sleep to continue the dream but you can't. It's gone forever, but the emotion lingers." A tear rains down my cheek. "I came here to get away from her. To wake myself up properly from that dream, but it's not working. I don't miss Kevin. I miss Stella."

"That's a lot," Mom says. "Phew." She leans over and pats my knee. "You've been carrying that load all on your own. No wonder you're exhausted. No wonder I believed you were depressed."

"I'm just in love with someone I can't be with." My shoulders slump. There may be some relief in sharing, but the outcome remains the same.

"How does Stella feel about you?"

"We haven't really talked about it. It's a bit too confronta-
tional, I guess, but from what I gather, she may feel the same."

"I wish I could tell you what to do. Give you some motherly
advice, but this is a really tricky one."

"I know. It's impossible."

"Nothing's impossible, darling," Mom says. "Just untried."

CHAPTER 36
STELLA

"I slept with my brother's wife," I say to Faye Fleming. We are halfway through a bottle of fine wine—most of it drunk by me—in a swanky London hotel room, when I just blurt it out. Before she can react, I hold up my hand. "Worst of all, I think I may be in love with her."

"You're in love with your brother's wife." Faye's famous eyebrows are knotted together. "Am I hearing that right or was there too much applause after the premiere earlier and my eardrums have been affected?"

I joined Faye and the *Like No One Else* PR team in Europe two weeks ago because I was going mad at home with Kate gone and Kevin moping around and Mom not knowing what to do with herself, which is, quite possibly, most unsettling of all. As though she knows her family might implode any second.

"I don't know what to do."

"Have you tried falling out of love with her?" Faye says matter-of-factly. She seems rather unfazed by my confession. Maybe she thinks I'm just playing—just saying outrageous things to entertain her.

"When you fell in love with Ida and someone had suggested that, would you have been able to?"

"Me? Fall out of love with Ida? Are you crazy?"

"You met Kate. I brought her to that party at your house."

"Oh." Faye nods approvingly. "I remember Kate. Oh yes, I can see that."

"What does that mean?"

"She's not, um, not-hot." Faye grins.

"Oh, god," I groan.

"I say this respectfully, of course." She tilts her head. "Is this why your agent begged to have you join the Europe promo tour? You needed to get away from her?"

"That was to get away from my brother. He's staying with Mom and me and being around him is unbearable. Kate went home to spend time with her family because she had to get away from me and Kev."

"Sounds like one big happy family."

"Doesn't it just?"

"How did this happen? You just took a shine to her one fine day?" Faye takes a small sip of her wine.

I respond by taking a much bigger sip from my own glass.

Then I give her the broad strokes about Kevin and Kate's unfruitful fertility journey and how it destabilized their marriage.

"I feel for them. A lot." She chews the inside of her cheek. "It sounds very similar to what Brian and I went through and, as you know, our marriage didn't survive. I know what that kind of thing can do to a relationship. It's really hard to just continue afterward and find a new path without the children you wanted so much. As though they were the only reason you were ever together in the first place."

"I didn't know that. I'm so sorry, Faye."

"Look at me now. I'm married to Ida Burton and we have Leesa and Leroy, so... this is life and you never know what's going to happen. I had huge doubts about making *A New Day*. If I'd chickened out because it was too gay, I might never have gotten to know Ida better."

"If you put it like that."

"Ida wasn't married to my brother, though."

"Ouch."

"But, ever since Ida and I came out we've been bombarded with the message that love is love and maybe that applies to much more ways of loving each other than same-sex couples."

"That's a dangerous can of worms you're about to open there."

"Why? You're two consenting adults."

"I know what it feels like to be cheated on. My girlfriend left me for my best friend. They had an affair for months before I knew anything about it. I don't want to do that to my brother."

"That sounds awful. I'm so sorry you had to go through that. How long ago was this?"

"Three years."

"Well then, three years later, when you look back, what was the most painful: that they were sleeping together behind your back or that they fell in love?"

"Both."

"Are they still together?" Faye asks.

"They're getting married." The fact that I can say this without flinching is revealing to me.

"Are you okay with that?"

"It's not my thing to be or not be okay with anymore. It's just how it is. They're each other's soulmates or something like that."

"What if Kate is *your* soulmate?"

"She can't be."

"Because of your brother?"

I nod.

"But your brother presumably loves you and wants you to be happy."

"Sure, but not with his wife."

"Well, not at first. That's too much to expect of even the most enlightened human, but given some time…"

"I haven't told you the best bit yet, Faye." I have to chuckle. In its own twisted way, it's kind of funny. "My mom walked in on us."

"Oh, no. This just keeps getting better and better. That's a movie right there, Stella. We need to get Charlie on this as soon as possible."

"It's one hell of a soap opera." What else are we going to do but laugh? It's a lot more fun than crying over what I can't have. "The point is that my mother knows, and she begged us to not let it turn into anything for all of our sakes. For the family's sake."

"What about your and Kate's sake?"

"There's no such thing. It's just too impossible. Too painful. Too difficult."

"How does Kate feel about you?"

I shrug. "Last I heard, she has feelings for me, but that was three weeks ago and a lot can change in three weeks. We haven't been in touch. By design."

"It's complicated all right, but ever since I fell in love with Ida, I will always try to make a case for love. No matter what. Because sometimes the price of not pursuing it is higher than what you think you'd give up for it in the first place."

I've had a little too much wine to get that without letting it sink in for a second. Then my phone beeps. What time is it back home? Mid-afternoon, probably.

"Speak of the devil, that's probably my mother."

"I can't even think about that, Stella. Your mother walked in on you." Faye obviously thinks this is a massive hoot. It would be funny if it wasn't so mortifying. Out of guilt more than anything, I grab my phone so I can text Mom back that I'm doing okay, which, in her mind, is probably code for me swiftly forgetting all about Kate.

"Oh," I say when I see who the message is from. So much for not being in touch. But maybe Kate has come to the end of her exile. She's bored in the Des Moines suburbs and she's just notifying me of her impending return to LA.

I know we agreed not to contact each other but damn it, Stella, I can't stop thinking about you.

"Oh, Jesus," I mutter under my breath.

"What is it?" Faye asks.

"It's from Kate."

"What does she say?" Maybe her impromptu little speech earlier made Faye invested in this more than she ought to be.

"That she can't stop thinking about me." I gaze at my phone screen. "You know this is all your fault, right?" Making more jokes is the only way I can deal with this right now.

"Me? What did I do?" Faye's eyes go wide.

"Kate and I have this running joke that she's 'gay for Faye'. That's you."

"Flattered as I am, I still don't see what that has to do with me." She flutters her eyelashes.

"You made her gay, Faye." I burst out laughing. "She saw us kiss in the movie and it… did something to her."

"Millions of people have seen *our characters* kiss in that movie and I'm fairly certain that for most of them nothing much has changed."

"It started out as a joke. Until it spiraled out of control."

"If you need someone to blame all this on, go ahead, blame me, but the real question is: what are you going to reply? Does Kate know you're in my hotel room knocking back all my expensive wine?"

"She'd probably go nuts if I told her that."

"Maybe that's exactly what you need. Some levity," Faye offers.

"I can't reply with a joke right now. God knows what she's

going through out there in the sticks? With no one to talk to and all that spare time to mull things over. Miles away from her life —and me."

"It's pretty obvious you can't stop thinking about her either."

I let my head fall back. "How long does it take to get over someone? Weeks? Months?"

"Depends on the intensity of your feelings for them."

"I'd just hoped distance would speed up the process, do what time can't. Make it go faster. Make it so I can just get on with my life without considering ruining my brother's. Because, just hypothetically, say that, yes, love is love, and Kate and I are entitled to love each other. We choose each other. Then what? My brother stops talking to me. Mom will kick me out of the house. She'd be so angry and, worst of all, disappointed in me. I'll lose my family and I don't want that."

"But you'd gain Kate."

"Our potential happiness is not worth all that pain."

"But what if it is? You'll never know if you don't try."

I shake my head. "I won't do that to my family. I just won't."

"That may be so, Stella, but hearing you talk about Kate, it sounds to me as though part of you already has."

"That's not true." I hold up one finger. "We chose each other fully sober exactly once. We had one night of weakness, that's it. That's still excusable. We ended it right after, when we came back to our senses. Now we just have to wait until our feelings go away."

"Good luck with that." Faye points at my phone. "You're not going to reply to her at all?"

"What can I possibly say?"

Faye scrunches up her lips as though she's seriously considering my mostly rhetorical question.

"If you think she's not worth it, then say nothing. Then you shut it down. Send the only message you can. That it's over."

The wine I drank over the past hour threatens to make its

way back up, that's how devastating Faye's statement sounds. Cold. Heartless. Ruthless, even. All the opposite emotions to those that run through me when I think of Kate.

"Maybe she's laying her cards on the table. Maybe that's the wisdom distance has brought her. That she wants to be with you." Faye's not letting it go just yet. She must have spotted the devastated look on my face just now.

"But it's imposs—"

"Stop saying it's impossible, Stella. Talk to your family. Tell them how you feel. Be honest and take it from there."

"Have you met my mom?"

"I don't think it's your mother you should be worrying about the most."

Poor Kevin. All the guy's ever done is look out for me. And now I have to tell him that I'm in love with his wife? How's that for sisterly love?

"Are you serious about all the things you just said?" I examine Faye's face. "You're a mother. Imagine if something like this happened in your family."

"My kids are far too young for this kind of drama. Thank goodness." Faye's face practically melts when she mentions her children. "I'm an outsider. I'm not part of your family and I don't know the dynamics of it. But from what you've told me, which is only one side of the story, but it's all I've got to go on, your brother's marriage isn't doing well, and you and Kate are in love. Either you hurt him now and he will suffer for a while, be angry with you, cut you out of his life for a bit. Those are all real possibilities. Until he comes around, because he's your brother. He's your family." Faye pins her gaze on me. "Or you and Kate hurt yourselves and miss out on something possibly amazing."

"If we hurt Kevin, we hurt ourselves as well. Either way, we hurt ourselves. It's an easy enough equation. If Kate and I are going to get hurt anyway, we might as well keep Kevin out of it."

HARPER BLISS

"Oh, sure. If only love were that easy. If only you could choose who you fall for. If only you could not fall in love with your brother's wife. Press the delete button on the hard drive of your heart." She exhales deeply. "Unfortunately, it doesn't work that way."

"Maybe we just need a little more time away from each other."

"Maybe." Faye refills my glass, emptying the bottle. "Maybe not."

———

Back in my room, Faye's words echo in my head. So do my own. But I've had enough of thinking this through, of turning it over again and again, trying to find another outcome that doesn't exist. Most of all, I just want to hear Kate's voice.

She picks up after the first ring.

"Hey." All it takes is for her to say one word, for me to hear her voice for a split second, and all the things I've been trying to push away engulf me again.

"Hi," I say.

"It's so good to hear your voice," Kate says. "How are you?"

"You're never going to believe who I was hanging out with when you texted me earlier."

"It would help if I knew where you were."

"I'm in London. With Faye."

"F-faye Fleming?" I wish I could see Kate's face. I should have video called her, but it seemed like too much.

"The one and only. I owe you a huge apology, by the way, because I told her exactly how gay you are for her."

"What?"

"I also told her about us," I say on a sigh.

"Oh, my god. What are you doing in London?"

"Working. European promotion tour for *Like No One Else*. I had to get out of LA. I was going mad… without you."

"You were?" Her voice wavers.

"Yeah. They even put me up in the same swanky hotel as Faye. She's just next door. She poured me a glass of wine too many and you know what I'm like when I've had a few. All boundaries out of the window."

"Stella." Kate's voice is suddenly sharp. "Are you okay?"

"I'm fine. Just surprised to get that text from you. How are things with your family?"

"I told my mom about us. I had to tell her. I couldn't keep it to myself any longer. She was quite understanding about it."

"She was?" My turn to be surprised. Kate telling her mother is much more profound than me telling Faye.

"At first she thought you had brazenly seduced me, but I made sure she knew that's not how it went." She pauses. "Although you did take off your top in the hot tub that night."

"I didn't do that to—" She's playing, trying to ease the tension, I do know that.

"Oh, Stella, it doesn't matter. I—" I only hear her the inhale and exhale of her breath for a few seconds. "What I texted you is true. I can't stop thinking about you. I should be thinking about a million other things, like how to save my marriage, but I can only think of you. It's like instead of making it easier, the distance has made it harder. Because I don't want to be away from you."

"I don't want to be away from you either," I blurt out. "When are you coming home?"

"I don't know. I'm dying to get back to LA, but only if you're there. When are you back?"

"Next week."

"Would you mind if I came back next week as well?"

"I would love that, but, um, Kate…" I can't believe I'm about to say this. "Maybe it's time we told Kevin."

CHAPTER 37
KATE

My heart flings itself against my ribcage as I ring Mary's doorbell. I've lost the right to use my key. I've been gone for a month, and it's been an excruciatingly slow month and an insanely fast one all at once. As though taking the outside perspective on my life here has sped up my decision-making process, but the only way to get there was by slowing down. By endless hours spent on my parents' porch, staring into nothingness. By long walks with my mother during which we didn't say much at all but our presence, our arms hooked together, said all there was to say. By taking a long hard look at myself and daring, for the first time ever, to find the courage to ask myself the only question that matters: what is it that I really want? There was only ever one answer.

Stella.

It took me a long while to get there, to fully admit this to myself, to find the energy within me to start this fight. Because it's not going to be easy. But it's the only right thing to do. I have to tell my husband that I'm in love with his sister.

That's how I manage to keep my spine straight when Kevin opens the door for me. When he looks me in the eye, he knows, because he knows me, that I've made a decision that might not please him.

Kevin may be Stella's brother, but he's my husband. I asked her not to be here for this, because it's my duty to tell him and mine alone. I married him. I vowed to be there for him always.

"Hug?" Kevin asks as he ushers me in.

I nod and we curl our arms around each other, maybe for the last time ever. We engage in some nervous chatter as we head to the backyard.

"We're alone," he says. "Mom and Nathan are at work and Stella's not back until tonight."

I don't tell him that I know more about Stella's schedule than he does. That we agreed, from a distance, that before Stella and I could even see each other again, I had to tell Kevin. It's the very least we owe him.

"How are you?" I ask as he pours me a glass of water. I sink into a chair and let my gaze wander over Mary's magnificent garden, over the pool house, the hot tub.

"Been doing a lot of thinking… soul searching, if you will." Kevin sends me a shy smile.

"And?"

"And… we need to talk. I may not know much, but I know that." He pauses. "Or no, I also know that it was good to take a break. For you to go away for a while. To have some breathing room. I needed that too. You should know that I don't begrudge you that. It was a wise move."

"Okay." I take a slow sip of water. "Have you come to any conclusions while I was away?"

"Truth be told, I've mainly been driving myself crazy by trying to figure out who it is you have feelings for. You don't have to tell me, if… it's not something you want to talk about. If you choose me."

My heart's breaking already. "Do you want me to choose you?" I no longer see it as a matter of choice, but I'm not Kevin.

228

"Of course I do. I know we have issues. But we can still have kids, Kate."

"Let's not even talk about kids right now."

"You're right. We're not there yet. I get that."

"Did you miss me?"

"What?" He runs his hand through his hair. "Of course I missed you. You were gone for a month."

"Please be real with me, Kev. Words don't mean all that much to me now. For months you've been saying one thing and doing the opposite. You may say that you missed me but I can no longer take your word for that."

"Did you miss me?"

"Yes…"

"But?" He shuffles in his seat the same way Mary does when she's nervous.

"There is someone else." The only way to say it is to say it. I can beat about the bush for another hour or I can, finally, just come out and say it. "I've tried to forget about them, but I can't."

"Damn it. I knew it." He tilts his head back and rubs his palms over his face. "Will you at least tell me who he is now?"

Oh, fuck. I swallow hard. "I will, but before I do, I need you to really hear that we tried to stop it. We tried for your sake. We tried to put you first, but… it didn't work, because, um, we fell in love."

"We? Who is we? What does this other dude even care?"

"Kev, it's not some dude. It's… It's, um… It's Stella."

"Stella?" His face is all confusion. "What do you mean? Not my sister?" He scoffs. "That's just not possible."

"I know how it sounds, but it's true. I'm in love with Stella." Nothing feels good about saying this. There's no relief. There's no catharsis. There's most certainly no redemption. Having to tell Kevin this is the most terrible thing I've ever had to tell anyone.

"Stella?" His voice shoots up. "But you don't even like her.

You've always said she's spoiled and taking advantage of Mom while chasing some pipe dream of acting. What are you even talking about? Also, Stella's a girl." He jumps out of his chair as though he's going to walk away. "Where's my phone? I need to call her."

"Kev, please, sit. Let me explain."

With a sigh, he sinks back into his chair. "How can you be in love with Stella? She's my sister!" His gaze skitters away, as though he can't bear to look at me—as though what I've just said is starting to sink in.

"She and I spent a lot of time alone here and... it just happened."

"What happened? Did she try to kiss you or something? I don't understand."

"I kissed her. She stopped me, and rightly so. We thought that would be the end of it, but it wasn't. It was only the beginning. I'm so sorry, Kev."

"What about Stella? She's in Europe." He slaps his palm against the side of his head. "I can't believe this. I asked her, point blank, if she knew who you had a crush on. I'm not totally ignorant. I did notice that you and Stella suddenly got a whole lot closer so I figured she might know. She lied to my face. To her own brother."

"What was she supposed to say?"

"How long? How long has this been going on?"

"Not long. Just a few weeks before I left."

"A few weeks?" He breathes heavily. "I thought it was just a crush and now you're suddenly in love with her?"

Some things, I can't tell him. Like how I fell deeply in love with Stella that night in Topanga, but it was impossible to acknowledge at the time. Like how us coming together that night was so much more than sex. How it felt like coming home to someone I didn't know had been waiting for me all along.

"I know it's a lot to take in." I try to keep my shoulders square, but it's a hard thing to do when the man you've loved for more than a decade is falling apart in front of you because of what you're saying—because of what you did.

"A lot? It's ridiculous, Kate. Can you even hear yourself? Do you realize what you're saying?" His hands shake.

"I do and I'm sorry." In an instinctive gesture of comfort, I almost reach for him—but I can never comfort my husband again.

"Did you sleep with her? Did you have sex with my sister?"

"Yes."

"But you're not even gay."

"How about bisexual?"

"But you never said."

"I didn't know. I—it's been confusing." All I really know is that I'm in love with Stella and I'm destroying the life I once knew.

"I'm trying to wrap my head around this but it's not really working." His breathing has calmed down.

"Look, Kev, you and I… it wasn't working anymore."

"For a while, but it could have worked again. We could have made it work. That's what you do when you're married. You work on your marriage. You go through tough times, wait it out, until the good times come around again."

"That's not how it's going to go for us and I'm really sorry about that. I'm the one ending things, but this isn't a unilateral decision, Kev. I think you know that."

"Oh, so now it's my fault that you slept with my sister."

"It's not your fault, but… you made it perfectly clear you didn't want to be around me any longer. Sometimes actions speak much louder than words and they hurt much more as well."

"That's why we were on a break, to sort that out—Oh, I see it now. That's not the reason. The reason is that you had to be with Stella. With my sister." Tears well in his eyes.

"I haven't been with Stella. I haven't seen her. We've tried to be as respectful as possible, even though it's impossible. I've asked myself what the right thing to do was so many times and the only conclusion is that there is none. I could have chosen to stay with you, but then what?"

"Then we could have tried again. You could have chosen not to tell me. I don't need to know this, Kate. You and... Stella. No. I'm telling you now that I will never accept this. Have you thought about what this is going to do to Mom? Has Stella? You were right about her in the end. She is a selfish brat who only takes her own feelings into consideration."

"Mary knows. She caught us and we had to tell her."

His eyes go wide. "Mom knows? No fucking way." He shakes his head. "What a fucking nightmare. I might have been gone a lot and been too self-absorbed, but to have this go on right under my nose, with everyone knowing? What's next? You and Stella having a three-way with Nathan?" He gets up again. "I'm going out. I need to, I don't know, process the shock. I think it's better if you're not here when I get back."

"Kev, don't go. We have to talk about this more."

"About you sleeping with my sister? I don't think so. We're done." He closes his fist around the hem of his shirt. "And if you're looking for possible ways to hurt me more, there are none. How's that for the right thing to do?" He storms off. I wait until I hear his car drive off to move. I had never intended to stay at the house after telling him. I've arranged to stay with Skye, just as Stella has made plans to stay with Hayley tonight. After the bomb has been dropped.

CHAPTER 38
STELLA

When I switch on my phone after the plane has landed at LAX, I have a voicemail from Kate and a dozen missed calls from my brother. I listen to Kate's message. I wish I could relish in the comfort of hearing her voice, but I know what she's going to say.

"Kevin knows. It went pretty much as expected. He's shocked and hurt. Expect the worst." Her tone is resigned. A pause in her message. "I'd really like to see you. Call me, please."

I close my eyes and inhale deeply. I wish I could get on another plane as soon as I've gotten off this one, but it's time to face the music. It's time to face my brother.

I've barely exhaled when my phone starts buzzing in my hand. It's Kevin. But this is not where I want to have this conversation.

With rising anxiety, I make my way out of the airport. Arriving home is usually a joyful occasion, and getting out of LAX something to do as quickly as possible, but I take my time. For once, I indulge in the LA traffic, grateful for the extra time it allows me. When I arrive at the house, all the cars are in the driveway. Everyone's home. Great.

The front door swings open as soon as I get out of the car. Mom hurtles toward me. Her eyes are puffy and her cheeks blotched red.

"You promised me, Stella. You promised you wouldn't do this," she says. No chance of a welcome-home hug, then, even though I've been away a few weeks.

"I'm sorry." I drop my suitcase in the driveway. It suddenly feels too heavy. Everything does. Kevin appears behind Mom. He glares at me but it's not his anger that stands out—it's his sadness. And I was perfectly able to predict this. I knew everyone would be mad at me and Kevin would be hurt, but predicting it is not the same as living it. As standing here between the rubble, between the consequences of what I've done. I stole my brother's wife. There is no excuse. Faye can go on about how love is love all she wants, but this, my family's utter disappointment in me, might not be worth it.

"Can I talk to Stella alone, Mom?" Kevin says.

"Of course, darling."

Mom hurries into the house. I follow her, dragging my suit-case behind me. I close the door. Kevin crashes onto the bottom step of the stairs in the hallway. Maybe I'm no longer welcome beyond this room. Maybe this house that has been my home for my entire life is now forbidden territory because it has no room for traitors.

"I just don't understand," Kevin says. "When did all this happen? And how?"

I should have called Kate on the way over, but I couldn't. I had to do this first. The whole point of going through this ordeal is so that I can talk to Kate—be with her—as much as I want afterward.

"We didn't do it to hurt you, Kev. That's the very last thing either of us wanted." Awkwardly, I lean against the staircase. "I'm so sorry about this and if there was any other way, I'd—"

"Of course there's another way. The way in which you don't do this. That you don't sleep with my wife. That she doesn't leave me for you—for my fucking sister. It seems pretty damn straightforward to me."

"I'm not doing this for fun. This hurts me too. It's been tearing me apart for weeks. But I'm in love with her and she's in love with me and we want to be together."

Kevin shakes his head. "Can't you just wait until it blows over? Because it will. This is just another one of your Stella things where you just take what you can get, whatever it is you want because that's how it has always been. Maybe it's my fault, you know? I let you get away with everything, said you could be anything you wanted, that you could have whatever you wanted. Just for the record, that did not include my wife."

"I know this is painful and that you feel betrayed, but... none of this happened in some sort of magical vacuum, Kev. You and Kate—"

"Oh no. You don't get to judge my marriage and use that as justification for what you've done. You simply don't get to do that. *You* did this. You and Kate. I'm not going to be your absolution. If you want to be with her, and she wants to be with you, I guess I can't stop you, but know that I'm no longer your brother because I don't want someone like you as my sister." A tear rolls down his cheek. "She's my wife, Stella. We've been married for ten years. We might have hit a rough patch, but that doesn't give you the right to swoop in, to make her feel better about herself for a minute, and have her believe she loves you now." He scoffs. "So, fuck you. I hope you're very happy together." His voice drips with venom. "Maybe you can have a bunch of babies together." He rises and without saying another word, walks up the stairs.

I sink onto the step Kevin just left and let out all the tears I've been keeping at bay. I drop my forehead onto my knees and cry. It was always going to be like this, but to feel my brother's hatred and disdain for me as something palpable in the air, to see a wall going up between us that may very well be there for the rest of our lives, is not something I'm equipped to deal with.

Someone knocks on the door from the living room.

"Can I come in?" Mom asks.

"Yes," I say between loud sniffles.

"Oh, darling." She crashes down next to me and puts her arm around me. "Oh, god. What a mess."

"It was Nathan's fucking tequila," I whisper.

"What's that, darling?"

But I can't blame anyone else for what happened. Kevin's right. Kate and I did this.

"I have to ask." Mom squeezes my shoulder. "Do you really love her so much that you have to do this? That you have to rip this family apart?"

"Would I be doing it if I didn't?" I reply, loudly enough so she can hear. "Maybe there are no excuses for what we did, but, to us, it somehow makes perfect sense."

Mom sighs. "I really have no clue how I'm going to make this better. How this family is going to get past this."

"It's not on you to make things better, Mom."

"I will not have my children hate each other. I simply won't allow it."

"Kevin's going to hate me for a good long while. Maybe forever." Tears stream down my cheeks again.

"He may surprise you. He's a lot more like your father than like me in that respect."

I'm not sure what she means by that exactly, but I'm too exhausted to ask. All I want to do is cry on her shoulder, but I'm not sure I can still do that.

She pulls me close. "Kev said he doesn't want you to stay here, but this is my house and you're my daughter. This is *our* house and your home. I need you to know that this will always be your home and I'm not kicking you out because your brother wants me to. Okay?"

"Thanks." My mother's kindness only makes me sob more. My family have always supported me in everything, Kevin's right about that, and this is how I repay them? "I'm going to stay at Hayley's for a while. I think it's for the best."

"Sure, darling." Her voice breaks and then the floodgates really open. The last time I witnessed my mother in this kind of pain was when my father died.

CHAPTER 39
KATE

I jump at the tiniest sound. My gaze has been glued to my phone for the past hour—since Stella's plane landed. Thiago fusses on my lap. He's tired but he doesn't want to sleep. I'm glad I can focus some of my attention on him because I'm going out of my mind wondering what's happening at the Flacks' right now.

"I'll take him." Skye opens her arms for Thiago. "He needs to go to bed."

I kiss Thiago goodnight and reach for my phone, willing it to ring. Wanting it so desperately to bring me some good news, which is the most insane case of wishful thinking because Kevin's not going to suddenly accept me and his sister being in love just because a few hours have gone by, or because his sister repeated what I told him.

Roland is helping Gabriel with his homework. The twins are upstairs, being told by Skye to be quiet from now on because their little brother is going to sleep. It seemed like a good idea at the time to stay with Skye, to have my best friend near while my marriage crumbles, but to come to this place of chaos, this house full of children, after the calm of my parents' home, and the ordeal of facing Kevin, was another big mistake. I should have just booked a hotel and have Stella meet me there. Because I want to see her. I need to know, when I look into her eyes, that this was not for nothing. That we didn't break Kevin's heart on a foolish whim.

I unlock my phone and book a hotel near our office. I shouldn't have asked Skye if I could crash here but, when Stella and I had our long-distance phone conversations planning this, it was as though we couldn't see past the huge hurdle of telling Kevin. It felt wrong to suggest booking a room for the two of us, let alone an Airbnb, which would be much more convenient, but we can't just move in together. That's not how this works. Although none of this has gone according to any conventional plans. It's all a big mess so we did the only thing that made sense: lean on our friends. But Skye is busy with her family. She doesn't have time to process this with me and it's not as if she didn't warn me, it's not as if she's ready to give her best-friend blessing to Stella and me.

I thank Skye and Roland profusely for having me over for a few hours, then get out of there. Darkness falls as I drive to the hotel and a sense of sadness settles over me because this is who I am now. A woman who has left her husband, driving to a lonely hotel room. But was I really better off before? Kevin and I stopped choosing each other months ago. Maybe, if Stella hadn't lived at Mary's, I'd still be there, alone and sad in the pool house, waiting for Kevin to come back to me. Maybe I'm the one who officially left him, but he'd already left me, without having the guts to tell me, long before any of this happened.

When my phone does finally ring, I nearly jump out of my skin. I pull over and take Stella's call.

"Hey," is all she says.

"Hey," I echo. "How did it go?"

"He's so angry and hurt and shocked, Kate."

"Yeah. Where are you?"

"On my way to Hayley's."

"I booked a room at The Rayburn. Can I see you?"

240

"Oh, fuck, yes. I'll be there in thirty minutes," Stella says.

————

I wait for Stella in the lobby, pacing, my heart rate skyrocketing, my mind scrambling to understand what we've done. But in a few minutes she will walk through those sliding doors and it will all make sense. All the hurt we've caused will at least have a reason. But what if it doesn't? Is there even plausible justification for us choosing each other, choosing ourselves over someone else? From going to the firm no we gave each other to two resounding yeses? Are the feelings we have for each other big enough to pull us through?

The doors open. Stella walks in and then I know the answer to all my questions. Because we wouldn't have blown everything up if we didn't believe, with every fiber of our being, that we wanted to be together. That we wanted to try something untried. Her hair is a mess and her clothes are disheveled and she has clearly been crying, but she's still the most arresting person in this space.

I haven't seen her in four long weeks and to finally open my arms to her, to feel her body against mine, is what I've been waiting for all this time. If there's no justification for this, then so be it, because this, folding my arms around Stella and knowing in my bones that what we have is special and profound and beyond any reason for justification, is more than plenty. When you know, you know. And oh, how I know.

"Come on." We take the elevator up to my room—our room —in silence, holding it all in until we have absolute privacy. Her body is hot behind mine as I hold the keycard against the lock and the sound marks the transition to a brand-new episode in my life. A new chapter. Not a new me because I will always be the woman who can't have children and whose marriage failed because of it. But I'm about to add a new layer to my former self, find a place inside myself to shelve some of the pain of the past few months and years, to not let it be the focus of all my actions any longer, to give my mind some reprieve from always thinking about all the things I will never be.

I take Stella's hands in mine and look into her eyes. I've never seen her this shattered, this reduced to a teary mess, this fragile.

"Maybe the hardest part is over now," I say.

"Maybe." She curls her fingers around mine. "At least we're together now."

"Fuck, it's good to see you." I can't stop looking at her, trying to take in every last feature of her face.

"And you." Her expression softens, as does her grip on my fingers. She lets go, then runs her fingertips over my arms. "I spent most of my time with Faye Fleming, but I still missed you like crazy." A hint of smile.

"You must really like me, then."

"Like you?" She steps closer. "I love you, Kate."

Fireworks explode inside me. All the anxiety I've been carrying in my muscles floods out of me. All the reasons for not choosing each other disappear. Because, sometimes, you have no choice.

I cup Stella's jaw in my hands. "I love you too," I say, then, finally, touch my lips to hers.

Her body melts against mine. Her hands disappear in my hair. The kiss goes from tentative to full-tilt in a matter of seconds. Our hunger for each other has multiplied with time and distance.

"I absolutely need to shower," Stella says when we break from our kiss.

"How about I join you?"

"As enticing as that sounds, I just need a moment to wash it all off me."

"Of course." I plant a soft kiss on the tip of her nose. "I'll be right here waiting."

"Telling Kev about us is the hardest thing I've ever done. To hurt my brother like that, it's, um… it breaks my heart into a million pieces. It hurts way more than when Toni left me for Sheena. It's different, because he's family and we're supposed to have each other's back. The things he said to me were awful and I totally deserved them."

Tension seizes my muscles again.

"But I had to do it. I had no choice, even though there should always be a choice. But, when it comes to you, Kate, I don't feel like I have one."

I nod. "Same." I swallow hard. "It's excruciating, but…" But what? I have no more buts. After all's been said and done, Stella and I are standing in this hotel room together, choosing each other. For now, it's all that matters. And we're not cheating on Kevin any longer. We did the hard thing of telling him. Of course I considered my options when Skye told me to do the hard thing and forget about Stella, to fall out of love with her. I might have even managed it, given time. I could have gone back to Kevin, but it wouldn't have been the honest thing to do. And sometimes, the most honest action is the hardest one to take.

CHAPTER 40
STELLA

The water rains down on me, and I let it wash away the tension from my body. I wish it could wash away the worst of my sins, because isn't stealing your brother's wife the biggest one of all?

I'm over the moon to be here with Kate, to have her waiting for me in the next room, but the ambivalence in my heart is killing me. Because I know two things for absolute certain: I want to be with Kate and I don't want to lose my family. I can stand in this shower as long as I want, I can scrub my skin until it's raw, but it's not going to bring me the solution of how to accomplish my two mutually exclusive goals. To be with Kate, I had to cause my brother pain. And the joy of being with Kate is inextricably linked to the agony of telling my brother. One does not exist without the other.

Sometimes, we hurt the people we love the most and it's because we love them that it hurts so much, the sharpness of the pain a measure of our love. But I have no choice. I need to put Kevin out of my head for now. Because Kate is out there, the woman I love—the woman I chose over everything else. This isn't merely agony and it's time to focus on the flip side now, if only for tonight. Although, this time around, we have

HARPER BLISS

much more than one night together. We have all the time we want—and we already paid the price.

So I lather soap on my skin and wash the past off me—after today, I'll never be the same person again. Just like I was never the same after Toni dumped me, and after my father died. Some events change you forever, alter something to the chemical state in your body, make your neurons fire differently from then on.

I may not know what the future holds for Kate and me, but I do know that I have made the ultimate sacrifice for her—for us. That should tell me all I need to know.

Suddenly, I can't get out of the shower fast enough. Every minute with Kate is precious because we had to fight so damn hard for it, first between ourselves and then against my family and, in the end, the fight will return to us again. But at least we'll have each other. We won't be alone.

Skin still dripping, I hurry into the bedroom. My hair sticks to my cheeks in wet strands. Kate is sitting on the bed and breaks into a smile at the sight of me. I reach for her, push myself onto her, throw my arms around her. Fully naked, I straddle Kate, who is still dressed, my blood already thumping wildly for her. Because my body, my deepest self, knows I made the right decision, no matter the cost.

Her hands travel up my back, leaving my skin covered in goose bumps. She pulls me close, and I look down into her chocolate brown eyes. The tips of our noses touch and there's nothing left to say now, only the things our bodies can communicate, the emotions beyond the words that can only be expressed like this. This isn't mere lust shooting through my body—it never was, because with Kate that was impossible from the start. We didn't just indulge in a one-time sin of the flesh, because for us, that doesn't exist. There were always so many emotions wrapped up in our actions, so many feelings rioting beneath our skin.

"Oh, Stella," Kate groans. One hand disappears into my hair while the other keeps pressing me close, as if she never wants to let go. I don't either. I'd like to stay in this perfect bubble in this hotel room forever, shut out the outside world and pretend it doesn't exist. Pretend it's just me and Kate in the universe, and this warm, luscious, exhilarating sensation in our hearts.

This is also what it feels like when you choose each other. Unequivocally right despite the consequences. If this is how Toni felt when she first kissed Sheena, I can no longer hold her cheating on me against her because I understand. But Toni has nothing to do with this. It's just me and Kate now and we get to take our time. We get to do this properly. We get to make love to each other knowing that we choose each other fully for the first time.

Kate loosens her grip on me and, slowly, her hand travels to the front of my body. Gently, she cups my breast on a sharp inhale of breath. Her thumb flicks along my nipple. She swallows hard but keeps staring into my eyes.

I trail the back of my fingers along her cheek, on the way to unbuttoning her blouse. I want her naked too. I want to see all of her after so much time apart. For a few seconds, my thumb rests on her neck and I feel how frantically her pulse races —for me.

Kate's hold on my breast intensifies and so does the look in her eyes. Then we can't stand it any longer. We have to break eye contact because not another second can go by without our lips meeting, without us kissing. To feel her lips on mine is like coming home after a long, uphill trip. Like being reminded of where I belong. Her tongue slips into my mouth and a pinprick of tears stings behind my eyes. But these are not tears of sadness or frustration or guilt. They're the opposite. So I don't stop them. Just like the water rained down on me earlier in the shower, I let my tears rain down my face because these are the happiest tears I've ever shed. They're the kind of tears you cry when you're reunited with someone who makes your life complete. When you know you're about to embark on the most amazing journey and you can already taste the happiness that lurks just around the corner.

We kiss and kiss, and I somehow manage to open her blouse before I tumble onto her, before she's on her back beneath me and staring up at me with eyes so full of lust I can feel it between my legs.

She blinks once and it's as though that minute gesture flicks the switch between us again, brings us onto the next level of what we're doing—the total and complete expression of our love. I wasn't lying or grandstanding or exaggerating earlier when I told Kate I loved her. If I didn't love her, I wouldn't have broken my brother's heart.

Kate wrestles out of her blouse and bra while I tug at her jeans, leaving her dressed only in a flimsy pair of panties.

"Come here," she whispers, and I think she's drawing me in for another kiss but, instead, she pulls me all the way up, until I'm straddling her face.

My legs are wide for her and if that's a reflection of what's happening in my heart, then it makes perfect sense, because my heart's all the way open for her, my entire body an extension of how I feel. My muscles taut with lust, my flesh buzzing with desire.

Maybe Toni wasn't the love of my life, after all—how could she be when she fell in love with someone else? Maybe the great love of my life is Kate and life had a funny way of bringing us together.

When Kate's tongue touches my clit, I no longer consciously know anything, but I feel it all the more. Her fingertips dig into the flesh of my behind while she tastes me, all of me, while her tongue licks me straight into seventh heaven.

My body, my resolve, is no match for this lust between us, for how I feel when I'm with her, for when her tongue touches me like that. I happily surrender, my cheeks still wet with tears, my hair still moist from the shower, my sex dripping with lust for her. I come at Kate's tongue and it's so much more than a quick orgasm in a hotel room. It's the conclusion of the choices we made and the beginning of our future together. It's so many things, I think, as my body slides down, limp and satisfied, onto hers.

"I missed you so, so much," Kate says as she holds me near, as she buries her nose in my hair.

"I gathered." My body shakes against hers as I chuckle. When I kiss her, I can smell myself on her, all my desire for her —all my love for her.

CHAPTER 41
KATE

"What are we going to do?" I ask Stella over breakfast in bed. "On a practical level."

"I don't know." Even though we barely slept, and Stella's jet-lagged on top of that, she looks more gorgeous than ever. Maybe because we can enjoy the simple act of having breakfast together now—of discussing pragmatic details of our immediate future without being racked with too much guilt. "Maybe we can just stay here for a while. Just for a few nights until we get our bearings."

I nod. "See what happens?"

"I can't go home. Not for the next few days. We all need some time," Stella says.

"I'm going to have to get my own place eventually." I sigh at the prospect of all the things Kevin and I have to sort out, legally and emotionally. "And a divorce lawyer."

"All in good time." Stella drinks from her coffee.

"Yeah." Part of me wishes time could pass already, but the other part of me doesn't want to miss a moment of how things will evolve between Stella and me.

"Maybe the hardest part is really over now." Stella puts her cup down. "I'm not saying it's going to be easy from now on, but, you know, we faced Kev. Nothing can be harder than that."

I nod. It's not as though I've suddenly stopped loving Kevin because I'm in love with his sister. But he pulled away from me at the worst possible time, which is not an excuse, but it is an explanation. We will never know whether we would have found our way back to each other. Kevin and I are over. I will need to grieve the end of our marriage as well, although I feel like I have already done so much grieving for the other things that didn't work out. One look at Stella is enough to pull me out of my funk. And I have no way of knowing whether she and I will make it, whether this is a real thing or just a rebound reaction, a complicated means of making myself feel better. Am I just burying my real emotions, my pain for not being able to conceive, underneath a layer of sexy euphoria? Only time will tell. And time, we have.

"What are you doing today?" I ask.

"Being with you." She flashes me a smile, and inside me, a glimpse of possibility flares up, because time is not the only factor that will let me know, loud and clear, how things will go between us. Last night, we professed our love for each other, and maybe that will count for a lot more than time and the circumstances of life. "I should see Damian at some point. Give him a debrief of my time in Europe." She falls back onto the bed. "No more auditions for me," she squeals. "I'm a working actor."

I remember her absolute anguish when she first got turned down for this part and I can't help but wonder if we would even be here if that hadn't happened. It's impossible to say and, of course, I wish that Stella hadn't had to go through the pain of rejection again, but that rejection kick-started this—us. Or maybe it all started when she took her bikini top off in the hot tub. Or when she whisked me to Faye and Ida's party. Maybe there's no point in wondering. Maybe we should just enjoy each other's company from now on.

"You are Nora Levine's co-star." It's so easy, delightful even, to get wrapped up in this with her. "You might regret no longer being single once your show airs," I say, painting on a smirk.

Stella pushes herself up and shoots me a funny look. "No regrets. No matter how hard it's been and it might still be, I have zero regrets about choosing you."

"Neither have I." I push the breakfast trays to the side so I can hug Stella for a good long while.

———

Later, Stella and I venture outside for the first time as a couple. We stop by the office to assure Skye I'll be back in full force tomorrow, although I already told her yesterday. But I want her to actually see me with Stella. Skye's my best friend and I haven't always given her the best updates on Stella. To her, Stella was always just my husband's annoying little sister whom I didn't much care for. The wannabe actor who never acted. The girl who, in my hyper-judgmental view, never amounted to very much. It just goes to show how things can change and how you can get people totally wrong, because what I didn't see back than was that Stella was persevering most of all. She had the privilege to do most of it poolside in her mother's beautiful backyard, but she still had to do it. She had to find the strength inside herself to not give up again and again. She had to believe in herself when others, like myself, had given up on her a long time ago already.

"I'm not going to pretend this isn't freaking me out, okay?" Skye's never been one to mince her words. "Because it damn well is."

"We know," I reply. "But sometimes life's just freaky like that."

"It's going to take me some time to get used to this new arrangement." Her gaze skitters from me to Stella.

"Take all the time you need."

"Let's hope time has the same effect on me as it did on you," Skye says. "So you both went away and came back knowing that you just had to be together?" She almost stares Stella down, but Stella's not that easily fazed.

"That's right," Stella says. "Although Kate made the first move."

"Guilty as charged, but in my defense, I wasn't living it up in Paris and London with Faye Fleming. I was doing some serious introspection in the suburbs of Des Moines."

"The point is." Stella squares her shoulders in that way of hers, as if she just got injected with an extra shot of confidence. "When you know, you know. Even when it's inconvenient at best and plain hurtful to someone you love at worst." She pauses. "I've been there. I know what it feels like to be stabbed in the back by someone you love. My girlfriend left me for my best friend," she explains to Skye. I might have mentioned it at the time, but it wouldn't have been a huge topic of conversation between Skye and me—another token of my ignorance.

"That's awful," Skye says.

"There are no two ways about it. It hurts like hell. And 'the circumstances aren't exactly the same, but that doesn't change how much pain we caused Kevin. Yet, we're all going to have to find a way to deal with that. To learn to live with it and with each other again."

"Kev and I, we were pretty much on the rocks, although we hadn't exactly acknowledged that yet. But it was in the air," I say. "We had this huge divide between us and I honestly stopped seeing how we could ever bridge that. How we could come together again. I don't know." Plenty of anguish courses through me when I talk about Kevin. Plenty of guilt as well. But sometimes it has to hurt really badly for a while before it can feel better—like pouring alcohol on a wound to disinfect it.

"I'm not judging you," Skye says. "I'm your friend. It's my job to root for you. To support the choices you make, even when they seem totally crazy to me."

"Was that what you were doing when you told me to fall out of love with Stella already?" I reach for Stella's hand.

"Fat load of good that did." Skye shakes her head. "My friendly advice clearly was worth nothing to you."

"That's not true. I tried, but I failed." I gaze at Stella. "Spectacularly."

CHAPTER 42
STELLA

Eleven days have passed since I last set foot in Mom's house. I've run out of clothes, and I would also really like to see her. All we've done is exchange some brief text messages. But I'm a mommy's girl and I'm going to need my mother's blessing sooner rather than later. And I can't shack up in a hotel room with Kate forever. Besides, Kate's at work all day, putting in long hours to make up for the time she missed. Pre-production for my new show is still a few weeks away, and I already know the scripts I've been sent by heart. Truth is, I don't know what to do with myself when I'm alone. Too many thoughts crowd my brain. Kevin's voice won't leave my ear. "I'm no longer your brother," he said and that's not something I can easily shove aside. I can't pretend he didn't say it—that he doesn't hate me.

I let myself in because this is still where I live even though there's something awkward about it. It's late afternoon and I don't expect anyone to be home yet in my family of workaholics, which will hopefully give me some time to acclimatize. To just be at home on my own for a while, in familiar surroundings, before all hell breaks loose again.

"Hello," I shout, just to be sure.

"Hello," a male voice echoes mine. Panic seizes me for a moment at the prospect of another confrontation with Kevin, but it's not his voice.

"Hey, Stella," Nathan says.

I never thought I'd be this pleased to see him. This man I've taken for a gold digger at worst and a highly inappropriate choice of partner at best. I've done nothing but judge him from the start, from that first time Mom introduced him to me as though their relationship was the most run-of-the-mill you would ever encounter.

"Nathan. Hi."

"Glad you're back," Nathan says. "Will we be needing a bottle of tequila today or not?" He grins.

"Oh, god, Nathan. You and your damned tequila." His presence takes the sharpest edge off my discomfort. When I just let things be, and stop trying to fight the idea of him and my mom being wrong for each other, he's one of the easiest people to be around. Laid-back and always with a warm smile at the ready.

"Sure. Blame it all on me." We walk through the house together and naturally settle at the kitchen island. "Can I get you a beer or something else?" He's walking to the fridge already.

"I'm driving, so just some water, please." It's strange to have Nathan fetch me a drink in my own home.

He grabs a bottle of water from the fridge and hands it to me. "How are you coping? Are you okay?"

"I'm okay. How are things here?" I settle onto a stool. "How's Kev?"

"He's back at work so I guess that's good. They've got that big project in Washington. Kevin's supposed to be in charge but Mary's not sure he's up to it now." Nathan pauses. "But none of this is for me to say, really."

"I wish there was a way I could make this better, but that's all it is: wishful thinking."

"As much as I'd love to be a fully signed up member of this

family already, for various reasons, I'm often still more of a bystander which affords me a more objective view," Nathan says.

"I'm sorry for all the times I made you feel like you weren't a part of our family."

"I get it. It's easy enough to believe I'm some dude hustling your mom. That it took you some time to see that I'm anything but. That I simply adore her for who she is." He leans his elbows on the countertop. "My point is that, from where I'm sitting and as far as I can tell, this will not be the end of this family. You've been through worse. I'm not saying it's easy and that Kev's just going to wake up one day and decide to forgive you, but I spent some time with him and… he knows he's not blameless in this. He knows he let Kate down. And when push comes to shove, he's just a good guy who loves his sister very much."

Tears sting in my eyes. Of all people, to have Nathan say this to me is unsettling, but of course he sees things. He's lived in this house for a while and he has eyes and ears. I may have chosen to ignore him as best I could, but that hasn't stopped him from picking up vibes about us.

"In my opinion, it's good that you came. You need to speak to each other. Kick-start… something," he says.

"How's Mom?"

"You know Mary. She's the strongest person I know. No doubt. But… you're her kids. Her soft spot. Of course, she's going to suffer when you and Kev are fighting."

"Is there any way I can make this easier on anyone?" I ask Nathan, as though he has all the answers.

"Talk to each other. Hash it out. Don't avoid the painful stuff because it's too difficult." He looks me in the eye. "As I said. It's good that you came home."

I take a few sips of water, hoping that it will stop the tears from escaping my eyes.

"How's Kate holding up?" Nathan asks.

A drop spills down my cheek at the mention of Kate. "Okay. She's back at work. Keeping busy. But there's a lot to sort out, of course."

"I bet." He sends me a warm smile. I do get why Mom couldn't resist him—and who am I to judge anyone for not being able to resist someone who, at first blush, might not be the best choice for them to be with?

"Just so you know," I say. "You are a fully signed up member of this family. I'm so happy Mom has you."

Nathan nods, then tips the bottle to his lips.

The front door opens, and my heart skips a beat. I hope it's Mom. I could do with a motherly hug before I face my brother. A few moments later, Kevin bounds into the kitchen. His face is ashen, his cheeks hollow. He looks like he has aged about twenty years in the past few days.

"Is it just you?" he asks when he sees me. "No Kate?"

"Just me," I reply.

His rigid posture slackens a fraction. "Thank fuck," he says on a sigh. "I can't bear to see Kate right now." He inhales sharply. "Are you still… with her?" Kevin asks, his voice trembling.

From the corner of my eye, I see Nathan slide silently out of the kitchen.

"Yes." I swallow hard.

"Is it really a thing?" Kevin slumps onto a chair. "Like really serious?" He rubs his palms across his face before running his hands through his hair.

"It is."

"Fuck." He loosens his tie, undoes the top button of his shirt. "Deep down, I knew I was going to lose her, that I was no good for her anymore. I just never in a million years thought I'd lose my wife to my sister."

I can't tell him that's not really what happened, although it might appear that way.

"I'm sorry, Kev."

He shakes his head. "I'm sorry for saying that you were no longer my sister. You will always be my sister, Stella. Always, no matter what. I made that promise to dad before he died. That I would never let anything get between us." Tears stream down his cheeks and he doesn't even bother hiding them. "I keep wondering what he would think of all this, but I don't know." He rubs a finger under his nose.

"I haven't made it very easy on you." My eyes are moist with tears as well.

"If it were easy…" he starts to say, but doesn't finish. "Kate, she's…" He fishes a handkerchief out of his pocket and blows his nose. "You know she wants kids. I don't get why she's with you if she wants kids so badly. If that's the thing that drove us apart."

I don't know what to say to that. Kevin and Kate going through round after round of grueling fertility treatments put the thought of having kids on my radar, but I always figured I'd just be the fun aunt, not the mother.

"What Kate's been through I wouldn't wish on my worst enemy," Kevin says. "She did that for us and I will always respect her for that. She deserves that and she's… she's a hard person to lose. I don't know what I'm going to do without her. Maybe it doesn't feel that way to her, but she's my rock. She's so strong and I—all I did was leave her to deal with the fallout on her own. If this is my punishment for abandoning her when she needed me most, then I'll take it. Then, maybe, it's my turn to be strong now."

"Kev, it's not punishment. Please, don't think of it that way."

"Maybe that's the only way I can think of it. The only way I can make it bearable for myself, by spinning it as some sort of logical cause and consequence."

But life is chaos, I want to say. There's no logic when your father dies when he's only forty-seven. There's no logic when all around you couples are having children, like there's nothing to it, while you have to go through one degrading procedure after another just for the smallest chance at getting pregnant. There's no logic and it's not fair. But who am I to deny my brother his reasoning? Who am I to deny him anything?

"Okay," I say. I wish I could give him a hug, but we're definitely not there yet. "Whatever you need."

"I'm going to D.C. for a few weeks to work with the local authorities on the Bernheim project."

"Oh."

"Can you tell Kate I'd like to talk to her before I leave. Sort some stuff out."

"Sure."

"I can't handle seeing the two of you together. I don't know when or if I'll ever be able to."

"I get it."

"First, I need to find out how to put my life back together." He looks at me briefly, his gaze neither hard nor soft, then gets up and exits the room.

I leave the house without waiting for my mother to get home, because I can't stay yet and just hang out here, in my home, with Kevin hurting upstairs. I guess that's my punishment.

CHAPTER 43
KATE

I meet Kevin at the house we lived in for the past ten years. The house he built for us and where we were happy for a long time. Where we dreamed of having kids—at least two, three if possible—and living the kind of life we'd both believed we were destined for. Getting married. Building a house. Having children. All the traditional ingredients for a happily ever after. But, as it turns out, life can have vastly different plans than the ones you draw up for yourself. A bit like this house that Kevin designed all those years ago and felt he had to rebuild, as though life, in the shape of this house, was giving him the chance of a do-over, of undoing the mistakes he made at the first try. As though knocking down a few walls and rearranging some rooms could undo all the pain we experienced here.

I let myself in, surprised but relieved his car isn't in the driveway yet, and sink into a chair in what used to be the dining room. What hasn't been covered with sheets is layered with dust. When Kevin first started remodeling, there were never any talk of us having to move out, but everything got out of hand, as these things tend to do. We stopped talking. He started doing his own thing, making decisions without consulting me, and I let him do it because I believed it would help.

I hear his car pull up and I brace myself. Stella said Kevin looked much more resigned than angry, but these things can change quickly. His reaction to me, the woman who betrayed him, might be very different than to Stella, who will always be his little sister first.

I stand as his footsteps approach. Something coils in my stomach as he opens the door, but it's not as grueling as I had anticipated. I don't feel completely crushed by guilt.

"Hey." Kevin toys with his keys. "Thanks for coming. Sorry about the mess."

He looks skinnier, no longer filling his suit jacket the way he used to. His appetite's always been the first thing to go when he's stressed or sad.

"It's good to see you," I say.

"Is it?" He chews the inside of his cheek.

I nod.

"We should probably sell this place. It's nowhere near done, but I can't bring myself to finish it now."

"You don't have to finish it." I can't think of anything crueler for him to do to himself—finishing the house we'll never live in. "I can take over. Bring in some workers. Make it look good before we put it on the market."

Kevin huffs out some air. "Do whatever you want, Kate. I don't care about the house anymore." And this from a man who cared about nothing but this house for the past few months. "I'll be in D.C. for a few weeks or maybe even months, depending on how things go. It's a big project, something I can really sink my teeth into."

"That's good."

"Stella can move back home. You can come around, have dinner with Mom and Nathan. Be one happy family." His voice is sharp, but his demeanor is deflated.

"You don't have to leave town, Kev."

"Oh, I do. I very much do." He takes his key ring and fiddles with it, removing one of the keys. He holds it up. "Do with the house what you want. I know you'll get a great price for it if you work your Kate magic. We'll split the money and possessions then we'll be done." For a second, I think he'll throw the key at me, but he's not the type—never has been. He bridges the distance between us and gives me the key. "I don't have it in me to go through a drawn-out, messy divorce. Let's just get some lawyers on it and divide our assets evenly." He scoffs. "Good thing we don't have kids."

Even though I no longer want children with Kevin, it hurts to hear him say that.

"Sorry," he says. "That was below the belt."

"It's okay." We've both said and done things that are unacceptable.

"There's one thing I don't get…" He shrugs. "Or no, that's not true. There are many things I don't get, but, the past few years, we put all our time, energy and money into trying to have a baby… and now suddenly you don't want that anymore?"

"What do you mean?"

"I thought having kids was what you wanted most in the world."

"I can't have kids, Kev. It's about time I came to terms with that. We, you and I, couldn't have kids and our marriage didn't survive because, as you just said, we put everything we had, emotionally and physically, into reaching that goal, and it didn't work. But damn, we tried. I'll always be grateful to you for never giving up on my dream."

"It was my dream too." Kevin's voice breaks.

"I know." Here we stand in our house of broken dreams. "I'm sorry it didn't come true." I'm saying sorry for so much more than that, but it's much harder to say that I'm sorry for falling in love with his sister. "Are you sure about this?" I show him the key he just gave me.

"Unless you want to live here," he says. "With my sister."

"I don't." This hasn't felt like my house since I was driven away from it. "I need to start fresh."

"This is it? No more Kate and Kevin? Just like that?"

"It was never 'just like that', Kev."

He nods. "I'm sorry for not being the man you needed me to be."

I shake my head. "Things… happened. Life happened to us, Kev." I pocket the key.

Suddenly, Kevin reaches out his hand. "You," he says. "You were such an amazing thing to happen to me."

I take his hand, curl my fingers tightly around his. "We had a few really good years."

"Fuck, yeah." Tears stream down his cheeks. He pulls me close. "I love you, Kate. I can't just stop loving you. I know I didn't treat you right, but it was never because I didn't love you anymore."

"I love you too." I let him hold me. I fold my arms around his waist and put my cheek against his chest, possibly for the last time ever. This chest I know so well. These arms that were my one true home for a decade. "And I'm so sorry for… for Stella. But I'm—" I can't say it, not while he's holding me like this, that I love his sister too.

"Be kind to my sister," he whispers. "She's much more fragile than she looks." He's probably referring to himself. He looks plenty vulnerable today.

I nod, my chin bumping against his chest. I inhale his specific Kevin scent one last time, before extricating myself from our hug.

"About you and Stella…" He wipes the wetness from his cheeks. "I don't know how to deal with that. I just… don't."

"Of course." People are not meant to deal with something like that. "It's going to take the time it takes."

"That's what we said about us," he says.

"Yes, but, if we're being truly honest, I think we both know we were well on the way to being broken beyond repair, whereas with Stella…" With Stella, everything's new and fresh and exciting, I don't say. With Stella, everything's still easy and thrilling and hopeful.

"I'm sorry too, Kate. For all the things I couldn't be. I need you to know that."

"I know." I reach for his hand now. "I'm sorry for hurting you. I will always be sorry for that. You're such a great person, Kev." I wave my free hand about. "We had such good times here."

"I guess we'll be seeing each other." He actually manages a chuckle. "At Thanksgiving and Christmas."

"Maybe it's about time I spent some more holidays with my family in good old Iowa."

"Yeah." He gives my hand one last squeeze. "I'm not sure what's left to say at this point."

Maybe the fact that we don't have anything left to say or discuss or declare is more evidence of how we kept our marriage afloat on hopes and dreams more than based on some-thing real, like a shared view of our future and realistic plans to try again. This is by no means easy, but it would have been so much harder if either one of us knew, in our heart of hearts, that we were still destined to be together.

"Bye, Kate." His hand drops from mine. He gives me one final nod, then leaves the house.

I slump back into a chair and let my tears stream freely. I cry for my failed marriage, for the kids I will never give birth to, for hurting my husband in the most unacceptable way, for this house I will never live in again—for being human and doing what humans do. For trying and sometimes succeeding and lots of failing in between. Then I call Stella.

CHAPTER 44
STELLA
ONE MONTH LATER

I'm driving home after the first day on my new job as Nora Levine's co-star. The table read was like a dream come true. To sit next to her behind a nameplate with Stella Flack printed on it. To read my lines with her. To meet the rest of the cast and some of the crew. The show runner is a woman whose—my phone starts ringing. Kevin's name lights up the screen. The nerves I felt before going to work with Nora Levine for the first time are nothing compared to the ones tearing through me now. I haven't spoken to my brother since he left for Washington almost a month ago. I pick up and, just to be on the safe side, just in case it took him a month to prepare a litany of insults to hurl at me, I pull over and park my car.

"Hey, Kev." I try to sound upbeat—it's not that hard after the day I've just had.

"Hey. Just wanted to see how your big day went today." Because my phone's connected to Bluetooth, his voice takes over the entire space of my car. It's almost like he's here with me.

"It was great." I don't want to sound too elated. For very selfish reasons, him leaving town has made things much easier for Kate and me, but that doesn't mean we've forgotten about what we did to him.

"Just great?" He sounds surprisingly cheerful.

"Amazing. Astounding. Like all my dreams were coming true all at once." He's still my brother, the guy who has always believed in me, but for obvious reasons, my demeanor around him, even on the phone, can no longer be the same.

"Awesome. I'm so happy for you."

Is he? "Thanks." Good thing I parked the car because I'm welling up again. "How are you? How's Washington treating you?" Mom's in daily contact with Kevin and she gives me the occasional update, but it's not the same as hearing it straight from him. It's not the same as actually talking to my brother.

"It's pretty great. Despite all the red tape to cut through, but we'll get there. It's good that I'm here to help move things along." There's something about his voice I can't decipher.

"Are you coming home any time soon?" He missed Mom's birthday last week. Although she didn't grumble about it too much, it was easy enough to see she missed having her son at her house for the celebration.

"We'll see. I just need to do my thing here first. Get this project on the rails." The thought of my brother going home to a lonely hotel room, no matter how swanky, breaks my heart a little. But I can hardly suggest I go visit him—and not only because I'm a working actor with a tight schedule to adhere to now. "Look, um, Stella, I wanted you to hear this from me. It's very early days, but I met someone. Her name's Bridget and she works for the city. She's recently divorced and we just sort of clicked. She's an architect, too, so we have a lot to talk about."

"Oh, wow, Kev. That's so wonderful."

"Don't go telling Mom yet, okay? I want to tell her myself. I want to introduce her to Bridget when she comes to D.C. next week."

"My lips are sealed." I can't help myself. "What's her last name?" I need to google this woman who has swept my brother off his feet to such an extent he was able to call me today. What did he tell her when they first met? If I look a little glum, it's only because my wife ran off with my sister.

"I'll tell you that when the time is right." Even though I can't see his face, I know he's smiling. "She has two kids. Two boys. Three and five years old. I haven't met them yet because it's way too soon for that, but, um, maybe you could tell Kate? I don't know how to tell her any of this."

"So, I'm allowed to tell Kate?"

"Duh."

"Sure, bro. I'll tell Kate."

"Mom said our house will be going on the market soon."

"Yep. All your stuff's at Mom's."

"Look, Stella," he pauses. "We both know how short life can be and I don't want to hold a grudge forever. Look at Dad. He didn't even make it to fifty. I don't want to spend the short time I may or may not have on this earth hating you and Kate." This Bridget must be some emotional miracle worker. Maybe she moonlights as a life coach or something, because Kevin's not usually this talkative when it comes to how he feels. But a lot has happened and we've all had to face some harsh truths.

"Thanks, Kev." I swallow hard. "And don't you dare die in your forties. I'd never forgive you for that."

"I'll do my best," he says. "I've got to go."

"Okay, but, Kev… Will you call me again?"

"How about you call me," he says.

"Will you pick up?"

"Try me," he says, and in his tone his yes is loud and clear.

———

Although it's killing me not to be able to tell my mother about Kevin meeting someone, I could at least tell her that he and I spoke on the phone. Her lack of surprise makes me believe she might actually have had something to do with that. Maybe she's been lobbying for me behind my back with Kevin all this time.

As expected, she insisted on a family dinner to celebrate my first day at work—although Kevin can't be with us. But the fact that he called me makes up for that a lot.

In front of my family, Kate and I minimize the displays of affection, but tonight, when she arrives, she walks straight toward me and hugs me in front of Mom and Nathan.

"How's my TV star?" she whispers in my ear. She still draws the line at kissing me in front of my mother, and rightfully so.

"Feeling extremely starry," I say, despite not having been near a camera yet. "Also, Kevin called."

"He did?" Her eyes light up for a split second.

"To ask how today went. He sounded good. Better." I'll tell Kate about Bridget later, when we're alone. She's renting an apartment close to work, where I spend a fair amount of my time, although I still officially live with my mother.

"That's so great to hear." She gives my hand a quick squeeze, then sinks into a chair.

"I'd like to say something." Mom taps a spoon against her glass before holding it up. "A toast. To my children, both wonderful in their own, very unique ways."

"Thanks, Mom." I brace myself while I send her a big smile.

Nathan hands Kate a glass of wine so she can toast with us, although, from looking at her face, I can tell this sort of thing is still awkward for her—it's only normal.

"As a mother, my most important job is to believe in you," she says. "And I always did, darling. Always. And here we are. Can't wait to see you on TV every week. Maybe you'll be better behaved on screen than in real life." She chuckles. "It's not because I always believed in you that you've made that easy on me. But that's your job as my child and I, too, have made plenty of mistakes along the way, but don't we all?"

She pauses. "Before he passed away, your father made me promise that I would let you be a child. You were only nine and he didn't want you to be forced to grow up all of a sudden just because he died." She arches up her eyebrows. "Some might say I took my promise a bit too literally, that I let you be a child for too long, but I don't care if I spoiled you, because look at you now." She sends me a smile. "This family's been through some tough times." She casts her gaze to Kate. "But who else can have their daughter-in-law remain such a close part of the family after a separation?" Her next chuckle is a bit more nervous. "All we can do is the best with what we have and, all things considered, we Flacks have been blessed with a lot." She reaches for Nathan's hand. "Your brother's not here, but he loves you, and he will come back to us when he's ready—of that I'm sure."

Mom doesn't know yet that Kevin might have a very compelling reason to stay in D.C.

"Here's to you, darling. Well done." She lifts her glass again and looks me in the eye. What a woman. Throughout this entire saga, I've never lost her support. It was only natural that, when she found out, she disapproved of Kate and me getting together, but that never stopped her from being there for me, and putting in a good word for me with my brother.

I walk up to my mom and give her the tightest hug I can— she deserves about a million more.

CHAPTER 45
KATE
ONE YEAR LATER

I watch Mary's adorable flower boys, and, for a split second, I catch myself thinking that those should have been my kids —the kids Kevin and I had. But Kevin and I didn't have any kids, and Mary's lucky that she now has two step-grandkids at her second wedding. She wouldn't have been so lucky if Kevin and I had stayed together—if I hadn't gone and fallen for his sister.

The whole thing is a peculiar state of affairs and maybe luck has nothing to do with any of it, because it would be pretty insane to chalk today's configuration of family members up to good luck alone. There's been plenty of drama and bad luck along the way as well. And I'm still not a mother. My new partner didn't come with an instant family—unlike Kevin's.

Stella and I sometimes talk about kids, and she knows how much I want them, but we've only been together a little more than a year.

Stella's her mother's maid of honor. Kevin is giving his mother away. A smile tugging at my lips, I remember how Stella railed against how traditional Mary wanted her wedding to Nathan to be, how 'stupidly patriarchal'—*Does she really need a man to give her away to another man? Are we really that stuck in the seventeenth century?*—but Mary wants what Mary wants, and Stella couldn't argue with that.

"You do whatever you want at your own wedding, darling," Mary said, and that was the end of it. It made me wonder if Stella and I would ever marry. Kevin's asked Bridget to marry him, although, in his case, he's not only asking her to be his wife; he's also asking her kids to officially become his step-kids. I'm happy for him that he met a woman who made all his dreams come true.

I keep my gaze on Stella, who is not a gown-wearing kind of woman, but she's dressed in one today, for her mother. Because Mary asked, Stella said yes immediately, even though it would make her feel uncomfortable for a day. Because Stella adores her mother and the day she—finally—moved out of Mary's house, only a few weeks ago, to move in with me, was surprisingly emotional—and not just because we were taking the big step of shacking up together. Even though she's almost thirty, Stella has lived with her mother her entire life. When I call her a mommy's girl, she takes it as the biggest compliment. So there she is, looking dazzling in her glossy pastel-yellow dress, complementing Mary, making her mother look good. I couldn't take my eyes off her if I wanted to.

From my front row seat, I witness how Mary and Nathan say 'I do' to each other. How they vow to be loyal and all the other things that marriage seems to require, but rarely lives up to. It's a little disconcerting to think that the next wedding I'll go to is my ex-husband's.

Mary's beaming. Nathan looks at her with so much love in his eyes. Eleven years ago, I said 'I do' to Mary's son. Stella was there, but I don't have any recollection of her at our wedding. Although she certainly didn't agree to wear a dress back then, not that her brother would have asked her. Kevin's always just let Stella be Stella.

Most of all, today, I'm happy for Mary—that she gets her happy ending, too. It's hard to forget how Stella disapproved of

Nathan at first, how she called him Keanu—which isn't the worst of names to call someone, but it was still disrespectful. How it took her time to get used to him, but not as long as she might have expected, because Nathan's sweet and caring and he makes sure there's always tequila at the house. But, in the end, Stella also accepted Nathan because her mother loves him. Just like Mary accepted that Stella chose me, because Stella loves me. And I love Stella.

I find her gaze. She looks at me with those big blue eyes of hers. They're moist and she looks a little flustered. In response, tears prick behind my own eyes. Kevin and I are no longer married, but I never stopped being a part of this clan. They're my family, too, as convoluted and unlikely as we may be together.

I send her a smile and, in return, she blows me a kiss.

———

To say it's easy and free of any awkwardness to share a table with Kevin and Bridget would be a flagrant lie. Although Kevin lives in Washington now, we have seen each other at the occasional Flack family gathering—and when we settled our divorce —but Mary's wedding is of an entirely different nature.

Kevin and I have so much history together. We shared more than a decade of our lives with each other. We went through so many ups and downs. Maybe it would be different if I didn't have anything to do with the Flacks anymore, but that's not the case. I may no longer be called Kate Flack, but I'm still part of the family. I look at my ex-husband and maybe it's a blessing that we're forced to remain part of each other's lives, albeit in a very different capacity. Because I don't want to forget Kevin and all the adventures we had together. All the peaks and valleys that make for a life. I've never had any reason to hate him and I'm so glad that he hasn't ended up hating me—and his sister. He might have been so hurt, so broken and humiliated, that his only option was to hate me, but, perhaps, deep down, I always knew he wouldn't, because that was not the kind of man I married all those years ago.

One of the boys tugs at his arm.

"Pleeeeaaaaase," he says, "Kev, will you come with me. I said please. Please, please, please."

Kevin's face lights up in a way that I haven't been privy to in a long time. In a way that it couldn't light up anymore when we were together.

Kevin hoists the boy—his name's Cooper—onto his lap. "Why don't you sit here with me?" He bumps Cooper up and down on his knee and the boy squeals with delight. He whispers something in Cooper's ear next and it must be hilarious because Cooper bursts out laughing.

Some men are meant to become fathers. Kevin became an architect and a husband—and he was a kind of surrogate father to his little sister for a long while—but all he ever really wanted was to be someone's dad. Even though I couldn't give that to him, I can be happy for him now.

Bridget ruffles a hand through Cooper's hair, then lovingly folds her arm around Kevin's shoulders. If you didn't know any better, you'd take this for a table representing the picture-perfect family that's always been there. But with so many things in life, not everything is what it seems.

I feel someone's hand on my neck.

"Damn it," Stella whispers in my ear. "I can't wait to get out of this dress. What am I? Some sort of human doll that only exists for the sake of—" I shut her up by kissing her on the lips in front of everyone. We can do that now. Everyone knows that we love each other.

"No one asked Kev to wear a dress," she says, as soon as I stop kissing her.

"Babe," I say. "It's what your mother wanted."

"My mother wants so many things." Her features soften

when she looks at me. Her eyes narrow. She digs her front teeth into her bottom lip.

"Your mother has everything she could ever dream of," Mary chimes in. "I'm serious." Mary's voice is low enough so only the people at our table—her family—can hear what she says. "A dream of a husband. Two kind and smart children. Two lovely daughters-in-law." She swallows hard. Her gaze cuts from me to Bridget, then back. Mary looks me in the eye. This mother Stella and Kevin share is, for a large part, responsible for who they have become—for the two people I've loved and love most in the world. "Thank you for making my children so happy."

While I return Mary's kind gaze, I hold Stella's hand in mine.

CHAPTER 46
STELLA
TWO YEARS LATER

"**F**or crying out loud," I shout in frustration. "They measured me for this suit only three days ago."

"Aw, babe." Kate looks up at me from the bed. "I'll give you a hand."

A hand? She gave me much more than a hand. It's for that very reason I seem to be gaining a full pound in body weight every other day.

Kate rises and puts her hand on my protruding belly. "Are you nervous?" she asks. "Because you have that glow about you. If you ask me, Nora's the one who should be worried, because there's no doubt you'll be outshining her tonight."

"You would say that and none of this is helping." I stare at Kate's hand on my belly. "Why didn't I go for stretchy pants?"

"Because you're stubborn and you can't stand being told what to do, even if you're given the best advice ever." Kate moves her thumb along my belly.

"It's the premiere party of my show. I can't wear stretchy pants." Up until now, I believed falling in love with my brother's wife would be the most irrational thing I'd ever do—but try being twenty-two weeks pregnant.

"Don't worry." Kate looks me in the eye, then heads into the walk-in closet. "I had the designer send over something more appropriate for someone in their second trimester."

"You did?" I want to cry and kiss Kate at the same time.

"Of course." She sticks her head out of the door. "How many times do I have to tell you that I have your back every step of the way?"

"A million would be good," I joke. "A billion would work as well." I hold out my hand to her. Kate rushes in my direction. "Thank you for being three steps ahead all the time."

"It's my job and also my absolute pleasure." She quickly kisses me on the lips, then puts a hand on my belly again. "Is Little Miss excited about tonight's event?"

"If she is, she hasn't made it known." Even though it's been five months now, most days I still can't believe a new person is growing inside of me. Me. The person who, for the better part of her life, only had her own best interests at heart—who lived with her mother until she was almost thirty. I'm going to be a mother myself. Thank goodness I still have four months to prepare for actual motherhood—and that Kate is going to be some sort of super-alpha mom. "She's probably going to be one of those jaded LA kids who turns away from the fake glitz of Hollywood," I say.

Kate chuckles. "With you as her mother? I don't think so."

"Me? You mean you, obviously."

"Don't be silly, babe. Have you not noticed how casual I am about tonight's premiere? Stella Flack's going to be my baby mama. I'm no longer that easily impressed."

"Yeah right."

"Are you sure Faye and Ida aren't coming, though?" She flashes me a toothy grin. "I'd love to have another chat with Faye."

"You'll have to make do with Nora."

"Is she bringing a date?"

"Nora? A date?" I purse my lips. "With her you never know, but it would surprise me if she did." I've worked with Nora for two years now and I'm still none the wiser about her personal life. She's approachable and friendly to a fault, but there's something ungraspable—something fundamentally unknowable —about her.

"We'll find out in…" Kate checks her watch. "Oh, damn. We'd better get a move on, babe. With all your antics, you're making us late to your own premiere."

———

Kevin and Bridget have flown in from Washington, without kids, for my big night. Mom and Nathan are there with bells on. Nora hasn't brought a date. She has only invited her two best friends—the ones she seems to hang out with almost exclusively as far as I can tell. We just watched the first episode of the second season of our show together.

"Here you go, babe." Kate hands me a colorful mocktail. Predictably, she has brought one for herself. Sometimes, I wish she'd take the edge off a little with a small glass of something— not a shot of tequila, of course—but there's no such thing as being casual about our pregnancy for Kate. She stopped drinking on the same day I did. But I get it. The only thing she wants more than this baby is having carried it herself, but that was not an option.

We all hold up our glass.

"To Stella," Mom says. "Can I go talk to Nora now?"

"Mom, we've talked about this."

"I know, darling, but I just get so excited."

"Let her come to you," I whisper. "She will, eventually."

"Speaking of," Kate says. "She's coming over right now."

Even though my part on the show is equal to Nora's, she's still—and will always be—the bigger star.

"Oh, god, Stella," she says. "I still can't believe you're going to have a baby."

Playing one of the main characters on a popular TV show

didn't make planning for pregnancy easy—not that it ever is. Just ask Kate. Ideally, I'd have been pregnant a month earlier, but there are some things that making TV will always come secondary to—although not according to some of the producers. But this is Hollywood and tweaks to the schedule can always be made.

Nora pulls me away from the little group I'm standing in.

"I just wanted to take a moment to congratulate you on another job well done. You were a real star this season, Stella. I've had a front row seat at seeing you become better and better. Great stuff."

"Thanks, Nora. That's so sweet of you."

"Eh, I have my moments," she says on a sigh. "God, I hate these things. It's lovely to have a moment with everyone who worked so hard all year, but I'm just so tired now." She gives me a once-over. "How are you even still standing? You're carrying another person around with you."

"I hate to state the obvious." I shoot her a grin.

"What? That you actually like parties?" Nora's face has gone all serious.

"No, that I'm about twenty years younger than you. Although I do love a good party."

Nora nods. "Rub it in."

"Just a heads-up, my mom's about to make a move on you. You can still escape if you want to."

"I always have time and energy for Mary. You know that." Nora paints on a smile in that way that she has. It looks plenty genuine, yet there's still something contradictory about it that doesn't ring entirely true—not an issue she ever has when a director calls 'action'. Nora Levine's one of the best actors in the biz.

While my mother is all over Nora, Kevin and Bridget walk up to Kate and me.

"Can we talk for one quick sec?" Kevin asks. He can be around Kate and me without qualms now. Time and distance have worked their magic. And he's much happier now than he was at the end with Kate. "We're only telling Mom and Nathan tomorrow. Obviously, I didn't want to steal your thunder tonight." He shoots me a wink. "But, um, Bridget and I are pregnant and we wanted you to be the first to know."

It must be because of the pregnancy hormones running through my veins, because instantly, my eyes fill with tears.

"Oh, god, Kev," Kate says, her voice shaky. She holds her arms out for Bridget, my new sister-in-law, who I have no intention of taking from my brother. "Congratulations," Kate whispers in Bridget's ear.

Gingerly, because he thinks I've become breakable just as much as Kate does, Kevin throws his arms around me. "You have no idea how happy I am," my brother says.

"I think I have a pretty good idea." There's plenty of space between us for me to, ostentatiously, rub a hand over my belly. "Congrats, bro."

"Two more little Flacks in the world," he says. "That can only be a good thing."

"We'll have to see about that."

"You're right. Our child could very well be a little troublemaker like her Aunt Stella."

"You should be so lucky," I joke.

"True," my brother says, his eyes on me, a smile on his lips. "I should be so lucky."

Kate slips her arm around my waist. "We should all be so lucky," she says.

GET THREE E-BOOKS FOR FREE

Building a relationship with my readers is the very best thing about writing. I occasionally send newsletters with details on new releases, special offers and giveaways.

And if you sign up to my mailing list I'll send you all this free stuff:

1. An e-book of *Few Hearts Survive*, a Pink Bean Series novella that is ONLY available to my mailing list subscribers.
2. A free e-book of *Hired Help*, my very first (and therefore very special to me) lesbian erotic romance story.
3. A free e-book of my first 'longer' work, my highly romantic novella *Summer's End*, set on an exotic beach in Thailand.

You can get *Few Hearts Survive* (a Pink Bean Series novella), *Hired Help* (a spicy F/F novelette) and *Summer's End* (a deeply romantic lesfic novella) **for free** by signing up at www.harperb liss.com/freebook/ or scanning the QR code below

GET THREE E-BOOKS FOR FREE

ABOUT THE AUTHOR

Harper Bliss is a best-selling lesbian romance author. Among her most-loved books are the highly dramatic French Kissing and the often thought-provoking Pink Bean series.

Harper lived in Hong Kong for seven years, travelled the world for a bit, and has now settled in the Belgian countryside with her wife, Caroline, and her photogenic cat, Dolly Purrton.

Together with her wife, she hosts a weekly podcast called Harper Bliss & Her Mrs.

Harper loves hearing from readers and you can reach her at the email address below.

www.harperbliss.com
harper@harperbliss.com

Made in the USA
Middletown, DE
05 January 2024

47252218R00175